BAD BLOOD

DC BROCKWELL

Print ISBN 978-1-913419-95-0

ALSO BY DC BROCKWELL

DAY 1
FRIDAY, MAY 18TH

1

Myles Jackman felt tugging at his feet. More than that, he felt the cold beneath him. When he tried to move his hands, they wouldn't move. A cold breeze blew over him; it was then he realised he was naked. Naked and outside.

There was another tug at his feet, followed by a tug at his hands. He was afraid to open his eyes. He felt movement in his bowels. Fear. He wasn't alone. He didn't want to see who was with him, who was tugging at his feet and hands.

"Wake up, you piece of shit!"

He felt the slap that snapped his face sideways. It stung.

Why was he here? The last thing he remembered was opening his car door in the underground car park... Oh, wait! Then he'd felt a hand over his mouth.

Fingers pried his eyes open.

They adjusted to their new stimuli. Glaring down at him was a set of eyes; it was only eyes because the rest was Shadow, towering over him. Although he was lying on the ground, Myles could tell how big Shadow was; tall and butch, the kind of person he'd steer clear of. "Please, what are you doing?"

Myles looked around him, desperately searching for a

reason why he was here. To his left was a storefront. He could make out a name: Whyte and Sons. He was in a hardware store car park! When he looked to his right, he could see the white lines of parking bays.

Shadow didn't answer him; instead, tugged at his feet. Pulling his head up, Myles looked down his body. His hands were tied together with rope. The rope from his hands was in turn tied to the rope binding his feet. "What are you doing? Why are you doing this to me?" His voice sounded desperate, even to him. "Please, I'll do anything you want, just let me go."

He panicked when he saw Shadow tying the rope to the bumper of a pickup truck. "No! Please, you can't do this. I haven't done anything wrong."

Myles recoiled when Shadow stopped tying the rope, and stood still – eerily still – before turning around and marching back towards him. Shadow loomed over him and glared down, the eyes black pits of pure hatred. "What?" Myles' voice was placatory. "Tell me what I've done, and I'll stop doing it, please."

Shadow reached into a pocket and pulled out a photograph. Crouching and shoving it under Myles' nose, Shadow replied, "It's too late for that."

In that moment, Myles knew he was a dead man. "That's not what it looks like, I promise you. I wasn't even there."

"Don't lie to me!" Shadow stood and placed the photo back in the pocket. "You have to answer for what you've done. And when you've made amends, your 'friends' will pay their dues, too." The way "friends" was said carried a level of disdain Myles knew only too well.

"I beg you, please, if you let me go, I promise I won't do it again." He tried to untie his hands. "And I'll stop my friends, too," he added, using the term "friends" loosely. They weren't his friends; they were his club members.

"Like I said, it's too late." Shadow squatted and pointed at the storefront. "Look up there. Say hi!" Shadow waved up at the cameras above the front doors, with such confidence, relishing it. "They're going to play this back over and over again. Who knows, I might even make you famous."

Myles panicked when Shadow went back to tying the rope to the truck's bumper. "Help! Please, someone – anyone – please help me!" he screamed as loud as he could, in the vain hope someone might hear him.

"Scream like a woman if you want, but we're in the middle of an industrial estate at two in the morning. There's no one around for miles."

"Don't go! Please." Myles knew the sooner Shadow got in the truck, it was over. His desperate pleas were ignored, as his captor opened the driver's door and got in, slamming the door shut. "Wait! Wait! Wait!" Myles' bladder gave way when he heard the engine start, the warmth of his urine pooling around him. "Pleeeaaasssee! I don't want to die!" He heard the truck's engine rev.

The truck inched forwards, dragging Myles three metres along the tarmac, Myles trying his best to hoist his body up, but unable to, the tarmac tearing into his back. He yelled out in pain, blood squelching beneath him, as the truck stopped. He'd never felt pain like it before. "*Fuck you!*" He writhed on the floor in agony.

Shadow revved the truck's engine again.

Myles knew his back couldn't take any more. He didn't have time to think about what else to do before Shadow accelerated forwards again, this time six metres. Shadow was enjoying it, thought Myles, his back taking another onslaught. When the truck stopped, he could feel the warmth of blood beneath him again, only a lot more of it. "Please, stop! You're going to kill me!"

In front of him, he saw an arm extend out of the driver's window, the thumb up. Myles could barely see through the free-flowing tears. He was in so much pain, he just wanted it to end. "No more, please." Even if Shadow stopped and let him go, his back was permanently damaged.

Gulping at the wheelspin, the smoke emanating from the tyres, Myles knew the split-second before Shadow accelerated that his time was up. He could smell the burning rubber as the truck leapt forwards.

2

———

With a groan, Alicia Weekes rolled over and switched off her shrill alarm clock. For the first time in at least three days she hadn't woken drenched in sweat, reliving the moment a rocket had blown up her Humvee, as she'd been walking alongside it, taking with it her left lower leg. More to the point, she hadn't watched five of her unit engulfed in flames in her dream, either, which she was grateful for.

Nearly every night for the last three years, she'd heard their screams like she was right there. It was a frightening, sickening sound; it was one she wished she could exorcise from her memory forever. It seemed the only thing that prevented her from dreaming was alcohol. She'd tried everything else she could think of: cannabis, sleeping pills. Nope, none of them worked, only alcohol.

Sitting up in bed, she pulled the duvet back, revealing her left residual limb. Even after three years, it took a couple of moments to register that she no longer had a lower leg, made all the more confusing each morning by the fact she could still feel it. She could still wiggle her toes, move her foot up and down, and even tense her calf muscle. According to the doctors, it was normal for amputees to feel their phantom limbs. Using her hands as support, Weekes turned and dangled her right leg over the bed, while she reached for her prosthetic limb and attached it to her stump. Feeling the suction, she stood, made sure it was on tight and walked through to her bathroom across the hall.

After brushing her teeth, Weekes put on her jogging bottoms, T-shirt and trainers and went for a leisurely jog, knowing she had hours before she was due at the station for her first day on the job. Having left the academy only a fortnight earlier, she knew today was going to be a steep learning curve, for how could it not be? She was going from front-line soldiery, to detective constable. The two jobs were so very different. On the way around her block, Weekes thought about her life, her family... her ex-husband.

She couldn't blame him for divorcing her; she wasn't the easiest person to know. However, she could blame him for taking away her little girl, her Hazel, named so after her mum. That, she couldn't forgive him for. Now she only saw Hazel at weekends. And her daughter lived over an hour away by car, with Nevan and his girlfriend, Erin. Weekes wished she could bring herself to hate her, too. Erin was too kind and selfless to hate; she volunteered at a soup kitchen twice a week, for Christ's sake, how could she hate that? No, Weekes knew she was at least partly to blame for their marital breakdown.

Before the incident, she was deployed twice to Iraq, on long tours. Nevan had handled it so well, looking after Hazel in her absence. She'd missed her family so much it hurt. What hurt most was video messaging them from the desert, only to have to click off. On more than a couple of occasions, she'd cried herself to sleep missing her beautiful family.

Then, after she'd had her leg blown off, Weekes had had a hard time adjusting to her new life. Nevan and the rest of her family were so patient with her, which made her mood swings worse. Not feeling like she deserved their support, she would fly off the handle at the slightest provocation. Yeah, she'd hated herself for so long, she couldn't remember a time she didn't. And Nevan's patience was awe-inspiring. The mere thought of him touching her made her recoil, not because she didn't find him attractive, no, because she thought she was ugly, unworthy of his attention, his love.

It seemed his patience had limits. And eighteen months earlier, he'd dropped the bombshell that he thought they should separate. Weekes had cried, apologised, begged him to reconsider. It was pointless, she'd realised, when he confessed he liked someone else. He promised her he hadn't done anything, hadn't cheated on her; he admitted he was attracted to her, the other woman. At that point, Weekes knew it was over. It took him a full year before he introduced Erin.

It was Hazel she felt sorry for, not herself. Weekes knew how important it was for a little girl to have her mum around, and visits at the weekend weren't enough. She and Nevan had been amicably divorced for a year. Divorcing him was her one big regret in life. And as she rounded the last bend after doing two laps of the block, drenched in sweat, she thought her new job might be a blessing in her otherwise tragic life.

Out of breath, she ran up the stairs, reaching her front door on the first floor, waiting until she recovered before letting herself in. She jumped in the shower, standing beneath the warm jets of water, and unwound herself. Life had been shitty, to say the least. After all the negative shit in her life, though, she was a pragmatist at heart. Weekes should've known Nevan would leave her eventually. Marriages were fragile; they broke easily, and if you weren't around both physically and emotionally to repair them... Well, it was curtains, wasn't it?

After drying herself off, she went to the kitchen and made herself a fry-up, a firm believer in breakfast being the most important meal of the day. It had been beaten into her by the military. Her entire life was governed by the army. When she thought back, she'd followed rules and orders her entire life; there were her parents' rules; there were her schools' rules; her college's; then there was the military's rules. Yeah, one way or another, she'd followed rules since she was born. Sometimes she envied free spirits, people who could do whatever they wanted, whenever they wanted. Because it certainly wasn't her life.

Her plate washed, Weekes looked up at the clock on the wall. It was time to get ready. She was supposed to report for duty at nine and hated being late. Changing into her new grey two-piece suit and black shoes, she checked herself in the mirror and walked towards the front door when her mobile rang. "Hello darling, how are you? Of course you're staying here tomorrow. It's just like any other weekend." She listened. "Just because I'm starting a new job, doesn't mean anything changes with our visits, sweetheart. Now, stop worrying and get yourself off to school like a good girl."

Nevan came on the line and she talked with him for a couple of minutes, until she saw it was time to go. Making her excuses, she said goodbye to him and left for her first day at work.

3

―――――

Mina clapped while grinning. "Are we really going to look at puppies tomorrow, Mummy?"

Nasreen glanced at her daughter in the rear-view mirror. "We sure are. A deal's a deal." The turning for Mina's school was up ahead. Nasreen indicated left, slowed, turning her attention to the road, even though she knew the area. "And you get to choose which puppy we bring home."

"Yay!" Mina jumped up and down in her seat as much as the belt allowed.

"Now, before you go getting all excited, you know the rules, right?" Nasreen turned into the school road. When she heard Mina huff, Nasreen asked, "And what are they?"

"Me and Katerina are to walk him every day. Only feed him once a day. He's not allowed on the furniture."

"Good girl." Nasreen pulled up outside the school. Her four-and-a-half-year-old was too clever, sometimes for her own good. Nasreen was always so proud of Mina's command of English. Her daughter read at a grade twice higher than her age, which was why she'd caved in at getting a puppy. Nasreen had never been allowed one growing up, so when Mina asked, Nasreen played hard to get, knowing that if her daughter continued to pester her, she would eventually relent. In all honesty, she wanted a cute furball around the house, too. "Right, we're here." She turned to her daughter in her seat. "And we're going to Uncle Terrence's tomorrow for a barbecue."

There was another loud "yay!" from Mina.

Nasreen thought Mina was about to explode with excitement, and pitied her teacher having to calm her down. Nasreen got out of the car, walked around to Mina's door, opened it and helped her out. Walking towards the school, she nodded at some parents, while saying hello to others. At the gates, she bent down and gave Mina a kiss on her lips; then she watched her daughter walk through to the safety of the playground.

Back in her car, Nasreen looked at the time. "Oh shit!" She started the engine. The previous day, she'd been sent an email asking her to meet Chief Superintendent Bukhari in his office at nine, sharp. She was cutting it fine. "Come on, get out of there!" she yelled at a car trying to parallel park. "Some of us have to work, you know."

Changing partner was stressful; she didn't know what to expect of Alicia Weekes. When she'd been informed of the news, Nasreen had dug around, trying to get the low-down on this year's top recruit. Being ex-military, Weekes' performance had been nothing short of exemplary in every area, apparently. Even with a prosthetic leg, Weekes had outshone her classmates at the training centre. Academically, she was equally superior, achieving nearly full marks in every subject.

Nasreen had endured enough stress lately. It seemed like a lifetime ago that she'd been handed Danny's missing persons case. It had tested her to the limit. When the investigation was shelved after only two days, she'd continued working it in her own time, which didn't go down well with the top brass. And after hearing her superintendent on the phone talking about her, she went rogue, hunting her attacker until she'd found his brother and he'd given her the address of the Harrisons' farm, where Danny and twenty-four other people were being held hostage, and where Beatrice Harrison had sliced open her cheek prior to Stephen Dyer saving her life. She'd nearly been fired for that one.

And then there was Cara Mooney, her last major case. Eight murders in total. Nasreen felt sorry for her more than anything. Betrayed by pretty much everyone in her life, including her parents, it was little wonder she snapped. It was through sheer luck and intuition that Nasreen and her team had located Cara before she murdered her ex-girlfriend, Lucy. Nasreen only wished she'd found Cara before she'd brutally murdered her victims. Unfortunately, that wasn't how it worked in the real world.

Pulling into the station car park, Nasreen found the nearest space she could to the building, parked, flew out of the car, and through the main doors. She used her security card to gain entry, then ran to the lifts, banging on the button impatiently. About to run up the stairs, the lift arrived, and she stepped inside. Jiggling her leg nervously, she cursed the lift for being so slow. With only two minutes to get to Bukhari's office, she was risking it.

On her super's floor, she waited for the lift doors to open. When they finally did, she ran along the corridor to his office. Before she reached his waiting area, she slowed to a stop. There was no way she was going in looking like she'd been dragged through a bush both forwards and backwards, so she took a minute to brush her suit jacket down.

When she felt calmer, she looked at her watch: 09:00 exactly. She'd just made it. Fluffing the bottom of her hair with her hands, Nasreen took a deep breath and walked towards the office door. As she walked through, she caught sight of a woman sat on one of the chairs outside his office on her left.

Nasreen noted she had bobbed shoulder-length brown hair, held an upright posture and a deadpan face. She could be an uptight secretary, she thought, looking at her as she walked past. Of course, it could be her new partner. Looking down at her legs, she tried to identify a prosthesis beneath the trousers. Nope, no false leg under there, she thought, the woman disappearing from view.

"Oh, Nasreen, you're here," Bukhari's secretary said. "I'll let him know. Please, take a seat." She had the air and tone of a gatekeeper.

Obeying orders, Nasreen sat down on a seat two down from the uptight, suited woman, smiling at her as she did so. Nothing in return, just the deadpan expression she'd seen a moment before. Nasreen thought the woman had rolled her eyes, but it could've been her imagination. "Like waiting for the dentist, huh?" Nasreen said, trying to lighten the mood, to which the woman simply nodded, no smile, nothing. She hoped this snooty woman wasn't her new partner.

The door to Bukhari's office opened. "Ah, Nasreen, please come in," he said, holding the door open for her.

Inside, she took a seat while Bukhari closed the door and sat down behind his large, swamped desk. This was the second time she'd met with Bukhari since he'd joined as Chief Superintendent, taking over from Clive Adams, who'd been murdered in the driveway of his home, shot to death. And Bukhari was just as dashing today as he had been a couple of weeks earlier. "I understand you're breaking us up, sir?"

"Reassigning you," Bukhari corrected. "Terrence is going to continue working the skip body case, but something's just come in. I think it'll be just the case to break in your new partner, Alicia Weekes. As you're a sergeant now, it seems redundant to keep you and Terrence together, so I'm giving you the chance to prove your leadership skills."

"And that's her outside, is it, sir?"

"That's her," he replied, official in his tone.

Nasreen tried her best to keep her feelings hidden; she didn't even notice the roll of her eyes, so when he asked if that was okay, she put on a brave front. "Of course, fine. A new partner, I'm really looking forward to getting to know her." And she hadn't meant it to sound sarcastic, either.

"I'm sensing you're not happy about it. Is there a problem I should know about? If there is, tell me now and I'll change things up."

"No!" she said, not wanting to cause trouble; she hadn't given Weekes a fair go yet, although her gut was telling her Weekes was going to be a handful. "There's no problem."

"Good, then it's settled. I hoped her reputation hadn't put you off."

"Reputation, sir? I haven't heard anything about her."

"Yeah, she's ex-military, so she's a bit stiff, should we say. When I interviewed her for this position, I thought you'd be perfect as her probationary sergeant; you'll iron out any creases, I'm sure. And this will be good for you; you'll be demonstrating leadership qualities, which will look good on your file, if you should ever want to go for inspector."

"I'll do my best, sir." Nasreen was saying all the right things, yet deep down she didn't want to be Weekes' probationary sergeant. Then again, she may be doing Weekes a disservice; her new partner might be lovely beneath the starchy surface.

"I know you will." Picking up his phone, Bukhari spoke to his secretary.

The door opened.

"Detective Weekes, please come and meet your partner, Nasreen Maqsood."

Nasreen stood, turned and faced Alicia Weekes. Up close, she was prettier than Nasreen had first thought. She had lovely soft dark brown hair, a dainty little nose and high cheekbones. These features were drowned out by her intense, dark eyes. "I'm pleased to meet you." Nasreen held her hand out. Weekes had a strong handshake, too, which was always a bonus. When Weekes smiled and said, "Likewise," Nasreen found her to be sincere.

Sat next to her new partner, Nasreen listened to Bukhari welcoming Weekes to the department. Nasreen smiled at all the right times, listening to Weekes trying to impress her new super. It was irregular for a constable to meet with such a senior officer, so she guessed Weekes was milking it for all it was worth. Because their department had been hit so badly with budget cuts, injury and illness, Bukhari had managed to talk the top brass into allowing him to recruit, which he was in the process of doing. In a couple of weeks, their department would have a full contingent.

"Right, back to the business at hand," said Bukhari. "You have a new case. I'm afraid you're being thrown in at the deep end, Detective Weekes. A body's been found in a hardware store car park. I do hope you have a strong stomach. SOCOs are there now, and the pathologist's en route. Here's the address."

"You don't have to worry about me, sir," Weekes said, standing. "I saw plenty on tour. I doubt there's anything that'll make me squeamish."

"Good to know," Bukhari replied.

"On our way, sir." Nasreen took the address from him. It said Whyte and Sons, which was situated in the middle of an industrial estate. It was Friday morning. She groaned inside, thinking about the crowds that would have gathered by the time they arrived. And the press, the vulture press. "We'll leave your guided tour until this afternoon, if that's okay with you?" she asked Weekes, who smiled and nodded.

"That's fine," Weekes replied. "But I would like a moment with Superintendent Bukhari, if you don't mind?"

Unusual, thought Nasreen, shrugging her indifference and leaving Weekes with her super. Outside in the waiting area, she sat down, thinking how sweaty her hands were, wiping them on her trousers. It wasn't like her to get clammy hands; she used to around Ashraf, when they'd first met. Oh good grief, she thought, it was Ashraf all over again, only this time she had a crush on her superintendent. How embarrassing!

"Anyway, thank you for your time, sir," Weekes said, as she stepped out of the office.

Getting up, Nasreen met Weekes and walked along the corridor with her. "So, it's Alicia, isn't it? All the guys here call me Nas," she said, smiling up at her taller partner. "It's good to meet you." Her icebreaker was met with a mere nod and, "Uh-huh."

"And by guys, you mean officers?" Weekes said.

"Huh?" was all she could think of to say.

Weekes stopped walking.

Nasreen stopped in front of her and turned, looking up at her.

"They're called officers, or detectives, Detective Maqsood," Weekes continued. "You can call me Detective Weekes, or just Weekes, if it pleases you."

There was nothing Nasreen could respond with; she stood there with her mouth open, anger welling up inside her. It was more than anger. Rage, bubbling, boiling. Who did this woman think she was talking to?

"Look, *Detective Maqsood*, I believe in starting as I mean to go on, so I'll be upfront with you. We're not going to be partners past today anyway. I've asked Superintendent Bukhari to partner me with someone I can actually learn from, and I'm afraid that someone isn't you."

Nasreen felt a smile forming. "Oh? And why's that?" She hoped Weekes couldn't see her shaking. And she *was* shaking; she could swing for her.

"You're reckless. You're in this for personal glory, and that's dangerous. You have no regard for rules, or regulations. They're not there as an obstacle to be overcome, you know, Detective Maqsood; they're there because they save lives."

Still speechless that her new partner would speak to her this way, Nasreen was about to retort, when Weekes continued.

"I think it's shameful that you were taken back. You should've been fired just for carrying out an unofficial investigation, much less going AWOL and breaching that farmhouse. The top brass should be prosecuting you, not bowing to media pressure."

"Are you finished? Good! You've had your say, and that's fine. If you want to change partners, then that's more than fine with me, too." Nasreen saw a couple of her colleagues walking towards her. Once they'd walked past, she continued. "You've obviously done your homework, as have I."

Weekes folded her arms. "Go on! I'd like to hear this."

"Alicia Mary Weekes, you spent twelve years in the army, during which time you've done two tours in Iraq and one in Afghanistan. With two medals of honour to your name, you were a rising star until you had a change of heart. You wanted to really help people, so you joined a private security company, whose main job was to accompany aid convoys through enemy territory, where your unit was attacked, your Humvee blown up, and where you lost your lower left leg. Since then, you've been in rehab, where you demonstrated great resilience and courage in the way you handled your new situation. And last year, you applied to become a detective. In training, you were top of your class in every subject, both physical and academic."

"Next you'll be telling me what my favourite colour is," Weekes interrupted.

Nasreen ignored the sarcasm. "You'll find I always do my homework, but you have to understand something: here, in the field, you know exactly nothing, nada. You're no more than a sponge waiting to be filled with knowledge. So, do yourself a favour, shadow me and you'll learn something today."

"I doubt that," Weekes replied, her arms still folded.

"You don't have a choice." Nasreen made to walk towards the lift. "I'm your partner today, whether you like it or not." She stopped walking, checking if her new partner was coming. Closing her eyes, she took a deep breath. "Let's just get going; we've got a body to identify." Her job was hard enough without this, she thought, heading to the elevator.

4

———

"What's that face for? Your audience awaits." Weekes grinned.

In frustration at not being able to fly at her partner, Nasreen pulled up the handbrake, hard. All she wanted was to get away from her; she was so disagreeable to be around. "When they see us, they'll ask us for statements. Just say 'No comment', okay?" Without checking if Weekes was even listening, Nasreen unclipped her seat belt and opened the door.

"Not if I take a leaf out of your book," Weekes replied, following suit.

On their silent journey over to the crime scene, Nasreen vowed to ignore Weekes' snippy comments. What she hadn't considered was how hard it was going to be. In front of the car, she waited for her partner to join her. "On second thoughts, leave the talking to me."

They headed towards the growing crowd cordoned off by three uniforms.

As they approached the throng, several reporters turned and started asking her questions. "No comment," she kept saying, squeezing through the crowd.

Behind her, she heard Weekes say, "When we have something to report, you'll be the first to know." Almost imperceptibly, Nasreen shook her head.

At the cordon, Nasreen showed a uniform her ID. He lifted the crime scene tape for her to duck under. Waiting for Weekes to join her, she surveyed the scene. It was a car park out front of a hardware store. The only difference with this car park was the blood; there were streaks of it everywhere; swirls, circles, and lots of it. In front of the store itself was a tent. There was a smaller tent to her left, which meant there was a severed body part, a limb, she guessed. SOCOs were busy photographing a heap of clothes over the far side. In the distance, she saw a CCTV camera above the main entrance to the store.

The coroner, in her protective white coveralls, emerged from the tent carrying two sets of protective clothing for them. Even though the pathologist's face was hidden, Nasreen recognised her as Sheila Gorman; she could tell by her height and walk, having worked with her on a few occasions. "Here she comes now," she said to Weekes. "Before she gets here, talk me through the seven stages of crime scene investigation."

"Oh good grief! Really?"

Nasreen nodded. "Uh-huh!"

"Let's see, it's been a while since I studied it," Weekes replied, sarcasm oozing over every syllable. "Secure the scene, separate the witnesses, scan the scene, photograph the scene, sketch the scene, search for evidence and finally secure evidence. Am I right?"

"Good enough. Now let's see how good you are in practise."

"Morning, Nas," the pathologist said through her face mask. "Here, put these on. You'd better prepare yourselves, this one's bloody. Who's this?"

"Sheila, this is my new partner, Detective Constable Alicia Weekes. Detective Constable Weekes, this is Sheila Gorman, the best pathologist we have." There was no handshaking. Nasreen obeyed the orders and stepped into her coveralls, putting on her face mask. "Right, shall we take a look?"

"The SOCOs have been here a while now," Sheila said, as they walked towards the main tent. "They've pretty much wrapped up, and we already know who the victim is."

"Who found the victim?" Nasreen asked.

"Some poor guy from the factory next door. He comes in early sometimes, drove past and saw the body lying in the car park, although he didn't know it was a body at first. He phoned it in. Sergeant Zahari is interviewing him now. He was the first and only witness to see the body before the car park was cordoned off."

They arrived at the door to the tent.

"I hope your food's settled, Detective Weekes." Sheila unzipped the doors. "I know I don't have to worry about you, Nas. It looks like Mr Jackman was dragged around for quite some time, judging by the extent of tissue damage."

Nasreen heard Weekes take a deep breath. "You okay? If you want to hang back, it's fine. This shouldn't be your first crime scene." She heard the zip open as Sheila stepped inside the tent. Nasreen thought she was being nice.

"I'm fine, really. I've seen my share of nasty shit."

Sighing, Nasreen followed her partner inside. "Don't say I didn't warn you," she muttered, knowing that if Sheila thought it was bad, it was worse. The first thing Nasreen noticed was the smell; it was vile, an assault on her nostrils. Looking to her right, she saw Weekes having trouble keeping her breakfast down.

The stench was equalled by the view. The body was barely recognisable as a person; it looked like a lump of bloody meat. There were two arms and one leg, a head, which was misshapen, face down. It was dark red and moist, the skin destroyed by the tarmac, leaving only muscle, bone and blood. Nasreen could see the bones in the victim's back. "Who is he?" she asked the pathologist, taking out her notepad and pen.

"His name's Myles Jackman. Whoever did this doesn't care if we identify him, or not. They left the victim's wallet and phone here, along with his clothes. I was about to turn him over. Do you mind?"

"Where's his other leg?" Weekes was breathing heavy, bent over.

Sheila raised her eyebrows. "This really is your first day, huh?"

"In the other tent." Nasreen bent down to help the pathologist turn the body over. It was squidgy to the touch, even through gloves. "You okay, Weekes?" She could hear her partner's breathing grow heavier.

She wished they hadn't turned it over. Myles Jackman's corpse had no face. While being dragged around the car park, he must have gone face down at some point. There was no nose. All the skin had been scraped away, leaving a bloody, pulpy mess.

Nasreen hadn't seen anything this savage before. "If you feel queasy, Detective–"

"Oh my God! I'm going to–" Weekes turned and bolted for the door.

"Go out the other door." Sheila pointed to where Weekes should go. "They'll be snapping away out there now."

"She'll learn." Nasreen smiled beneath her mask. Standing up, she regarded the body. "Poor bastard," she said, feeling the blood on her gloves. "What a horrible way to go."

"Oh, I nearly forgot." Sheila turned and grabbed a bag from a table behind her. Handing it to Nasreen, she said, "We found this next to the body. We figured the suspect cut it out. It's Myles, according to Zahari. The suspect's sending a message?"

Nasreen didn't doubt it. "It looks that way." She studied the cut-out picture of Myles Jackman smiling. There was something troubling behind the victim. "Please don't be a serial," she said into the ether. There was an arm around Myles' neck, obviously part of a larger group photo.

"I don't think we should jump to conclusions, Nas."

"You saw the arm behind him?"

Sheila huffed. "Yeah, I saw it; I just didn't want to think it meant there might be more to come. The eternal optimist, me. And we don't know this is part of some serial agenda. Until we do, we treat it as an isolated murder case, yes?"

"Agreed," Nasreen replied, hope in her voice. After Cara Mooney's killing spree, the last thing she wanted was to be hunting another psychotic killer. Please be just the one, she thought, looking at the arm behind Myles Jackman. Deep down she knew there would be more. The killer enjoyed it. "Right, I think we need to see the footage. I'd better see how Weekes is getting on first."

Outside the tent, the paparazzi were busy filming Weekes hunched over, throwing up the contents of her breakfast. Nasreen put a comforting hand on her shoulder. "You all right?" she asked, only for her partner to put her hand up, warning her to keep away. "It's nothing to be ashamed of, you know. I threw up on my first case."

"That's not it. Must be something I ate."

Oh really? A grin crept over her while Weekes had her head down. "You should've said so earlier. I'd have sent you home sick."

"What?" Weekes looked up at her, still hunched over. "I'm not sick enough for that. Give me a minute, I'll be right with you. It must've been the smell in there, reacting with my stomach, or something."

"Oh, okay. Take your time. We need to go take a look at the CCTV from the store, but I can wait until your stomach settles."

"How can you not react to that? The stench alone was bad enough, much less the body. Have you ever seen anything that bad before?"

"Worse. A couple of weeks ago, we were given a body to identify in a skip on a construction site. Now, that was disgusting. Dead for over a month before it found its way to the skip. The smell was bad, but not as bad as the maggots."

"Oh God, no!" Weekes heaved.

Nasreen could hear the journalists behind the cordon talking about Weekes throwing up. It would end up in the national rags, she thought with glee. It served her partner right for being such a pain earlier. Nasreen could almost see the deserving headlines now.

5

———

Assistant Commissioner of Police of the Metropolis, Peter Franks, opened the office door to find he was the last to arrive at the meeting. The Home Secretary, Suzanne Embry, stood behind her desk, beckoning him in. "Sorry I'm late," he said, closing the door behind him. "I've been sorting tomorrow's dawn raids with one of the commissioners."

Embry motioned for him to sit down next to Harold Thomas, Franks' immediate boss. "And everything's ready to go? So soon?" she asked, sitting behind her large desk. "I didn't think we'd be going ahead for a few weeks."

"We're good to go." Franks noticed how lovely she looked in a pink blouse, with her long dark hair tied in a ponytail. Facially, she was beautiful. Of all the female politicians he'd met, she was easily the most attractive. "We've got eight properties under surveillance. Our intel's good, and if anyone asks, it was all down to our network of CIs."

"Excellent!" she replied, looking at Harold Thomas, as if asking why he hadn't informed her earlier. "That's great news, Peter. Good work."

Without looking at Harry, he replied, "I thought it was about time we hit the headlines. The more high-profile arrests we have, the better. And this is just the start."

"I have to say, you're certainly on the ball." Embry picked up her small, circular glasses and put them on. "Do you have anything to add, Harold?"

Franks didn't look at Harry, who Embry called Harold; she always called everyone by their extended names. He stared straight ahead, waiting for his boss to speak. When he didn't, Franks broke a little smile. Harry was his immediate superior in name only; he knew it and Embry and Gary Holmes, the newly elected NCA Director General, knew it.

"Only that we still need to be cautious," Harry said, finally. "The Garvey threat may have been contained, but we still don't know if he's sent copies of his files to anyone. It's been a good couple of months, I know, however we need to be vigilant; there's no knowing how much he had on us."

It was true, Garvey had threatened to send copies of his files to someone. Franks had been worrying about it for weeks, since Darius – one of Maggie Hughes' guys – had phoned him to let him know that Maggie had killed Garvey. Now there was no knowing who had the files. "I agree in being vigilant, ma'am, but I do think the files would've surfaced by now. I think we can get on with the job at hand."

"Good," Embry replied, sitting back in her high-back chair. "Let's proceed... with caution. Tell our people to keep their eyes and ears open; we can't have anyone getting wind of it." Leaning forwards, elbows on the desk, she added, "Very well, Harold. Good point. Now, Gary, how's the Rothstein investigation going?" She turned her attention to the Director General of the NCA. "Are we going to get any blowback from it?"

"Not that I can see, ma'am," Holmes replied. "There's one potential disaster waiting to happen, though, if I may?" He waited for a nod of approval from Embry. "It's the doctor. All the survivors are describing the same man. We've got a good picture of what he looks like now, so it won't be long before we identify him. And when we do, there's no knowing how much he'll know."

"About the project? He won't know anything," Franks scoffed. "The guy was there to see to the captives. I doubt he knew anything about the project. Rothstein wasn't even involved in the brothel, apparently; he left the running of it to his daughter and son-in-law. I can't see us having any problems with detaining him."

William Rothstein's daughter, Beatrice Harrison, and her husband, had run the brothel/slaughterhouse beneath their farm in the south-west. Over a sixteen-year period, the Harrisons had abducted countless sex workers up and down the country, and imprisoned them into a life of sexual servitude, until they outran their usefulness. When that happened, they auctioned their murder to the highest bidder. The true number of victims was still unknown.

Embry considered this. "Gary? Harold? Do you concur?"

"I trust Peter's judgement," Harry confirmed.

"As do I," Holmes seconded. "I had to put it out there."

"Very well, Gary, you may apprehend him," Embry replied. "The media's breathing down my neck about the whole Rothstein affair anyway. I think getting confirmation of who was murdered in that bunker will help keep the vultures at bay, don't you? At the very least we can give their families some kind of closure."

If he'd wanted to, Franks could've made Harry's position untenable. If he was vindictive, he could have let it slip that his boss had entered into a relationship with Amelie Desmarais, the high-class prostitute who was sleeping with Lennox Garvey, and working with him to expose the project. If he were so inclined, he could do that. Glancing sideways at his boss, he felt nothing but contempt for the man – he was weak.

"Is there anything I need to know before we get down to official business?" Embry asked, picking up papers from her desk. When they all shook their heads, she called the meeting to order. "Peter, you don't need to be here for this. I thank you for your time and commitment. Good luck tomorrow morning. I look forward to seeing the highlights."

"Thank you, ma'am," he said, getting up and walking out of the office. He was escorted by Embry's personal guards, who'd been waiting in the hallway.

6

———

"What's he doing?" Weekes asked, watching the CCTV monitor. She and Nasreen were sat at a desk with the store manager stood behind them. "Is that a photo?" The masked person was crouching down, showing the naked, bound victim something.

"I knew it! He's preaching."

Glancing at her sergeant, Weekes turned her nose up. "What are you talking about? He's showing him a picture, that's all. How is he preaching?" She'd only been with Sergeant Maqsood for a couple of hours, and already she was annoying her.

"There's obviously something incriminating in that photo," Nasreen replied. "The suspect's gone to a lot of trouble to abduct the victim, drive him out here and tie him up. Now he's showing him a photo. Myles Jackman's done something to piss him off."

It was a theory. "I guess we won't find out until we see what's in that photo, will we?" Her attention turned to the screen once more. The suspect was looking directly up at the camera, pointing. The pointing turned into a wave. "He's taunting us!"

Nasreen nodded. "He's enjoying it, too." She turned to the

manager. "I think it's best if you leave the room. I don't want you seeing this."

The manager left without complaint.

"We'll come and find you when we're done here," Nasreen said. "Thank you."

Watching the monitor, Weekes observed Jackman pleading for his life, while the suspect tied a rope to the bumper of the pickup truck. She'd already seen the body; she wasn't sure she could stomach watching the poor guy getting murdered as well. Then again, Nasreen was watching the screen intently, showing no signs of guilt, or squeamishness. No, she was stronger than this, Weekes said to herself, going back to the screen, where the suspect had hopped into the truck. Smoke billowed out of the exhaust. She saw the truck revving. "Snuff movie," she said, to the ether.

"Hmm?" Nasreen was still focused on the monitor. "What was that?"

"This is like watching a snuff movie," Weekes said, as the truck surged forwards by a couple of metres. She grimaced when she saw the victim dragged on his back, red smears forming from where the tarmac had shredded his skin.

"That's exactly what it is." Nasreen looked up at her. "It's just lucky we're the only ones who can see it. Something like this would get a million hits online."

The suspect revved the engine again, taunting his victim, who screamed in both pain and fear. Wanting to close her eyes, Weekes forced herself to watch as the truck raced forwards, dragging poor Jackman behind on his back. Blood trailed the victim. Turning around fast, Jackman's body rolled as it followed the truck. The pickup drove around the car park at high speed five times; by the third circuit, the victim was dragged face first.

The suspect slowed the truck to a stop finally, got out and walked over to the victim. Stood over him, the suspect took out a photo and a pair of scissors. Carefully cutting out the victim's face, the killer stooped down and left it by the side of the victim. And to her surprise, Weekes watched as the suspect pointed at the camera again, this time turning it into a gun shape, and pretended to shoot.

He went to the bumper and untied the rope, leaving it attached to Jackman's skinless corpse, walking through the lines of blood. "What's he doing?" she asked. The suspect was fiddling with the back of the truck.

"Oh shit!" Nasreen said, digging inside her suit jacket and pulling out her mobile.

"Is that what I think it is?" she asked her superior, who already had her phone to her ear. She didn't receive a reply.

"Yeah, sir, it's me," Nasreen said. "We've got a problem here at Whyte's. The suspect filmed the whole thing. He had a mobile attached to the back of his truck. Do you mind getting on to Cyber and asking them to look out for the film online? Thank you. The last thing we need is this getting out in public."

"You think he'll post this online?" Weekes asked.

"It's happened before. If he's doing this for some sort of cause, he'll need an audience. Unfortunately, this will go viral, if it gets out. The good thing is, if he posts it, Cyber should be able to trace its origins, so it could work in our favour."

"Look, the truck's closer," she said, squinting at the licence plate. "Can you make it out? It looks like it starts with an M."

"Could be an N," her supervisor replied. "It's too dirty. Even if we enhance it we won't get a clear picture. And if we do, I doubt it's the suspect's truck; it's probably been stolen."

"It's worth a shot, though, right? I'll ask the manager to send us a copy." Even if her supervisor didn't, she thought it was worth a try.

"Go ahead. Right now, though, we need to get back to the station. While I'm looking into Myles Jackman's background, I need you to liaise with the council. I noticed there were a number of CCTV cameras on our way here. We'll need to trawl through them to find out which direction the suspect headed in."

Weekes didn't like the sound of that. Trawling through hours of footage sounded soul-destroying. "I tell you what, I'll look into Jackman while you liaise with the council. I need experience using the PNC anyway. It makes sense."

"I'll tell *you* what, *Constable* Weekes, how about you do as I ask, and I won't write you up in my report?" Nasreen's eyes were narrow slits. "You need experience in following orders. It seems strange to me that you're so adamant about the importance of orders in the military, and yet seem incapable of following any yourself."

Without being given the chance to argue, Nasreen walked out of the office, leaving Weekes feeling a lot smaller than she had upon entering. Giving credit where it was due, though, Sergeant Maqsood was tougher than Weeks had originally thought. "I was just saying," she mumbled on her way out.

7

"How are you getting on?" Nasreen looked over Weekes' shoulder, noticing her rubbing her eyes. The monitor said it was 17:36. Her trainee had been watching CCTV footage for over four hours. "Have you managed to track it?"

"For about two miles, yeah. Then it just disappears. I know which direction the truck was heading, but after this junction, I can't find it. There's a slip road, here, which doesn't have cameras, and he could've taken a left, here, or a right, there." She was indicating the roads on a map in front of her. "I've asked the council for more footage, over a wider area, but they haven't sent it over yet."

"Good, it's a start." Nasreen felt sympathy for her prickly constable, knowing how awful watching footage could be. "Keep on it. We might catch him with the new footage. Oh, and if they give you any trouble, let me know and I'll talk to them."

Weekes turned her chair round and looked up at her. "I'm more than capable of talking to them myself, thanks." She then turned back, watching the monitor.

Nope, all sympathy gone, Nasreen thought, biting her tongue for the twentieth time. Rise above it, she told herself, walking to her desk. "How are you getting on, anyway?" She heard Weekes ask from behind the partition separating them.

In response, Nasreen stood and peered over the wall. "I found out a fair bit. He lives with his parents in a village about an hour's drive south of here, over the South Downs. He's thirty-two, runs his own IT consulting business from a summer house at the bottom of his parents' garden. He's been questioned for GBH and ABH, although never convicted."

"Sounds like a decent kind of guy," Weekes replied, sarcasm evident in her voice. "Do we know why?"

"Nope. I'm about to call his parents." It was the worst aspect of her job, speaking to the next of kin of victims. On the other hand, she always found the different reactions fascinating: some grieving parents ranted and raved; others broke down crying; some swore vengeance, while others wore deadpan, expression-less faces. "I'll try to get them to come in for an interview first thing Monday." She noticed Weekes looked relieved.

"Thank God; I thought you were going to say tomorrow morning. You know I can only work Monday to Friday, right? I have my daughter on weekends."

Why didn't that surprise her? Nasreen was beginning to wonder why Bukhari had hired her in the first place. Weekes didn't like following orders, even though she had in the army – lives depended on it, apparently – and now she wouldn't work weekends? "I do now." She sighed, sitting back down at her desk. A small part of her wanted to request a new partner, yet a larger part of her wanted the challenge.

As she was about to pick up the phone, Terrence Johnson and Inspector Arjun Gupta walked into the office. "Let me intro-duce you to Detective Constable Weekes," she said, getting up from her chair. They walked over to her. "Hey, how's it going? Any leads yet?" The skip body they'd been given a couple of weeks ago was turning out to be a total bust. She walked around to Weekes' desk, Terrence shaking his head, telling her they were no nearer finding any suspects.

To her frustration, Weekes got up from her seat and shook Gupta's and Terrence's hands, smiling softly, flattering them with how she'd heard so much about them at the training centre. She was so full of shit, Nasreen thought. She joined in their chit-chat, surprised at how cordial and attentive her new partner could be. "Any news from Cyber?" Nasreen asked Gupta, terminating the pleasantries.

"Not so far." Gupta had recovered from the knife wound he'd received, courtesy of Cara Mooney, whose body had been recovered from the bottom of the cliff she'd fallen from. "If it's out there, they'll find it. I'll let you know if they do."

And on that note, Terrence and Gupta said their goodbyes. As Terrence was walking away, he turned back and said, "Oh, Weekes, my wife and I are having a barbecue tomorrow, if you want to come along and meet everyone?"

"Ah, erm." Weekes scratched her head. "I'd love to, except I've got my daughter tomorrow. I'm so sorry!" She sat back down on her chair, looking awkward, like Terrence had just asked her out on a date.

"So? Bring her along. What's her name? How old is she?"

"Hazel, and she's six. Really, thanks, but we have plans tomorrow. I appreciate the invite, though."

"Suit yourself." Terrence handed her a scrap of paper. "If you change your mind, here's the address. It'd be good for you to meet everyone off duty."

Nasreen watched her partner accept the address and pocket it. After they'd gone, and she could speak to Weekes without ears listening, she looked down at her. "It'd be a good idea to come along," she said, the hostility in Weekes' eyes obvious. "It's a good way of meeting everyone. We don't have these social gatherings often, maybe once or twice a year."

"I said no, and I meant it." Weekes glared up at her. "I don't need guilt-tripping into it, thanks. I like to keep work and social separate."

Before she could say anything else, Weekes turned back to her PC.

"If that's your choice, so be it. If you want to be the outsider."

Back at her desk, Nasreen sat down on her chair, picked up her landline phone and dialled nine for an external line.

DAY 2
SATURDAY, MAY 19TH

8

Franks couldn't help it; he was excited. Looking at the bank of monitors in front of him, he saw several views from cameras on the raid teams' helmets. This morning's dawn raids were two years in the making, and the official starting point of Operation Cleansweep. His chosen dealers had delivered. The houses that the raid teams were waiting outside of were homes of drug dealers his chosen guys had handed over. "Are we set?" he asked Charles Norris, the Northumbria Police and Crime Commissioner responsible for the raids.

"We're good to go here," Norris, a large man with white hair replied. He filled up his immaculate uniform, and then some. "They're waiting on your green light."

"And we're happy with the intel? The merchandise is definitely there?" After he'd received the names of the dealers from the likes of Astor, Foster and Margaret Hughes, he'd set up surveillance teams to give them a paper trail. And in light of Margaret Hughes' family being in tatters, he'd thought it best to deal with her rivals in the north-east first. "I don't want to look stupid, Charles. This has to run smoo–"

"It's there," Norris replied, cutting him off. "In total, across the eight homes, there's cocaine, bags of ecstasy pills, copious amounts of cannabis, and MDMA. Like I said, we're good to go, Peter. Our CIs have confirmed it."

Looking at his watch, Franks saw it was just gone five. The sun was rising, which was the best time of day to raid homes. It caused maximum confusion. Looking through the window, the sky was dark blue, getting lighter with each passing minute. This was it, he thought, the moment he'd been waiting for. "Very well, order the breach," he said to Commissioner Norris, who in turn ordered one of his six control room personnel to radio the order through.

On screen, Franks watched as the heavily armed police officers used battering rams to break open the doors. There was no sound; there didn't need to be. When the officers forced open the doors, there would be an awful lot of shouting, bravado. He could do without listening to that first thing in the morning. Switching between the eight screens, Franks watched scumbags get forced out of bed and fall to the ground, hands behind their backs. Any day they managed to take dealers off the street was a good day, a proud moment. "Tell them to tear those houses apart," he ordered, leaning on the back of a chair, still watching the raids. "We need results."

Pacing back and forth for what felt like an eternity, he waited for confirmation from the assault teams. In real-time minutes it took forty-five for the first to be radioed through. "And?" he asked Norris, who had a grin on his face.

"Target one: four kilos of cocaine, and assorted extras," the commissioner replied. "Plus, three pistols, a shotgun and two machine pistols."

Breathing a sigh of relief, Franks blew out a lungful of air. It was only one target, one home. There were another seven. The haul would be bigger than even he'd dared imagine. "Good. Keep on it."

Commissioner Norris turned back to the monitors, his earpiece in place, ready for the upcoming transmissions.

Dumb, thought Franks, they were all dumb. Who kept drugs in their home? He had very little respect for the criminal fraternity of today; it seemed they didn't have a single brain cell between them.

"Target eight," Norris said. "Eight kilos of coke, three MDMA, ecstasy pills, cannabis. We hit the mother lode here. Four pistols. Three suspects in custody, awaiting transportation. And target three: Five coke, two MDMA, and an assortment of others."

"Holy shit! Keep going," he ordered Norris, who, again, turned back to the monitors. While the control room staff were busy conversing with the raid teams, Franks daydreamed about the pats on the back, the kudos he would get for the raids. Suzanne Embry was already impressed with how he was handling the project – unlike Harry, who was useless – and after this, Franks could expect his stock to rise in her eyes.

Watching these dealers fall like pins in a bowling alley was what made everything worthwhile. It made dealing with the likes of Rothstein, Garvey and Amelie Desmarais bearable. Franks wasn't overzealous; he knew that this was a mere drop in the ocean. It was well-known that when one dealer dropped, another would pop up in its place. The project was never designed to purge society of all dealers, just dramatically reduce them enough to persuade the public that the government's current drug policy was flawed. Legalising drugs was the cure to this particular disease. It had worked in other countries, even certain states in America, so why not here in the UK?

Franks was a career police officer and patriot. For over twenty-three years he'd seen crime rise sharply, mainly due to the Police and Criminal Evidence Act of 1984, after which his colleagues' hands had been, literally, tied behind their backs; it gave criminals the advantage. Back in the day, being able to threaten, intimidate and attack suspects had proven its worth.

Now criminals knew their human rights and played on them. Drug dealers, even if caught, were given such soft sentences that they weren't a deterrent. No, legalising drugs was the answer to their prayers. Project Cleansweep would demonstrate to the public how it could be done. In eighteen months or so, when they leaked the story to the press, they'd be able to show the difference they'd made.

"Target four," he heard Norris say.

9

Weekes could feel the hangover before she even opened her eyes. Her head was thumping. Opening one eye, she saw her on/off companion, Brian, lying next to her. He was snoring for the championship.

It wasn't just her head that hurt. Thinking about it, her good leg hurt, too. When she pulled the duvet back, she saw the scab on her knee. On their way home from her local, she'd fallen over, drunk. Spying her prosthetic leg, she reached for it, hoisted herself up and attached it. There didn't appear to be any damage done to it, which was a blessing, considering how much it had cost her parents. "Wake up," she said, too loud for her fragile ears. "She'll be here soon." Nothing. No response, just a louder snore. Hitting him on his back, she added, "Come on, get up! I'm not having Hazel seeing you crawling out of here."

He grunted, before pulling himself upright. "What were we drinking?"

"It's more suitable to ask what we weren't drinking," she replied, regretting going to the pub, although she'd had a laugh. Too many laughs, more like. "Get dressed! She'll be here in less than an hour."

Leaving him to get dressed, Weekes walked through to the bathroom and jumped in the shower, desperately trying to wash away the previous night. Feeling the hot water, she vowed never to bring Brian back home again. Last night was a huge mistake.

Hearing the glass shower curtain creak, she whirled around to find him trying to step in the shower with her. "What the fuck! Get out!" She glared at him. Pushing him back, Weekes again ordered him out. "Get dressed and get out of my flat!"

After he'd moaned about the way she treated him, she jumped out of the shower, walked up to the door and locked it, water dripping on the lino. Back under the jets of water, she asked herself why she behaved the way she did? She'd brought him back to hers a half dozen times and after each encounter she felt ashamed. And yet she kept doing it. Not anymore, she said to herself, washing him away.

Having dried herself and changed into civvies – light blue jeans and white vest top – she found Brian tying his shoelaces up sat on the sofa in her lounge. He was angry; she could tell by the exaggerated way he was looping the laces and pulling the bow together. "Last night was the last time," she said, arms folded.

"That's what you always say, Weekes," he replied, his eyes narrow. "Until next Friday night, that is." He stood and faced her. "I don't know why you treat me like this. You act like you hate me sometimes, you really do."

"I don't hate you." She recoiled when he stepped towards her.

"You sure act like it. I've been good to you, haven't I? Hell, I've walked you home more times than I can count. I know you've got a thing about your leg, but I keep telling you it doesn't bother me."

Weekes scoffed. "A thing? I don't have a thing."

Brian skulked past her, into the hallway. At the front door, he turned to her. "You're the one with the problem, not me. When you stop hating yourself, come find me. You know where I'll be."

"Yeah, in the pub with all the other losers," she said, as he opened the door.

Weekes cursed silently when she saw Nevan and Hazel stood outside.

"Nevan!" she said. This was the last thing she wanted. Hazel looked up at her with big, confused eyes. "Hello, my little nut." She wished a hole would open up and suck her in.

There was an awkward silence as Brian waited to be introduced to her ex-husband and daughter. "Brian was just leaving." She pushed him past Nevan and Hazel, into the hallway. "See you again soon, Brian." She watched him walk away.

Hugging Hazel, Weekes stood and looked at Nevan, averting her gaze after seeing the look of disgust in his eyes. "Go on through to the lounge, honey," she said to her daughter, "put whatever you want on the TV." After Hazel had wandered off, leaving her with her ex, she said, "Sorry you had to see that." Not inviting him in for the inevitable row that would follow, she added, "You're early."

"Seriously? You're giving that guy the shove of shame in front of our daughter and blaming me for being early?" His voice was an angry whisper. "It's half nine, Alicia; you could've chucked him out when you woke up, which judging by how you look, was only ten minutes ago. What's Hazel going to be thinking now, huh?"

There was another long silence.

"And you look like shit, by the way."

Weekes felt anger rising to the surface. "Don't stand there and judge me! In case you've forgotten, I don't answer to you anymore." She could punch him in his judgemental face. Knowing she only had herself to blame, she forced an apologetic smile. "You're right, though, I should've thrown him out first thing. It won't happen again, I promise."

"And you smell like a brewery, for Christ's sake." Nevan pulled an offended face, wafting the "stench" with his hand. "Go and finish getting ready, would you! I'll wait in the lounge with her."

Feeling like a chastised child, Weekes walked through to her bathroom, brushed her teeth for a full five minutes, sprayed some deodorant under her armpits and tidied up after herself, listening to Nevan and Hazel laughing at the cartoons. Freaking out that she hadn't tidied the kitchen, she rushed along the hallway only to find Nevan staring at the mess.

She closed her eyes, silently cursing to herself. When she opened them, Nevan was holding a near-empty bottle of cheap vodka, shaking his head in disappointment. In addition to the vodka, there were half a dozen empty cans of lager and two open and drunk bottles of wine sat on the counter, making her feel guilty. "It's not all mine. I had friends over last night."

Pouring the remnants of vodka down the sink, Nevan binned the glass bottle and leaned against the counter, his arms crossed. "You don't have friends," he said, more in truth than trying to cause an argument. "You've got a problem, Alicia," he said, his eyes sympathetic, the accusatory squint gone. "And I'm not letting Nut stay here unsupervised, not with you like this. If you have a problem with that, speak to my lawyer, but right now we're leaving."

"Nevan, please, don't do this," she begged, knowing his serious tone only too well. "I'm fine, honestly. I might be a bit hungover, but I'm good."

"You can't drive like this," he said, unfolding his arms and walking out into the hallway. "Hey, Nut, come on, we're going home." He held his hand out for her to take. "Mummy's not feeling well," he said to her, walking to the front door. "Say goodbye to Mummy!"

Feeling tearful, Weekes bent down and hugged Hazel so tight, she was in danger of crushing her. "I'm so sorry, darling," she said, rubbing her daughter's back. "I'll be better by next weekend, I promise." There was disappointment in Hazel's eyes. Standing up, regarding Nevan, Weekes said, "I meant what I said. I'll be better."

"I hope so," he said, opening the front door.

Watching her ex-husband and daughter walk along the hallway to the elevator, she smiled and waved them off, a tear escaping and rolling down her cheek. When they were out of view, she closed the door, leaned against it and burst into tears.

10

———

Holding the carrier, with help from Mina, Nasreen could see her car in the distance. She was beginning to wish she'd found a space nearer the main entrance to the rescue centre. The one-year-old King Charles Spaniel was heavy, especially when inside the cage she'd just bought. It didn't matter. Dot was the cutest thing she'd ever seen and seeing Mina so happy was worth the money and effort. "We'll just put her in the boot, honey," she said, Mina wanting to help her.

Dot was mostly brown on the body, with white legs and a big, white dot on her back. When she looked up at Nasreen with those big brown eyes, her heart melted. "Be a good girl, please," she said, putting her fingers through the cage for Dot to sniff.

After closing the boot, Nasreen helped Katerina put Mina in her booster seat. While she was strapping her daughter in, who was struggling to turn around in her seat to see Dot, her mobile went off. Leaving Katerina to it, apologising, Nasreen took the call, surprised to find Weekes on the other end. "Hey! I wasn't expecting to hear from you today," she said, standing up and watching guests come and go from the main rescue centre building. "What's up? I thought you had your daughter today?"

"I do," Weekes replied. "I mean, I did."

"Oh!" she said, not wanting to pry, not really caring. All she wanted to do was get Dot home before Mina exploded with excitement.

"I mean, she came down with some bug."

"I'm sorry to hear that," she replied, not wishing sickness on anyone, even Weekes.

"It's nothing serious, she'll be fine for next weekend."

"That's good," she said, wondering why her partner was calling. She wasn't easy to talk to at the best of times, much less over the phone when it was clear she was upset. "Are you okay? Do you want to talk about it?"

"No, I'm fine. Listen, the reason I'm calling is I'm free today, if you fancied taking a trip to that village? We could interview the Jackmans, make a start on the investigation."

"We're off duty, Weekes," she warned, thinking her partner was trying to bait her. "The last time I did that, I got suspended, so the answer's no, I'm afraid."

"I'm not talking about going there off duty. You've Inspector Gupta's number, haven't you? You could get permission from him. I won't go without it."

She could tell by Weekes' voice she was at a loose end, and actually felt sorry for her. Listening to Katerina struggling to clip Mina in, she sighed. "I've just bought a dog for the family," she said, trying to talk herself out of it. "I need to spend time–"

"Please. I couldn't stop thinking about Myles Jackman last night. His family deserve answers, don't they? And we're not going to get them by being at home."

Nasreen had to admit she'd been feeling guilty; she always did whenever she had free time during an investigation. The uniforms would be carrying out their roles, interviewing witnesses and informing the next of kin, although they didn't have a detectives' training. Things would invariably be over-looked. She watched Katerina struggling with Mina. "All right, I'll call Inspector Gupta, how's that? If he gives the green light to overtime, I'll come by and pick you up in an hour. But, if I do, we're both going to Terrence's barbecue later, deal?"

"Deal. See you in an hour."

Before she could tell Weekes it wasn't a foregone conclusion, her partner had hung up. "Shit!" she said, putting her phone in her bag. Getting into the back with Mina, she made a monster face, made her fingers look like claws and said, "Mina Maqsood," in a scary voice.

Her daughter looked up at her with wide, scared eyes. "Mummy, stop it!"

"Has Mina been a bad girl?" Her daughter squealed in both fear and delight, knowing a tickling was brewing. "This is what happens to bad girls." And tickled her under her armpits, loving Mina's laugh. Once the laughter had abated, she said, "Right, sit still so I can strap you in. We need to get home."

"You're working, aren't you?" Mina asked.

Her daughter was clever, a bit too clever. "For a bit, yeah," she replied, apologising to Katerina, "but we're still going to Uncle Terrence's for the barbecue. You don't mind driving her there, do you?" When Katerina said it was fine, she squeezed her nanny's shoulder in thanks. "I'm only going to be gone for a couple of hours, tops, I promise," she said to Mina, who looked mildly annoyed, crossing her arms.

Knowing Mina was strapped in, safe, she phoned Gupta, waiting for him to pick up. She was pretty sure she could've called Bukhari and asked him, however she didn't want to push any boundaries with him. Going to her immediate superior was best practise, and she was pretty much guaranteed a positive outcome with Gupta anyway. She spoke to him briefly, before he gave the go-ahead, saying he would call the chief constable there and let him know of her intentions. "Thanks," she said. "See you at Terrence's."

11

Assistant Commissioner Peter Franks usually hated press conferences. On any normal day he would do anything to avoid the photographers' flashing cameras, the noise and the endless questioning. Dressed in his immaculate uniform, he stood on a podium outside the city centre police station, waiting for his cue to start talking. He held his hand up, signalling the journalists to stop talking.

There were three main cameras focusing on him: Sky News, the BBC and ITV. He watched the Sky News cameraman's fingers work their way down from five to one. He'd spoken in front of the cameras countless times, yet he was still nervous.

When the fingers disappeared, he stared into the central camera's lens. "Good morning. I thank you all for being here at such short notice." He cleared his throat. "At precisely five o'clock this morning, the Northumbria Police carried out several raids on premises in and around this city. I'm delighted to report that our dedicated and highly trained firearms officers proved successful in apprehending twenty-five known drug dealers without firing a single shot. Narcotics with a street value of over five million pounds were seized during the raids on these properties around the city. A number of semi and automatic weapons were also recovered during the raids."

Franks picked up a glass of water and took two sips.

"This was a multi-force operation and it was in no small way thanks to our network of covert informants who brought us the information we needed to secure these apprehensions. We are indebted to these brave men and women, who risk their lives on a daily basis, and to the tireless efforts of our dedicated officers.

"Today marks the start of our war on illegal narcotics, and those who seek to distribute them. And to be clear, this is a war. That said, it's a war we're going to win. So, I have a message for any dealers out there: it's time to find another source of income, because your time is over. These raids are just the beginning." He let the last poignant sentence trail off, knowing it would have an impact. "I will now hand you over to Police and Crime Commissioner Charles Norris, who oversaw the operation."

Standing back from the podium, Franks let Norris step forward and take to the microphone. He listened to Norris reiterate what he'd already stated, only going into more detail on what was seized. The journalists were eating it up, taking notes in their paper pads and on their tablets, getting ready to write their stories for the Sunday papers, and broadcasts later in the day. Smiling behind Norris, Franks was ecstatic the raids had yielded greater results than he'd hoped; he'd expected a few kilos of cocaine, but nothing on this scale.

After Norris had finished speaking, he took to the podium again, the cameras flashing and the glint of sunshine hurting his eyes. "I have time for one or two questions."

The journalists rattled off questions, which Franks easily answered. They asked how the police had acquired a "network" of CIs? How long they'd had these CIs at their disposal? Why hadn't they used them before now? Who were their next targets? He had answers for every question, ready prepared.

He wasn't even breaking a sweat when a Sky crime correspondent asked, "Do you have any leads on the whereabouts of William Rothstein?"

A slight panic hit him. He gulped. "A full investigation is still ongoing at this time. And we're following up on every lead we have."

Another journalist, from the BBC, asked what happened to the drug dealer they'd caught on the marina a couple of months ago. "Lennox Garvey is currently in protective custody," Franks answered immediately. "He will be testifying against his former boss, William Rothstein, as and when the latter is apprehended. And that's all I have time for."

"One quick question, please, before you go, commissioner," a voice at the back of the mob shouted. "Do you know how many victims there were under the Harrison farm?"

"Detective Maqsood rescued twenty-four captives from the Harrison bunker. As for how many sex workers perished prior to the bunker's exposure, I'm afraid I'm not at liberty to say. The National Crime Agency is investigating this case as we speak. I've been assured by Director General Gary Holmes they'll leave no stone unturned; these facts will be discovered, and the loved ones of all those murdered will be informed. Given that the Harrisons lived at the property for sixteen years, the number is expected to be significantly higher than those rescued."

Taking a large gulp of water, he thanked everyone for their time again, turned and stepped down from the podium. Commissioner Norris signalled for him to follow. Franks obliged and walked back into the police station, while a couple of civilian employees brought in the wooden podium.

12

———

"You okay? You're looking a little peaky." Nasreen thought her partner might have been more communicative, since she'd just given up her Saturday afternoon on her request. But no, Weekes hadn't said much on the hour-long drive to the village.

"I'm fine!" Weekes was gazing out of her passenger window.

"You might've caught the same bug as Hazel," Nasreen suggested, noticing how jittery Weekes seemed; her knee was bobbing up and down, like she was nervous. Up ahead, she saw a signpost for the village. It was a nice drive along narrow country lanes. "We can always call this off, if you're not feeling well?"

"I said I'm fine."

Nasreen nodded. "Okay then." She caught a whiff of alcohol on her partner's breath. "Did you have a good night last night?" Her question wasn't subtle. They were going to interview the victim's parents, and she didn't want them smelling Weekes' breath.

"What?" Weekes asked, her eyes narrow. "Why do you care if I had a good night?"

"No reason. I'm just making conversation." Catching the same stale alcohol smell, Nasreen wrinkled her nose, concentrating on the sharp bend approaching. "We're going to be spending a lot of time together, you know. It'd be good to get to know each other, don't you think?"

"You've got a short memory – I already told you I've asked to be assigned a different training officer. I'm expecting Superintendent Bukhari to call me into his office any day now, so no, we don't need to get to know each other. Let's just get to the Jackmans' home, interview them and get this case started, shall we?"

Biting her tongue, Nasreen decided to focus all her energy on the case. She had neither the time, nor the inclination to win Weekes over. "You won't win any friends asking for a swap. The super won't like his orders being questioned, and if you do swap, who's to say you're going to like them?" Of course, she'd seen how Weekes had treated Terrence and Gupta, like they were rock stars.

"I don't care if people like me. I'm here to do a job, that's it. If colleagues become friends, so be it. It's not why I'm here."

Keeping her eye on the road, Nasreen asked, "Can I ask why you *are* here?"

"What is this? My interview?"

Sighing, Nasreen looked at her passenger. "Humour me. Come on, why'd you join the Force? I'm asking; I'm interested."

Weekes studied her. "Why did you join? You must get abuse all the time. Why do you do it?"

"Adrenaline junkie," she joked in response. "Nah, I've wanted to be a police officer for as long as I can remember. I joined the cadets when I was twelve, and I've been hooked ever since. I love it here. You get to meet some awesome people, and some awful ones, too."

"Like Cara Mooney, you mean? That awful?"

"Yep. She was one. If I'm honest, I felt more sorry for her

than anything. She had a terrible childhood. When I read her therapist's notes, I remember thinking if I'd had as awful an upbringing, I'd probably be as evil as she was."

"And what about Beatrice Harrison?"

Approaching the village, Nasreen glanced at Weekes. "What about her?"

"Was she one of the worst people you've met? I mean, I watched all your interviews, read all the articles. You must hate her for slicing your cheek like that, surely."

"I don't hate anyone. But she's as close as I've ever come to hating someone, yeah. I'm just glad I managed to get Danny out of there in time. Beatrice Harrison's paid her dues now." It wasn't entirely true. There were times when she looked in the mirror, wishing Beatrice Harrison was alive, so she could exact her own revenge, and not have Steven Dyer save her. "So? Why did you join?"

"It seemed like the most natural progression after leaving the army, I guess. What? Were you expecting a big 'to help people' speech? Look, I like helping people, sure, it's what I've done my whole career. But now it's about me and doing something I'm good at. I'll be a great detective, you'll see."

"I'm sure, if you can follow orders."

"You need to take a left up here, go a hundred metres up that road and hang right. It's at the end of the road," Weekes said, pointing. "And I can follow orders fine, by the way."

Three minutes – a left and a right – later, Nasreen slowed the car to a stop outside a gorgeous palatial country house. The property was protected by a perimeter wall and wrought-iron gates. She drove up to the gates, wound her window down and reached out, pressing the intercom button. "Detective Sergeant Maqsood to see Mr and Mrs Jackman, please," she said, as a buzzer sounded, and the gates opened automatically. She heard

Weekes whistle, impressed. "Yeah, I know," she said, looking up at the huge mansion while driving along the gravel driveway towards the front door. "How the other half live."

There were so many windows. Eight along the ground floor, eight on the first and four on the second. The house must be worth a couple of million, she guessed. Stopping behind a Bentley, she took the keys out and looked at Weekes. "You're here to learn, right? Let me do the talking," she said, opening her door. De-creasing her suit with her hands, Nasreen waited for her partner to join her. "This is always the most important interview in any investigation," she said, walking towards the red front door. "It's important to build a rapport with the next of kin, because they'll usually be the biggest help. If they're not involved."

To her surprise, Weekes didn't make a snide remark. She didn't need to knock, as a tall, wiry man with a tiny little moustache opened the door, dressed in a tuxedo. "We're here to see Mr–"

"Jackman, yes, I know," he replied, in the stuffiest of Her Majesty's accents. "Please, follow me. I'm afraid Mrs Jackman has been taken ill, so you will be meeting with Mr Jackman only, Detective Maqsood."

The interior was exquisite, like something out of *Downton Abbey*, she thought, taking in the winding staircase, the crystal chandeliers and obviously expensive red carpets. Upstairs, downstairs, she thought, following the "butler" through the reception room, taking a left, and stopping behind Jeeves as he knocked on a thick wooden door. Nasreen turned and looked at Weekes, her eyebrows raised.

"Detective Maqsood?"

Nasreen turned back to find a short, round man in the doorway. Expecting someone taller, she tried to hide her shock by holding out her hand. "Mr Jackman, I'm so sorry for your loss," she said, shaking hands with him, which wasn't how she usually greeted interviewees. She'd been caught off guard. "I know this is a really bad time, but we have a few questions for you about Myles."

Before she knew it, she was sat in what could only be described as a library. There were books everywhere. Every wall was a bookshelf. In the middle of the huge room was Mr Jackman's desk, a Victorian golden oak antique. Nasreen was sat in a comfortable chair in front of him, with Weekes sat to her left. "I need you to know we're doing everything we can to bring the suspect who did this to justice," she looked him in the eye, not daring to avert her gaze for a second, "but we need your help in order to do so."

Weekes took out a notepad and pen, resting it on her knee, pen poised. "Do you know of anyone who might want to harm your son, Mr Jackman?"

Wanting to roll her eyes, but resisting the urge, Nasreen watched Mr Jackman for his response. She could tell a lot about interviewees by their facial expressions. He looked puzzled. There was more to it; he looked tired, sad and uncomfortable.

"I've been thinking that myself all day. Wracking my brain. And I can't think of a single person who hated Myles. He was a good boy." Jackman's eyes glazed over. "Why would someone want to do this to him?" A sob escaped him, before he put a hand up in apology and took a deep breath. "I'm sorry!"

"Anyone he's had arguments with over the years?" Weekes asked, probing.

Nasreen shot her partner a glare. "It's okay, Mr Jackman, in your own time," she said, not wanting Weekes' eagerness to build a barrier. "I know it's difficult."

"Let's start with Myles being questioned over an assault," Weekes suggested.

"That? That was nothing. He got drunk, got into a fight at the pub down the road. It was over before it even began. He's friends with the guy. He's friends with everyone in this village. You won't find his kill... You won't find him here, detective." He picked up his tumbler of whisky and took a long sip.

"Can I have his name, please?"

Nasreen glared at her partner again, asked her host to excuse them and walked with Weekes out of the room, closing the door behind her. "What did I say just now, huh? Let me do the questioning," she whispered angrily. "You're destroying my rapport. You don't go marching in there asking hostile questions. You ask open-ended, probing questions first and build up to that if you need to. He's grieving, and co-operating." She put her hands on her head in frustration. "Go back to the car and wait for me, can you do that? Or are you going to find another way of wrecking this case?"

"All right, all right." Weekes held her palms out in a placating manner. "I was just trying to help. I'll meet you back at the car, keep your hair on."

Watching her partner walk away, Nasreen said, "Oh, and there's a packet of mints in my car door. I can smell the alcohol on your breath." She took a deep breath herself, before going back into Jackman's library.

"I apologise for the interruption," she said, sitting back down. "I had to send my partner on an errand." Feeling for him, she took out her notepad and a pen. "It would be really helpful if you could tell me what happened. If only to rule people out of our enquiries."

"I'm telling you, you're wasting your time with this." Jackman took another sip of his whisky. "It was stupid, really, a small scuffle in our local. Myles and Aaron are friends now; there was no harm done."

"Aaron?"

"Beckwith. His family live over the other side of the village. I can't believe we're talking about this. It happened four years ago. No one was charged with anything. You should be out there looking for the real suspect, detective."

"Humour me, please. So, what was the dispute about?"

"I'll give you three guesses," he said, placing his tumbler on the desk in front of him, "and you should only need one."

"A girl."

"You got it! Zoe was seeing Aaron at the time. Then she started seeing Myles, and Aaron found out. You can guess the rest. They both had separate groups of friends, who all got involved, and before anyone knew what was happening, the pub erupted. The police were called. Because no one was really hurt – Myles got a fat lip – they didn't take it any further. Honestly, detective, that's it! That's the story. Aaron and Myles are good friends now. Even Zoe and Aaron chose to remain friends."

"This Zoe? Is Myles still seeing her?"

"I think so, although we haven't seen her in a while, and it's Zoe Needham, by the way. She's got a flat in the city. Myles stays... Used to stay over sometimes during the week, but mostly she stays here at the weekend. She has a high-powered job in a finance company. I'm sorry! I should've asked if you'd like a drink."

"I'm fine, thanks. Was Myles staying over last night? Is that why he was in the city?" She was getting somewhere, she was sure of it.

"No, not last night. He was due to meet someone there. Business. I think a prospective client, or current client, I forget what he told me, sorry."

"I don't suppose you know where, or with who, do you? We're looking to confirm his movements leading up to two o'clock."

"Is that what time he...?" Jackman trailed off, not being able to say it out loud.

Nasreen affirmed his question. "I can't tell you, I'm sorry. But he might've written it on his calendar; he was very organised. Come, let's go take a look." He stood, grabbing a set of keys from his desk drawer.

13

———

Weekes reached over the driver's seat and fumbled in the door's pocket for some mints. She saw her supervisor coming out of Jackman's house carrying a laptop. Popping the mint in her mouth, she sucked on it, hoping the taste would cover up her alcohol breath. It wasn't good, being called out on only her second day on the job. "You were in there for ages," she said, as Nasreen sat behind the wheel. "Did you get much out of him?"

"Lots." Nasreen placed the laptop on the back seat. "We've got our next interview in the local pub around the corner. The guy he had the fight with was Aaron Beckwith. Myles' girlfriend's name is Zoe Needham; she lives in the city. Myles was meeting a prospective client there on Thursday night, apparently. We've got some leads, at least." She used the PNC on the dashboard to look up Aaron Beckwith. "Colourful."

"What is?" Weekes asked, reading Aaron's sheet. "Another nice guy by the sound of it. GBH, ABH, affray, breaching the peace. And there I was thinking village life was dull."

"Not a chance," Nasreen scoffed, putting the key in the ignition. "These little villages can be cesspools. Anyway, Mr

Jackman told me Aaron will be watching the FA Cup final in the pub. He said the lads always have a few beers before a match. Are you up for this? You can resist buying a drink, can't you?"

Ouch! thought Weekes. It was the kind of catty remark she would make herself; she was impressed. "I think so, unless I start thinking about you, then it's game over." She made sure she smiled when she said it. Fortunately, it seemed Sergeant Maqsood took it as banter. "Well? What are we waiting for? Let's go!"

On the way to the King's Head pub on West Street, Weekes watched the world go by, while Nasreen drove. It was a picturesque village, complete with its own church, convenience store, butchers and greengrocers. Weekes couldn't understand how a small greengrocer could survive in this climate, having to compete with the major supermarkets. The streets were cobbled, slowing traffic to below twenty miles per hour within the village perimeter. "The village seems nicer than its inhabitants," Weekes mused.

"Yeah. A couple of friends of mine grew up in villages just like this one. Everyone knows everyone else's business. Personally, I'd pass."

The pub appeared on their right. Weekes could see drinkers sat on benches outside the front. The car park behind the pub was a quarter full, making it easy for Nasreen to find a space near the back doors. Weekes was nervous, not knowing if Nasreen was going to write her up in her report. "Hey, before we go in," she started, as Nasreen switched the engine off and went to open her door. "You're not going to report me to Inspector Gupta, are you? I promise, it won't happen again – I've learnt my lesson."

"Of course I'm not." Nasreen sighed. "I'm no grass, Weekes. You made a mistake, that's all. And no harm done. But please don't let it happen again, or I'll have to."

"Oh, it won't. Thank you."

Nasreen shrugged. "Now, shall we go speak to Aaron Beckwith? Can I trust you to keep your mouth shut?"

Weekes mimicked zipping her mouth closed. Not having to worry about a blemish on her record so soon after starting her new job was a weight off her shoulders. While sat in the car waiting for Nasreen to emerge, she'd had a knot in her stomach. She was better than this, she thought, deep down knowing she had to sort her drinking out, and soon. "Let's go!" she said, opening her door.

Walking along the front of the pub, past a couple of groups of lads sat on benches, Weekes heard a couple of them comment on her looks, and not in a bad way. She smiled, liking the look of one of them, who was broad shouldered with his top off, pint of lager in front of him. It wasn't bad to like the attention, especially knowing they'd run a mile knowing she only had one leg. Beckwith wasn't one of the lads, she noticed.

Inside, she joined Nasreen at the bar. Leaning with her back against it, she scanned the open-plan room. Beckwith was sat on a table with five friends, three guys and two girls. The cup match was showing on a huge television hung on the wall. Chelsea vs Manchester United. "There he is," she said, nodding at his table.

Following Nasreen, she stood slightly back at Beckwith's table, listening to how her supervisor spoke to him. All she wanted to do was get stuck in.

"Aaron Beckwith?" Nasreen took out her ID wallet and showed him. "We'd like to ask you a couple of questions, please."

"About Myles?"

There was a palpable atmosphere around the table. Weekes noted the long glum faces. One of the girls had red puffy eyes, like she'd been crying, which was understandable. Unlike the lads outside, Aaron and his friends weren't there enjoying themselves.

"I'm afraid so. Let's go out the back. It's just a few questions, nothing to be worried about."

Out in the back garden, Weekes joined them on a rickety wooden bench that had passed its best by date. When Weekes sat down the table creaked.

"Is it true? Was he dragged around a car park?" Beckwith asked.

He was a good-looking guy, she noted, with dark hair and an impressive physique; he obviously worked out, when he wasn't at the pub. Weekes glanced over at Nasreen. How did he know the details of Jackman's death?

"Don't be surprised," he said. "This is a village. Everyone knows everything about everyone. Zoe called me last night, told me what the police said. Is it true?"

"It's true," Nasreen replied. "I'm sorry!"

Beckwith sniffed; he looked like he was about to cry. "I only saw him on Wednesday. We were supposed to be meeting up to watch the footy." He looked down. "I can't believe he's dead. I've never known anyone die before."

Nasreen put her hand on his on the tabletop. "We're going to catch this guy, I promise." She paused for effect. "But we're going to need your help, Aaron."

"My help? What can I do? I'm mates with him, sure, but I didn't know him that well." Something seemed to register in him. "Unless... You don't think... You think I had something to do with it? Is that why you're here? You think–"

"No. We don't think that, not at all. Your name came up on a police report from four years ago. We're just following up on it."

"That stupid fight! Look, we're friends now. Sure, we had a little bust up ages ago. We shook hands a couple of days after."

"It was over Zoe Needham, wasn't it? And Myles is still with her, right?" The tone was there, in her voice. "That must've pissed you off, huh?"

"You've got to be fucking kidding me!" he hissed. "Yeah, it pissed me off, it did. For all of five minutes. Zoe's a twat, okay? She uses blokes. You'll be hard pushed to find a guy around here she hasn't been with. I forgave Myles for fucking things up between me and Zoe. Since then, we meet up most weekends, watch the footy, go out for beers, the usual. I had fuck all to do with it."

Nasreen put her palms out. "It's all right, we're not accusing you. Can you think of anyone who might want to hurt him? Anyone he might've annoyed?"

"That could be a long list. I mean, I don't want to speak ill of the dead, or anything, but Myles could be a twat, too, which is why he was so well-suited to Zoe. Two twats together."

"What exactly does that mean? A twat, how?"

"He was a bully. I wasn't with him at school, but I've seen how he treats his ex-classmates. He bullies some of them, even now. Some of my mates were in the same year as him; they've told me stories. You've got ten, maybe fifteen people to question right there."

Weekes continued listening, watching. He seemed genuinely upset.

"What school did he go to?"

"Beacon Downs. Most of the kids in this village go there."

"Do you know any names? Are there any that stick out to you?"

"A couple, maybe. Irwin Landers; he's a local lad, drinks in here occasionally. And Richard Pryce. Yeah, he's a strange one, he is. Myles loved picking on that ret... Sorry! Mentally challenged one. He's a glass collector here, and he volunteers at the animal shelter. They're the two that stick out."

Weekes scribbled the names down in her notepad. It was

interesting listening to her supervisor asking Beckwith questions. Although he started the interview with his back up, Nasreen soon calmed him down, extracting as much information as she could. Weekes had to admit, she was impressed.

"It would be a big help if you could verify your whereabouts between 11pm on Thursday and 6am Friday," Nasreen said, to his nod of understanding. "So we can eliminate you from the investigation. And if you have someone who can corroborate it, all the better."

"I was here until half-twelve. I'll be on their CCTV. And then my girlfriend stayed over at mine. Will that do?"

"You live locally?"

"With my parents. But they were in bed by the time I got back, so they can't say if I was in or not. Paige's inside now, if you want her to tell you where I was?" He looked past Weekes, stood up. "Hey, grab Paige, will you?"

It had been an eventful afternoon. By the time she'd finished taking notes, Weekes had a good list of names to go on. Their list of potential witnesses and suspects was growing. Knowing that Myles Jackman was a bully opened up avenues of interest. There was a lot of bad blood in this village, she thought, thanking Beckwith and Paige for their co-operation.

"You're not planning on leaving the area any time soon, are you?" Nasreen asked both interviewees. She received two shakes of their heads. "Good. We might need you to come in for a formal interview. Until then, take my card. If you think of anything that might be important to this investigation, please call me. Any time, day or night."

Walking to the car, Weekes smiled at the guy on the bench outside the front of the pub. She heard more comments of how fit she was from his mates. "You were combative with him," she said to her supervisor. "Thought you said to start off nice?"

"He has motive. He's about the right height and build. He

knew the victim, lives in the same village. I don't think he's our guy, but I'm not ruling him out. What you don't do is get the next of kin's back up, without good reason. Do you understand? Mr Jackman will probably be our best source of information."

Weekes got in the car. "Where to now?" she asked, tapping on the PNC on the dashboard, waiting for Nasreen to give her a name to look up.

"Terrence's barbecue."

14

———

"Why did I agree to this?" Weekes asked. "I hate these things."

Nasreen put on the handbrake, switched off the engine and looked out of her window at Terrence's house. It was a lovely-looking four-bedroom detached home in a middle-class neighbourhood. Dominique Johnson, Terrence's wife, was an avid gardener, which was obvious when Nasreen admired the beautiful front lawn, complete with plants and flowers in beds around it. There was a trellis on the front of the house, between the windows, with ivy growing up it. "You'll enjoy it when we get inside. Come on, let's go!"

Having driven the police car back to the station, Nasreen had driven her own car here. She'd packed a change of clothing. Opening the boot, she took out her bag and met Weekes, before walking along the driveway towards the front door. "You'll like Dom; she's lovely," she said to Weekes, knocking on the door. "Really welcoming."

Dominique opened the door, dressed in a pair of dark blue short shorts, a white T-shirt and flip-flops. Her long, dark hair was down. Nasreen thought she looked stunning. "I hope we're not too late," she said, leaning in and kissing her host on both cheeks. "You look great, by the way." She was invited into the hallway, Weekes following her inside. "Dom, this is Weekes."

"Alicia, please." Weekes held out her hand.

"Okay, Alicia." Dominique kissed Weekes awkwardly on both cheeks. "Make yourself at home. We only have one rule at these barbecues: no case talk. Is that all right with you? This house is a crime-free home; I don't want Terrence talking about it, and I don't want his friends and colleagues talking about it either."

Nasreen, bag in hand, followed Dominique and Weekes into the kitchen, where a few of her fellow officers stood in small groups talking. "I'm going to get changed," she said to them both. "It's okay to use your bathroom, Dom?"

"Wait! You're leaving?" Weekes asked, terrified.

"You're fine here, Alicia." Dominique put her arm around Weekes' shoulder and walked her out into the garden, where the majority of her colleagues were.

Nasreen went upstairs to the main bathroom, locked the door and changed into her shalwar kameez, which was mostly grey with a mid-blue trim. The sleeves were blue with an embroidered pattern interwoven into the fabric. Satisfied with how she looked – bar the scar covering her cheek – she unlocked the door and walked downstairs, through the kitchen and into the large garden, where she saw Terrence manning the barbecue.

"Mummy!"

Nasreen bent down to accept Mina's great big hug. "Have you been a good girl for Auntie Dom and Uncle Terrence?"

"She's been great." Dominique stroked Mina's hair. "You've had fun with Dana and Vincent, haven't you, Mina?" Her host smiled. "Katerina stayed for an hour or so. She said she had to get back for Dot."

For a minute there, Nasreen had forgotten all about Dot, the poor thing. Taken to a new home and left alone for a few hours. She resolved to make it up to the wee dog the next day. "Thanks so much for looking after her," she said to her host.

When Mina went running off to find Vincent, Dom and Terrence's son, Nasreen looked for Weekes, hoping she wasn't stood in a corner by herself somewhere. Her question was answered when she saw Weekes' face in amongst a group of five of her workmates. She smiled at her partner, gave a little wave, but when Weekes held up a large glass of wine in salute, her smile faded. It felt like her partner was rubbing her nose in it.

15

———————

Nasreen couldn't sleep. Lying on her back, she stared up at the ceiling. Weekes had a nerve; she'd spent the rest of the evening getting more and more drunk. Her partner had sure been the life and soul of the party, making everyone laugh. Nasreen had been surprised at just how sociable Weekes could be; it was an eye opener. Being so stiff at work, Nasreen had never expected her partner to wow her friends and colleagues, and yet she had. Of course, they didn't know Weekes had a drinking problem.

There was a whimpering coming from the lounge. Knowing she wasn't going to drift off any time soon, she pulled the duvet back and sat up. Another whimper. Putting on her slippers, Nasreen walked out of her bedroom, along the hallway and into the lounge, where Dot was wagging her tail. "Hey, you," she whispered, sitting down in front of the cage. She carefully opened the cage door, trying her hardest not to wake Mina. "You're just the cutest thing," she said, when Dot hopped onto her lap.

"Can I join you?" Katerina whispered, in her pyjamas. "I can't sleep."

"Course you can." Nasreen was stroking Dot, who loved the attention.

"I want to stroke Dot, too."

Nasreen looked at her daughter in her pyjamas; she was too cute to say no to. "Come in, then, darling," she whispered to Mina, who ran in and sat down next to her, trying to garner Dot's attention.

"She's the cutest," Mina whispered, looking for her mum's approval.

"She sure is. Although, I think you might be the cutest one here. What do you think, Kat?"

"Definitely Mina. She's a lot less hairy for starters."

Mina chuckled. "Hey, why are we all whispering?"

"We're trying not to wake Mina up." Nasreen winked at her.

"But, *I am* Mina," added her daughter, her face straight, deadpan.

"Oh! There you are!" Nasreen replied, shocking Mina with a tickle under the armpits, Dot clinging on to her for dear life.

She spent the next hour making a fuss of the dog, while keeping Mina amused until she fell asleep on her lap.

It was an unexpected family moment. Nasreen was mindful of her job taking time away from watching her Mina grow up. And if she let it, her job would. There were always crimes that needed solving, and more worryingly, it seemed, always murders that required investigating. She would have the next day off, spend the whole day with Mina and Dot. Katerina was out all day. And then, first thing on Monday, it was on. She and her drunkard partner would start investigating Myles Jackman's murder.

DAY 4
MONDAY, MAY 21ST

16

———

Weekes sighed, watching footage of cars coming and going. Having messed up her weekend and shown herself up, she'd set her alarm early, even for her. After she'd paid for the taxi home on Saturday night, she'd thought it a good idea to go to her local. Of course she'd bumped into Brian, apologised profusely for her behaviour, and had spent the rest of the night with him. She was so stupid, destructive. And she'd paid for her stupidity on Sunday morning.

With a hangover, she'd visited her parents for Sunday lunch, where her dad told her she looked awful. And she did, with bags under her eyes, dry skin, chapped lips. It was at lunch she'd decided not to touch a drop of alcohol. True to her word, she hadn't. And last night, she'd tossed and turned in bed, finally falling asleep at around 2am. Her alarm went off two hours later.

Her focus was interrupted when she saw Nasreen walk in wearing a tailored grey suit, not unlike her others; this one was closer fitting. Weekes reached into her drawer and pulled out a pack of chewing gum, put one in her mouth and dropped the pack back in her drawer. "Morning!" she said to Nasreen, who sat down at her desk without saying a word.

It was going to be a long day, she decided. It *was* her fault, though. "I've managed to follow the truck for three more miles before I lose it again." She waited for Nasreen to walk around her desk and stand behind her.

"Show me on the map." Nasreen leaned in close to her, probably trying to smell alcohol on her breath.

"Here." Weekes pointed then ran her finger along the physical map, ending at a junction with four exits, which was paused on the screen. "It's worse now. He could've taken any route, and three of them lead to country roads with no cameras on them. Sorry! Looks like we've hit a dead end on this."

"It might not matter," Inspector Gupta interrupted from behind her. "Cyber's got us into the victim's laptop. Here's the password. And I've just got off the phone with a Sergeant Upton, who says he's found Jackman's car."

"Really?" Nasreen turned to Gupta. "At the prospective client's offices?"

"No, a multi-storey car park," Gupta replied. "And before you ask, it has CCTV. You can expect their footage sometime this morning." He handed Nasreen the laptop in a see-through plastic bag.

Weekes pulled out some latex gloves from her drawer and put them on, then took the laptop from Nasreen, placing it on her desk. When it was out of its bag, she lifted the lid and switched it on, waiting for the screensaver to appear. "Where do you want me to start?"

"Social media," Nasreen replied. "Facebook, Twitter, Instagram, whatever he's on. The suspect knows him. If I were a betting person, I'd put money on it."

Finding the Facebook icon, Weekes clicked on it and scoured Jackman's posts. It was a step up from watching CCTV footage, a bit more interesting. The screen was beginning to affect her eyes, which were grainy and sore from lack of sleep.

17

While Weekes was working her way through Myles Jackman's laptop, Nasreen sat down at her desk. She picked up her landline phone, dialled nine for an outside line and tapped in Jackman's girlfriend's number. It took four rings before Zoe Needham asked who was calling. Nasreen identified herself to the distraught girlfriend and spent a couple of minutes talking to her, before inviting her to the station for an interview. "Zoe Needham's on her way now," she said to Weekes, who was engrossed in the laptop.

In the meantime, she decided to check out Jackman's school: Beacon Downs Academy. Clicking on Google, Nasreen typed in the school's name. A colourful website popped up; it was a nice-looking site in purple and orange. Under the history tab, she read that the secondary school was once called Beacon Downs Community School, when it boasted the best attainment results in Sussex, up until the mid-1990s, when results dropped sharply.

It was then known as Beacon Downs College, extending its curriculum to seventeen and eighteen-year-olds. She read that three years ago, Beacon Downs College went into special measures, subsequently joining forces with a Sussex university, to become Beacon Downs Academy, where results were back up with the top private schools in the league table.

Picking up the phone, she dialled the school's number. When she got through to a receptionist, she identified herself and asked if there were any teachers there who would remember Myles Jackman. The receptionist replied there were three and gave the names.

Armed with that information, Nasreen booked appointments with two of them after school hours. The headteacher was relatively new, so no good to her.

Next, she looked up the two locals – Irwin Landers and Richard Pryce – that Aaron Beckwith had mentioned Jackman bullied at school. Both were clean, according to the PNC. All she could find on them were home addresses and vehicle registrations. Neither drove a pickup truck. Neither had priors, cautions, nothing. Her gut told her they weren't the suspect she was looking for. If experience had taught her anything, it was that violent criminals like The Dragger almost always had form. However, she was willing to concede that there were always exceptions; some people were great at concealing their true selves. "I've booked interviews at the school this afternoon," she informed Weekes. "Have you found anything?"

"Nothing. Jackman liked cats, is about all I can tell you. He's got about fifty funny videos of them. There's nothing of note here, though. He liked taking photos when he was out and about, loved showing people his food. No arguments with friends. It's pretty boring, actually."

"Your first interview's downstairs, Nas!" Terrence shouted.

"Thanks." Nasreen put her PC into sleep mode. "Come on, Weekes, you're in on this one." She picked up her suit jacket, put it on and walked with her partner through the open-plan office and into the hallway, towards the lift.

18

Zoe Needham was a pretty little thing, Nasreen noticed. Despite the bags under her eyes from crying herself to sleep, she still managed to look beautiful. It was amazing what a little make-up could do. With long, dark hair up in an attractive bun, a pretty face with a cute button nose and big, brown eyes, Nasreen could see why both Aaron Beckwith and Myles Jackman were attracted to her. She was so dainty, couldn't have been any more than five-three.

"Please help us find this guy, Zoe," Weekes pleaded. "You don't want him out there, free to kill someone else, do you?"

"I've already told you everything I know. How do you expect me to know who that is? He's wearing a scarf over his face." She threw the photo on the table. "Don't you think if I knew, I'd tell you?"

Nasreen reached across the table and held Zoe's hands. "It's fine, Zoe, honestly. My partner's just keen to find this guy, that's all. We know you're trying to help." She would have words with Weekes after the interview. "Has Myles ever told you about arguing with anyone? Anyone who might hold a grudge against him?"

"No, there's no one like that." Zoe sniffed. "Everyone loved Myles. Whenever we went out everyone was lovely to him. I mean, you know about how we met, right? I was seeing Aaron back then. There was a fight and all, but they were friends again a couple of days after. Since then, though, I've never heard him mention anything like that, honest." Her eyes beseeched Nasreen to believe her.

"Zoe, did Myles ever mention bullying his classmates?" Weekes asked.

"What?" Zoe turned her attention to Weekes. "Seriously? You think this masked guy's one of his classmates? Get real! You don't go murdering someone because they bullied you; that's crap."

"Some do, actually," Nasreen corrected. "Bullying can be a huge motivator."

"I was at school with Myles. And yeah, he picked on some people, but there's no way this is one of them. I picked on some girls at school, who didn't? It doesn't mean I'm going to get murdered by one of them."

"You know, there are more people in the photo this suspect showed Myles," Weekes said. "We don't know who's in it, or why he's after them, but that's what it looks like right now. I don't want to scare you, Zoe, but there could be more murders to follow. So, please, think, is there anyone at all you can think of who wants to hurt him?"

"Oh, great! Are you saying he could be after me now?"

"Until we know who else is in that photo, we honestly don't know," Weekes confessed. "Probably not, but–"

"Listen, this guy's holding all the cards right now," Nasreen interrupted. "He knows who he's after, and we're playing catch-up. Has he had any arguments with clients he's told you about? Anyone like that? It doesn't matter how big, or how small the row."

"Wait!" Zoe looked up, as if searching her brain. "This is probably nothing, but when we were at school, he had an argument with the IT teacher, Mr Sanders. He was almost expelled over it... And a couple of years ago, Myles did some work for him, but Mr Sanders refused to pay, saying he wasn't happy with his work. They reached a compromise in the end but Myles said he wouldn't work with him again."

Nasreen caught Weekes' attention. She nodded her understanding. "That's good, Zoe," she said. "In fact, that's great. He's one of our next interviews."

"Hang on, you don't really think this is Mr Sanders, do you?"

"Honestly, we don't know, but I'm putting my money on whoever this is knowing Myles in one way or another. I can tell you this: the more we know about Myles the better."

"Can you think of anyone else?" When Zoe shook her head, Weekes asked, "What about Richard Pryce? What can you tell us about him?"

"Dickhead Pryce?" Zoe smirked, then let the smirk drop. "Sorry! Force of habit. It's what everyone calls him. Either that or Pryce Winning Dick."

"Why did everyone dislike him, Zoe? What is it about him?" Nasreen asked, not feeling so sorry for her.

"No one disliked him, not really," Zoe confessed, retracting her hands. "He was just a bit weird, that's all. He was this awkward, painfully shy bloke, you know? Never at ease with anyone. At lunch he used to just walk around the playground on his own. Then Myles and his mates took a shine to him, teasing him. He didn't deserve half of what happened to him."

"And yet you still call him Dickhead Pryce," Weekes commented, disdain in her voice. "Myles and his mates are bullies, Zoe."

"I know," Zoe replied, eyes down. A smile formed, as she looked back up. "But they were so funny."

Nasreen tried to hide her disgust. Having been bullied relentlessly herself, she knew how hurtful it could be, and how bitter and hateful it could make the victim. "What happened to him? Tell us what your boyfriend used to do to him."

"Silly, childish stuff, you know?" Zoe cracked a smile. "One time, we were playing hockey, and we all heard a boy yell out. When we checked out the boys playing rugby, we saw Dick... Richard with his shorts and pants around his ankles. Myles pulled them down before yelling out." The smile vanished. "It was hilarious, everyone thought so."

"Do you know what happened to him after school?" Weekes asked.

"Nothing happened to him. As far as I know he still lives with his parents on that awful, scabby farm. Myles told me he volunteers at the animal shelter near the village. Oh, and he's a glass collector at the King's Head. He was voted the least likely to succeed; I guess we called him on that."

Nasreen had heard enough. At first, she'd felt sorry for Zoe, had wanted to comfort her. Now, having heard her meanness first-hand, she wanted out of this room. Thanking her interviewee for her time, she asked for more details of the animal shelter before excusing Zoe, and warning her not to leave the city, that she might be required to answer more questions. The worst part of it was knowing Zoe felt no remorse for how she and her classmates had treated Richard Pryce.

"I had more questions to ask," Weekes moaned. "We didn't ask her about Irwin Landers."

"I know; I wanted to ask her about him," Nasreen confessed, "but I couldn't watch her smiling any more. Did you see that? No guilt, no remorse."

"I wanted to smack her off her chair. If we weren't looking for a tall, stocky guy, I'd have bets on her being our suspect; she's cold enough, for sure." Standing up, Weekes looked down at Nasreen. "So, where to now?"

"We're going back to the village. I think we've just scratched the surface. I bet if we ask around, all kinds of stories will come tumbling out. And I'm really interested to see what this IT teacher has to say."

19

———

"Just tell us what happened, Mr Sanders," Weekes said, observing the tall, wiry man across his desk in the IT room of the school. From the moment she met him, she knew there was something off about him. He was too self-confident, too full of his own self-worth. "We know you had an altercation with Myles."

"Sure, we had a row," Sanders replied. "People have rows all the time. Did whoever told you about it mention that we reached a compromise? I bet they didn't."

"Actually, they did," Nasreen said. "They also said that your 'altercation' got physical. Where did the row take place, Mr Sanders?"

"I don't believe this." Sanders stood and glared down at Nasreen. "Are you trying to finger me for killing Myles? This is ridiculous. We had a row over services Myles delivered, or rather didn't deliver, I should say. I wasn't happy with it and told him I wouldn't pay until he came through. And yes, I pushed him, and he shoved me back."

"Where did this happen?" Weekes had her pen in hand.

"A café. I'll give you the name and address if you want?"

Weekes turned her pad around and handed him her pen. There was nothing she liked about Sanders; he epitomised everything she disliked about human beings, which was a long list. He was arrogant, conceited and patronising. He'd tried to patronise her earlier in the interview. "Thank you," she said, reading the café name and address. "Continue, please."

"Continue what? That's it. It got a little physical, someone in the café stood between us and we both calmed down. Ten minutes later we were sat at a table talking about how we could remedy the situation. I told Myles what I needed doing, he agreed to do it, and I agreed to pay him the full amount. It's what he should've done anyway. Two weeks later, he completed, and I immediately transferred the money across to his account."

"And that's it? That's the last time you saw him?" Nasreen asked.

"Yes! I probably shouldn't say this, but I didn't like him. He was always high. I don't know why I hired him in the first place." Sitting back down, he paused, studying Weekes. "That's a lie. I do know why: he was a first-rate programmer. He's easily the most talented student I've ever taught. In fact, he taught me a few things."

Picking up the notepad and pen, Weekes said, "He was always high? How do you know that? Earlier you said you hadn't seen him for years after he graduated."

"This is a small place, detective. He left quite a legacy. All the teachers hear rumours about him, even now. And the younger students talk about him all the time – they seem to look up to him, revere him."

"And what do they say, exactly?" Nasreen checked Weekes' reaction.

"The most popular story they tell is how Myles and his mates gave one of the teachers a nervous breakdown. And it's partly true; they hounded Tim until he quit."

Looking across at her supervisor, Weekes, poised with her pen, asked, "Tim?"

"McClennon. If you're looking for people who might want to do Myles harm, I can write a few down, if you'd like? But I'll need a bigger piece of paper than that. He bullied so many students here. In fact, I can show you." He pulled open a drawer in his desk and produced a yearbook. "Here! This is the 2001 graduation yearbook, the year Myles left."

Taking the book from Sanders, Weekes opened the cover. The first double page had small photos of the year group. There were eighty photos included. Finding Irwin Landers, she pointed at his photo, Sanders glancing down at it. "What can you tell us about him?" she asked, noting his raised eyebrows.

"Irwin?" Sanders sat back in his chair. "He made the fatal mistake of coming out at school. And when he did, it was open season on him. Myles and his lot were relentless; they made his life hell for the remaining three years. In his final year, Irwin was absent so much, he almost had to retake the year."

"Forgive me, but if you all knew this bullying was going on, why didn't you intervene?" Nasreen asked. "Why let him go through hell?"

"Knowing and seeing are two very different things. Myles wasn't stupid; he wouldn't overtly bully anyone. I didn't once see it happening. I heard the odd comment, sure, but never saw any physical bullying. I knew it was happening, and there was nothing I could do about it. I couldn't go pointing my finger at Myles, not with how scared the headteacher was of his dad; it would've been career suicide."

Weekes nodded her understanding. He was right: unless someone witnessed bullying, it was like it never happened. "Why? What's his dad to this school?"

"The biggest donor, and head of the board. Had I accused Myles of bullying anyone, my job would've been for the chop.

It's cowardly, I know, but I have bills to pay. If Mr Jackman finds out I'm talking to you about him, he'll have me fired. And I don't want to lose this job."

"Relax, Mr Sanders, he won't find out," Nasreen reassured him.

Weekes clicked the top of her pen, housing it inside her suit jacket, before packing her notepad in the opposing inside pocket.

"Just so we can eliminate you from our enquiries, can I ask where you were in the early hours on Friday morning?" Nasreen asked. "Between midnight and six o'clock in the morning? It will be a big help."

"Asleep. At home."

"Alone?"

"I knew you were going to ask that. And yes, alone. I have no one to corroborate my alibi, I'm sorry. I did go to my local convenience store just before I went to bed. About half eleven, I'd say. Is that any help?"

Weekes waited for Nasreen to take note of the convenience store's address and thank him for his time. Her supervisor handed him a card. Walking to their next interview along the corridor, Weekes asked, "Well? What do you think?"

"There's no way he's our guy. He's about fifty pounds too light. You saw the footage, the suspect's broad shouldered. He's too skinny to be our guy. Let's find out what Myles' other teachers have to say, shall we?"

20

———

Weekes put on her suit jacket. "I'm off home. Night."

Nasreen said goodnight, watched Weekes walk out of the office, and went back to her monitor. Her colleagues, including Terrence and Gupta, were sat at their desks, mostly preparing to leave for the day. The footage from the multi-storey car park where Myles Jackman's car was found had come through earlier in the afternoon. Looking up at the clock, she saw it was half past five. Already late, she phoned Katerina and informed her she'd be back to tuck Mina in.

The remaining two interviews at Beacon Downs Academy had turned out to be a waste of time. A flaky art teacher remembered Myles Jackman well, but she didn't recall him bullying any of the other students. In fact, she'd sung Myles' praises, telling her how talented and studious he was. She and Weekes had also asked her about Richard Pryce and Irwin Landers. She'd been complimentary about both, which didn't help.

Their third interview, Myles Jackman's history teacher, wasn't much better than his art teacher. He'd been less than helpful, not remembering much of anything, although Nasreen believed he was going through health issues. It was possible, she'd thought at the time, that he might be senile. How he taught history, which was all names and dates, she didn't know.

It didn't matter. They had more than enough to be getting on with. Sanders' interview alone had given them plenty of interviews to set up with most of Myles' year at school, especially Pryce and Landers. Then there were Myles' friends in the village to interview, plus his clients and family. It was a lot for the two of them to do. Knowing she would have to ask Gupta for extra manpower, Nasreen sighed, watching the footage.

The time at the bottom right of the screen said it was 23:36. The car park was lit with sparsely placed orange lights. It was difficult to see through the dark, but she persevered, squinting when she saw a figure approach Myles' car. It was Myles, dressed in a dark suit, the same dark suit they'd found in the car park of Whyte and Sons. "There you are," she whispered, watching him fumble in his pocket for his keys.

She moved uncomfortably when she saw a shadow emerge from behind the car next to his. The figure's arms reached out for him, grabbing his head and pulling it back, the hand covering Myles' mouth. Shadow's other arm came out, holding something. It looked like a needle, which would make sense, given that his body went limp inside a minute.

Making a note of the time on the monitor, she watched as Shadow dragged Myles' unconscious body backwards, to a truck. It dawned on her that she hadn't acknowledged the truck entering on any of the cameras. If she could find out the time of the truck's arrival, she'd be able to work backwards with nearby CCTV cameras. Watching Myles' abduction was as sinister as watching anything on film or television. This was real, not some re-enactment.

Knowing she had the details written down for future reference, Nasreen stretched and yawned. It was home time. Locking her notepad away, she shutdown her PC, took her suit jacket from the back of her chair and said goodbye to Terrence and Gupta.

DAY 7
THURSDAY, MAY 24TH

21

"You know, we could be looking at this all wrong," Weekes suggested. "If your theory's correct, and the suspect has a photo with other people in it, we might be interviewing all these people for nothing. It might not be connected to Myles Jackman at all. The connection might be with one of the other people."

Nasreen, concentrating on the road ahead, nodded her agreement. "Uh-huh," she said, listening, but focusing on an erratic driver in front. "But we don't have anything else to go on, until we have another victim. If we do, it'll be easier to find a connection in the victimology. Right now, we need to delve into Jackman's background."

"So, we're just working on the theory that ninety-five per cent of murders are committed by suspects knowing the victim? Okay, I get that."

"That and the forensic evidence. We've got uniforms checking all registered owners of 2005 Ford Rangers in Sussex, which should help narrow the search. At least we've got that much to go on. If we find that truck, we find the suspect."

There was no denying all the interviews they'd carried out so far might have all been for nothing, although they did know they had a lot of potential suspects. Jackman and his friends had bullied so many students at Beacon Downs School. That in itself wasn't at all convincing, though. Nasreen was intrigued at meeting Richard Pryce, which was where she was driving – a smallholding on the outskirts of the village.

Navigating the thin, winding country roads, the GPS on her dashboard told her to take a left. Following its instructions, she slowed and turned, continuing along a one-car lane until she reached a farmhouse in the middle of nowhere. Stopping in front of a gate with a "Pryce Is Right Labrador Breeders" sign on it, she got out and opened the gate, before climbing back in and driving through. "Here we are," she said, pulling up behind a Toyota Shogun.

As she got out, Weekes meeting her at the front of their car, she heard barking in the distance. The farmhouse in front was surrounded by what looked like acres of land. She'd been told it was a smallholding, but it wasn't that small to her.

"Hello there, can I help you?" a thin, tall man dressed in oily overalls asked. He came out from beneath a Shogun, which was up on blocks. "Are you here to see the pups?"

"No," Nasreen replied, taking out her ID and showing him. "We're investigating the murder of Myles Jackman." She saw the look of shock on his face. "We'd like to speak to Richard Pryce, please."

The man's demeanour changed. His face went from potential customer friendly, to a sneer. He kicked his leg out, hitting someone's ankle beneath the Shogun. "Boy, get your arse out here," he said, his tone hostile. "What've you been getting yourself into now?"

The pair of legs turned into a large man, about six feet tall and broad-shouldered. His face was dirty and round. She wouldn't say fat, just round. When he stood, he towered over her. "Richard Pryce?" she asked, in confirmation.

He looked down at the floor.

"You won't get anything out of him," clarified oily man. "He's dumb as they come, aren't you, boy? Now, what's this about?"

"We'd like to know where he was between midnight and six o'clock on Friday morning." Weekes glanced at Nasreen, letting her know he fitted the suspect's profile in height and weight. There was hope in her eyes.

"That's easy," oily man replied. "He volunteers at the animal shelter on Thursday nights. Stays there with Dr Chilvers from eight until eight. If you go over there, I'm sure they'll clear all this up. My boy may be dumb, but he's not a bad boy. He's more into animals than people. He loves animals, which is why I keep him on here."

Nasreen took an immediate disliking to the craggy old man. Calling his son dumb was bad enough; it was also the contempt he held in his voice, and the way he degraded his son that she found distasteful. "We'd like to speak with your son in private, if you don't mind?"

"What did I just say? He doesn't talk. And certainly not to strangers, detective. If you want confirmation of his whereabouts on Friday morning, I'll give you the address of the animal shelter. Will that do? Chilvers will clear all this up. It's too bad what happened to Myles, but he had it coming."

Nasreen glanced at Weekes. "Oh? Why's that, Mr Pryce?"

"He was an arsehole. Ask around. Everyone'll tell you, he was a bully, plain and simple. Because his old man practically owns this village, he thought he could get away with whatever he liked. It looks like someone thought different, huh?"

"He bullied your son, right?"

Pryce glared at Richard. "Everyone bullies my boy. Because he never stands up for himself. Even after I've given him boxing lessons in our barn, he still stands there and takes whatever's given to him. Sometimes I wonder if he's mine."

Nasreen could tell by the way Pryce Junior had his hands in his pockets, looking down at the floor, that he was scared of his father. She could imagine Pryce Senior teaching his son by unloading on him, calling it training. "When was the last time you saw Myles?" she asked Richard, not expecting an answer.

"You see? He doesn't talk," Pryce Senior said. "Let me show you around the farm, so you can see him with the animals. It's all he cares about."

Accepting his offer, she followed Pryce Senior and Junior around the rear of the property, where the kennels were kept. The puppy farm was huge, with a massive wooden barn at the back housing a mixture of at least thirty adult dogs and puppies. Pryce had five sets of Labradors of varying colours, which he bred. It smelt of dog in the barn; it was quite overwhelming. "It's just labs you breed here? There's no other breeds?"

"No need for any others. The most popular pups in the country. We sell to the public, and to organisations in need of guide dogs. This is a good source of income. And Richard looks after the lot."

The dogs adored Richard, she noticed, when he opened a cage and brought out one of the adult bitches. He lay on the floor with her, while she licked him and wagged her tail. It was obvious he had a way with them.

"Now I ask you, does this look like a murderer to you, detective?"

The answer to that was obvious. Nasreen couldn't see him dragging a naked Myles Jackman around a car park, any more than she could see Pryce Senior winning father of the year. "No, he doesn't," she conceded. "We'll take a trip to the animal shelter, Mr Pryce, and if this Dr Chilvers verifies his whereabouts you'll not see us again."

After thanking Pryce Senior for his candour, she said her goodbyes and headed for the barn doors. Having the address and directions of the animal shelter in her hand, she wanted to get the confirmation from Chilvers and move on.

Weekes turned back to him. "One final question, Mr Pryce. Can you think of anyone else who might have reason to hurt Myles Jackman?"

"It's a pretty long list, but I heard a rumour he had a run in with some lad a couple weeks ago, a real nasty piece of work. Drug dealer apparently. A big fight in the pub car park. I hear the dealer was sleeping with that slag girlfriend of his, that awful Zoe Needham. He came all the way down from the city to beat Myles up, or so I heard. I don't know if there's any truth to it. Ask that friend of his, Beckwith and his girlfriend. If anyone'll know, they will."

Nasreen couldn't believe it – no one had mentioned any of this to them. Aaron Beckwith and his girlfriend, Paige, hadn't, nor had any of the teachers – who would've heard something. None of the other interviewees either. "Thanks, we'll do that."

22

"I still like him for it," Weekes said, reading the sign for Brambles Animal Shelter. "In my experience, it's always the quiet ones. He's the right height and size, and he has a history with the victim. He's top of my list."

"That's not how I read him," Nasreen replied. "All I saw was some poor guy who's been bullied his whole life for being shy, and who loves animals. I don't think he's got a bad bone in his body, but if you want to look into him, be my guest. Of course, if this Dr Chilvers says he was there on Friday morning, it's null and void."

"Being bullied by Jackman gives him intent. But, like you say, if he has an alibi I'll drop it. There's something about him, though. I don't trust people who don't look you in the eye, call me old fashioned."

"Ordinarily I'd say the same, but he's probably on the spectrum."

Weekes tutted, knowing Nasreen was right. "Maybe," she said, as Nasreen turned left into yet another narrow lane, continuing along it until they came to a large property hidden by acres of land. From the outside, it didn't look like much, just a prefab.

It wasn't until she walked up to it, that she could see how far back it went; it was massive. "And you're sure this Dr Chilvers is in today?"

"I rang ahead. The receptionist said Chilvers is in on Thursdays; she volunteers Thursday days and overnight until 8am Friday morning."

"That's a long shift," she said, opening the front door and letting Nasreen enter first. On approach, she'd kept an eye out for cameras, noticing there were none. And on the drive here, she'd watched out for road cameras. None.

"Hi! I phoned just now," Nasreen said to a receptionist, a pretty little blonde woman wearing a dark blue uniform with Brambles Animal Shelter embroidered on the left breast of the fabric. "I'm here to speak with Dr Gillian Chilvers."

As the receptionist – Yasmin – picked up a landline phone, Weekes took in her surroundings, reading the leaflets pinned up on the noticeboard; they were info leaflets about what to do with injured birds, squirrels, hedgehogs and all manner of other wildlife. It smelt of animals, cleaning detergent and newly applied paint in reception. It wasn't an offensive smell; she found it welcoming.

"Detective Maqsood?" Dr Chilvers said from behind her.

Weekes stopped reading the leaflets and turned to find a tall woman in a white coat stood next to Nasreen. The veterinarian had long, dark hair tied in a ponytail, no make-up on, and a rather long nose, which didn't detract from her attractiveness. Estimating the vet to be about five feet eleven, she towered over the slight Nasreen.

"Yes, Dr Chilvers?" Weekes heard Nasreen ask, as she joined her partner. "I'm Detective Sergeant Nasreen Maqsood, and this is my partner, Detective Constable Alicia Weekes. We'd like to ask you a few questions about one of your volunteers, Richard Pryce."

"Please, come on through." Chilvers motioned with her arm. "Yasmin, join us, would you? She knows Richard as well as anyone. You don't mind, do you?"

Weekes followed Nasreen, Chilvers and Yasmin into a triage room, with a silver bench for assessing patients, filing cabinets, worktops with machinery and gadgets atop their surfaces. It was much like any vet's assessment rooms in the country, except this one accommodated wildlife instead of predominantly domestic animals. It smelt cleaner than out in reception, more like cleaning detergents.

"What would you like to know, detective?" Chilvers asked, stood to one side of the bench with Yasmin, while she and Nasreen stood the other.

"We're investigating the murder of Myles Jackman," Nasreen confessed.

Weekes noticed Yasmin's expression change. "Did you know him, Yasmin?" she asked, interrupting, for good reason. She noticed Yasmin glance at Chilvers for permission. "You look about the same age as Myles."

"We went to Beacon Downs together, yeah."

"What can you tell us about him?"

"Other than he was an arsehole, not a lot. I'm sorry! I shouldn't say that, I know, but he was. He was the biggest bully I've ever met. A really nasty piece of work."

"And you're local, too? You live in the same village?"

"A neighbouring village, actually, but I went to Beacon Downs. It was the best school, grades wise, so my parents wanted me to go there. And it might've been best for grades, but it was awful for bullying. I was picked on by Myles' friends, that awful Zoe Needham and Paige Roper. They were the worst. But Richard, he got it really bad. Myles and his mates wouldn't leave him alone."

The more Weekes heard about Myles Jackman, the more she

believed the suspect was one of his classmates. There was so much hostility towards him. And the picture the suspect had shown Jackman could have been a picture of him and his classmates, the bullies. "How does Richard get on with Myles now?"

"The last time Richard saw Myles, he was humiliated by him in front of the whole pub. Myles dropped a glass on the floor on purpose, made Richard come and sweep it up. Then, one of his mates, Aaron, poured a pint of beer over him, and that was just for starters. They carried on like that all day, while the footy was on. They loved it so much. It made me mad, having to sit there and watch it. Richard's the loveliest person you'll ever meet, I swear. He wouldn't hurt a fly."

"I got that when I met him earlier," Nasreen confirmed. "It seems he gets it at home, too. Do you know his father as well?"

Yasmin nodded. "The guy's a dick. He's as bad as Myles, mocking him, calling him dumb, stupid, a retard. And he beats on Richard, too. He says he's teaching him to defend himself, but he's not. He gets off on it."

"Did he speak to you, detective?" Chilvers asked Nasreen.

"No, not a word. His father did all the talking. He told us to come speak to you, that you'll corroborate Richard's whereabouts in the early hours of Friday morning? He told us Richard was here with you all night?"

"He was," the vet replied. "He volunteers every Thursday, from 8pm until 8am on Friday morning, just like he'll be here tonight. And I don't know what I'd do without him. Yasmin's right: he's the loveliest person you'll ever meet, if you're lucky enough to get him talking."

"He talks?" Weekes asked, surprised.

"Oh yes, detective. A lot. Once you get past his shyness, you'll find him to be quite the chatterbox. He loves animals so much; and he's brilliant with them, so kind and gentle. I swear he'd make the best vet."

"And you can vouch for his whereabouts on Friday morning?"

"Absolutely," the tall, impressive vet replied. "He was right here with me all night, looking after the animals out back. There's the logbook in reception. I can go get it if you'd like? He signed in and out."

Weekes was disappointed. If Richard Pryce was here, he couldn't be their suspect, and she liked him for it. Everything fitted, the bullying alone was reason enough in her book. "Yes, please, that would be great. I looked but I couldn't see any cameras out front."

"You'd like more proof?" Chilvers asked. "We have CCTV. Yasmin, be a dear and go get the logbook and go through the footage, would you?"

Damn it! They needed to go back to the beginning. "Thank you."

"If you want my opinion, you're barking up the wrong tree with Richard," Chilvers said, after Yasmin left the room. "He's one of the good guys."

"I believe you. But we need to eliminate him from our enquiries; I'm sure you understand," Nasreen said, in a reassuring manner.

"Of course, det–"

Chilvers pitched forwards, coughing.

"Are you okay? That's a nasty cough you've got there," Weekes said, hearing it rattle in her chest. "Would you like a glass of water?"

Chilvers put her hand up, recovering. "No, I'm fine," she said, wiping her mouth. "I'm getting over a nasty bug. It's nothing, really."

Out in reception, Weekes saw Richard Pryce's signature. When Yasmin had shown her video footage of Pryce parking at 19:55 on Thursday night and leaving at 08:10 on Friday morning, her suspicions were alleviated. It was official: they needed to look elsewhere.

Nasreen thanked Chilvers and Yasmin for their assistance.

"I hope you catch whoever killed Myles," Yasmin said. "I didn't like him, but he didn't deserve what happened to him. No one deserves that."

"Thank you," Weekes replied, resenting that Nasreen was right. She wouldn't get very far in this job by being wrong. Being ambitious, Weekes wanted to make sergeant within a year. It didn't look possible as it stood. "Could you get that video emailed over to us, please?"

"That won't be necessary," Nasreen overruled.

Outside in the car park, Weekes said, "Why did you contradict me like that? All we saw was Pryce parking up and leaving. He could've driven off in the middle of the night."

"Don't let your hunch cloud your judgement, Weekes," Nasreen replied, opening the driver's door. "He has an ironclad alibi. Let's move on, shall we?"

"But–"

"No ifs or buts, it's over. Get in."

After fastening her belt, Weekes glanced over at her partner. "Where to now?"

"The village. We're going to find out if there's any truth to Myles having a fight with Zoe's dealer friend."

23

———

Nasreen parked in a bay at the King's Head car park. "It's something you're going to have to get used to. We've all been there before. We've all suspected the wrong person." She killed the engine and opened her door. "Come on, let's go find us another suspect."

It seemed like the village pub was always busy. Even at lunchtime on a Thursday it was heaving with a mixture of youngsters and the elderly, either tucking into their lunch or stood by the bar, drinking. Didn't these people work? She walked up to the bar, Weekes following her. To her astonishment, Aaron Beckwith was behind the bar, pulling pints. And who was at the other end of the bar? Paige Roper, his girlfriend. "Well, hello again," Nasreen said to Beckwith, who mouthed, "Oh shit!". "Can we have a word, please?"

When Beckwith protested, citing being too busy serving to talk, she insisted, ordering him to join her in the beer garden. Beckwith asked one of the regulars to look after the bar while he and Paige followed Weekes outside.

Sat on a rickety bench, with Weekes next to her, Nasreen knew it was time to dig a little deeper, to scare her interviewees a bit, something she knew her partner would enjoy. "So, when we spoke earlier, you never told us about Zoe's new love interest, did you? Why not? Don't you think Myles having a fight with a drug dealer might be useful information for us?" She glared at them, in turn, gauging their reactions.

"Yeah, someone might think you have something to hide," Weekes said, her tone scornful on purpose, which appeared to have the desired response.

Beckwith shuffled nervously. "We couldn't tell you about that," he confided. "If Finn finds out I'm talking to you, he'll kill me. I'm not kidding; he's a proper psycho-nutjob."

"A psycho-nutjob? You haven't seen me when witnesses lie to me. I can be a psycho-bitch when I want to be, so you'd better tell us what we need to know. This Finn, what's his surname?"

Gulping, Beckwith glanced to his right, at his girlfriend. "Do you want to get me in trouble? I'm not kidding, he'll come back here and kill me if he finds out."

"It's Palmer," Paige interjected. "Finn Palmer, happy now? When we get assaulted by him and his mates, we'll be sure to make a complaint against you."

Nasreen could see how scared they were. "Just tell us what happened in the car park."

"Finn beat Myles up," Paige replied. "He drove down here after Myles and Zoe had an argument. Zoe dumped Myles, and when Myles started mouthing off that he'd kill Finn, that thug came down here and beat him up. That's it. The guy's a psycho. And he said that if Myles ever spoke to Zoe again, he'd kill him."

"Yeah, but he didn't mean it," Beckwith said. "It's just the kind of thing he'd say. I seriously doubt Finn dragged him around that car park... Please don't tell him we spoke to you. We don't want to get on the wrong side of him – he knows a lot of people."

"And this Finn lives in the city?" Nasreen asked, seeing the interest in Weekes' expression. If he did, she would like him for it. The guy had even threatened to kill Myles.

"Yeah, not far from Zoe, apparently," Paige said. "We only know about him through Myles. He was in bits after he found out Zoe was sleeping with Finn behind his back. He went on a big bender after that."

"Why the hell didn't it occur to you to tell us this before?" Weekes stood and stared them down. "If he murdered Myles on Friday morning, he's been free to roam for days, and that's your fault."

"You'd better pray he's not our suspect," Nasreen said, also standing. "And if you've omitted anything else, and we find out about it, you're in big trouble. Don't go anywhere, in case we need to ask you more questions, got it?" With urgency, she started walking away, towards the pub and car park.

"Don't tell him we spoke to you, please," Beckwith shouted.

"I can't promise that," she shouted back as she walked away, angry that they'd omitted such an important piece of information. It was a shame their pool car didn't have access to the PNC. Giving the keys to Weekes, she sat in the passenger seat and buckled up, taking her mobile out of her pocket, as Weekes started the engine. "We have a new suspect, sir," Nasreen said to Gupta when he answered. "We need everything you have on a Finn Palmer."

"You really think it's him?" Weekes asked, driving out of the car park.

"It could be," Nasreen replied, deep down hopeful. "I'll bet he has form. We know he has history with Myles and threatened to kill him. It's more likely than an animal loving, cripplingly shy Richard Pryce doing it, don't you think?" Putting her mobile on speaker phone, she noted Weekes shaking her head, concentrating on the road. Obviously not, she thought.

"I have his sheet here, Nas," Gupta said.

"Go ahead, sir," she said in a loud voice, drowning out the noise. "You're on speaker phone. Please tell me he has form."

"Oh, I think you could say that. GBH, ABH, assault, burglary, and that's just for starters. He was released eight months ago after doing a five year stretch for aggravated burglary; he robbed a couple at knifepoint, stabbed the husband in the gut. The husband didn't die, luckily. A career criminal, Palmer was charged with assault at the age of twelve, and since then his sheet's grown. If you're going after this guy, be careful."

"Thank you!" she shouted. "What's his address?"

Gupta reeled it off and Nasreen wrote it down, before entering the postcode in the car's GPS system on the dashboard. Thanking Inspector Gupta, she hung up and watched Weekes driving. "See? This is what it's about."

24

___

Trying to catch her breath after walking up fifteen flights of stairs, Nasreen finally found herself on Finn Palmer's floor, checking the number ensconced on the wall. "Do you need... a minute?" she asked Weekes, who seemed unfazed, even with an artificial leg. "I'm done in," Nasreen added, bending over and placing her palms on her knees. "Bloody lift."

"Crikey, you're out of shape," Weekes replied, eager to get on.

Nasreen stood up straight and followed her partner along the narrow, graffiti-covered corridor, noting the numbers on the many brown wooden doors. They were after "forty-two". Recovering by the time she joined Weekes outside Finn's door, she motioned for her partner to back away, reaching inside her suit jacket for her cosh. "Go ahead," she said to Weekes.

Weekes knocked.

There was movement from inside. Fortunately, there was no peephole for Finn to look through, which was good for them. Hearing the lock, Nasreen tensed, not knowing what to expect. When the door opened a crack, she saw a face appear. Holding her ID up for the resident to see, she asked, "Finn Palmer?"

The resident slammed the door shut, his heavy footsteps audible.

"You know what to do," she said to Weekes, who immediately kicked the door open. "Finn Palmer!" Nasreen shouted, following Weekes inside, adrenaline spiking. "We need to talk to you about Myles Jackman." She could hear movement in front of her.

Following the hallway to the living room, she saw Finn stood in front of a tatty couch, scared, ready to fight or flee. "We only want to talk to you," she said, hoping the reassurance was enough. Weekes was in front of her, closing in on him. "We need you to come with us to the station."

"I didn't do it," Finn cried, looking for a way out. "You have to believe me."

The closer Weekes came to him, the more he looked like he was about to run. "Weekes, back off! It's okay, Finn, we're just here to talk."

Weekes ignored her, edging closer to him.

"Oh shit!" Nasreen said, as he ran directly at her partner, pushing Weekes in the chest. Nasreen pressed the release button on her cosh and the metal bar extended. "We don't want this," she said to Finn, who was grappling with Weekes. "Come quietly, Finn."

Weekes fought with him, grabbing whatever clothes she could to keep him from fleeing. Nasreen watched as he forced her off, finding space between them to run towards her. With Weekes on the floor, she braced for impact, his sixteen, maybe seventeen stones flying towards her.

Sidestepping, Nasreen gave him the space he needed, whipping the cosh in front of his ankles. He cried out in pain, falling face-first. Seizing her opportunity, she jumped on his back, grabbing his arms and pinning them behind him, while he swore and spat. "I gave you the opportunity to come quietly," she hissed, taking handcuffs from Weekes, who was on her feet. "Now we're arresting you for assaulting a police officer."

"I didn't do it," he repeated. "I only beat him up, I didn't kill him, you have to believe me. Please, I didn't do it."

"If you can prove you weren't there, you have nothing to worry about, do you?" she said, clicking the cuffs around his wrists. With Finn on the floor, unable to move, Nasreen took out her mobile and called it in. They were going to have to search the flat for evidence, while he was being questioned. She had twenty-four hours to find something on him, before they had to release him without charge, or apply for an extension. Nasreen was sure they'd find something, either on his phone, laptop, tablet – which were all on the table behind her – or inside the flat in another form. "You're under arrest for assault. Weekes, read him his rights."

25

———

Peter Franks walked along the marina, towards *The Albatross*. Glancing to his right, he could see the Palace Pier, and a bit further along, the British Airways i360 in the distance. It was still light at eight o'clock. He loved the smell of the ocean and its gentle movement. If he wasn't meeting his boss, he might have looked forward to spending a couple of hours on board a luxury yacht. Alas, he was under no illusion, he was in for a frustrating night.

With his coat in hand, feeling the perspiration under his armpits, Franks approached the vessel, stepping onto the docking plank. Harry came out to greet him. "Evening," he said to his boss, jumping onto the deck. How did Harry have such a cool boat? It was the very picture of plush; everything about it exuded decadence, style and sophistication.

"Come inside, Peter," Harry said.

Inside the lounge, Franks joined Harry at the small bar, waiting for his boss to pour him a drink. He could be at home watching TV with his wife. Instead, he was here with Harry, knowing he was here to reassure him they were doing the right thing. Harry was coming apart. "Cheers!" he said, clinking

Harry's glass. "So, what did you want to see me about?" It was the most obvious question.

"Actually, I wanted to thank you." Harry held up his tumbler. "You could've made my job untenable, but you didn't, so thank you. You could've mentioned Amelie to Embry. Why haven't you?"

It was a good question, and one even he couldn't answer. "Why would I? We've a good thing going here. And I'm not after your job, Harry."

"I know that. But I wanted to say thank you in person. I've let the ball drop more than once recently. It's just–"

"Just what?" he asked, like he didn't know.

"It's just I can't stop thinking about her," Harry confessed, his head down in shame. "I could've killed her. I swear I would've had she not clocked me one. Now, every time I close my eyes all I see is her pretty face all contorted, staring up at me with these accusing eyes. I can't sleep; I can't eat. I can't do anything." He drank a mouthful of his finest whisky. "What have I become? I joined the Force to help people, not to become the very thing I swore to protect the public from."

Franks put his glass on the bar. "But you didn't kill her, did you?" He put his hand on Harry's arm. "She left here in one piece, so stop beating yourself up over it. That bitch was working against us, Harry. If she'd had her way, we'd be locked up right now. She deserved everything she got, don't you see that?"

"I know, but it doesn't matter. I was strangling her, with my bare hands, right here in this lounge. She was sucking at the air, trying to breathe, turning purple, and I was the one drawing life from her... Me."

Sighing, Franks saw the anguish in his boss's eyes. "Like I said, you didn't strangle her. She's gone, but it wasn't you. Whether you feel it or not, your hands are clean on this; you've nothing to worry or feel guilty about. Amelie was using you to get to the Project. Garvey should've warned her about what she was getting involved in and if she knew, well, it's her own fault. And if she didn't know, that's on Garvey."

"Do you know what happened to her?"

How should he respond to that? "I do. And trust me on this, you don't want to know. Just leave it at that, she's gone. Like she never existed. You're not going to get any blowback on this, Harry, so take solace in that. It's over. Amelie's gone; Garvey's gone. You need to suck it up and move on with your life." He could see it sinking in. "What we're doing is a good thing – it's going to save lots of lives and make people feel safer."

"I wish I had your faith. We need to rethink the Project, Peter. It's not worth it."

"Hey! You came to me with this, remember? We spoke about the pros and cons, didn't we?" he asked, feeling his temper fraying. "There were always going to be perils and pitfalls... And we can't cave in at the first hurdle."

"First hurdle? Clive was murdered outside his own home, for Christ's sake," Harry growled, his hand shaking. "And there's a trail of dead bodies leading back to us. We've got very capable detectives investigating these cases, Peter, have you forgotten that?"

"And they're never going to link it back to us, are they?" he replied, his voice louder. "I'm the one out there, guiding these investigations, not you. You've hardly contributed anything to the Project, have you? Unless you include getting involved with Amelie."

There was an angry silence between them.

"That's not fair," Harry complained, his voice calmer and low. "How was I to know she was in bed with Garvey? Don't say that. I want the Project to work every bit as much as you do."

Franks took a couple of deep breaths, checking his temper. "Look, I know you do, and I understand you're having second thoughts." And he did; there were times when he wondered if the Project was worth it. "But we have to see it through, don't we? We owe it to the country to see it through. Think how much safer people will feel with all these gangs banged up. Just think, by the time we're through, the Justice Department will need to build more prisons to accommodate the dealers we're going to be convicting... We need to hold our nerve, Harry, that's all."

He was relieved when Harry nodded and took another gulp of his whisky. It was obvious to him that his boss was having second thoughts; he had been for a while. And although his host seemed to be coming around, he thought he might have to take drastic action. He wasn't about to let Harry derail the most important project he'd ever worked on.

26

Nasreen slammed the phone down on the table in front of Finn Palmer. The screen showed a picture of Myles Jackman from a distance, walking along a road with Zoe Needham, his then-girlfriend. The date showed it was taken three weeks ago. "You'd better level with me here, Finn," Nasreen said, leaning on the table. "Why have you been taking photos of Myles, huh? Because, from where I'm standing, those look like surveillance pictures."

"It's not what it looks like, I promise," a scared Finn said. "I was following him, yeah, but not to kill him. He was giving Zoe shit, so I told her I'd sort it. I went to his village and staked him out. Then I confronted him in the pub car park. That's all I did, I gave him a scare, roughed him up a bit."

"It doesn't look good for you right now, though, does it?" Weekes intervened, also leaning on the interview room table. "I mean, if you had an alibi, we might be able to eliminate you from our suspect pool, but you say you were at home alone on Friday morning. That, coupled with these photos, and the fact you first beat him up, and then threatened to kill him, puts you right up there at the top."

Watching Finn sweat was satisfying. Nasreen thought they might have their man. "Plus, you're about the right height and build as our suspect, so, yeah, I'd say you're our prime suspect. It's up to you to convince us you're not, Finn. So, tell us why you're not our man. Your sheet's as long as your arm – ABH, GBH, aggravated burglary. You stabbed some poor guy in his own home, so why not murder Myles, hmm? I mean, he wronged you, he wronged your girlfriend."

"For fuck's sake, we've been here for hours. Look, I was at home all day Thursday and most of Friday; I was sick with some stomach bug. I was shitting for England. Don't you think I wish I was out? Because I do. I didn't speak to anyone all day; no one phoned. I spent the day in bed."

"Have you ever owned a pickup truck?"

Finn looked up at her. "Huh? Why? I wouldn't be seen dead in a pickup."

It was the only area they were lacking evidence. Without the truck they had nothing, only circumstantial, nothing confirmatory. "That doesn't mean a thing."

"Yeah, you could easily borrow a truck from a mate, couldn't you?" Weekes broke in. "Or in your case, steal one. And with your history, I wouldn't put it past you."

"When the fuck's my solicitor getting here? I've co-operated with you as much as I can. I waived my right to not speak, given you everything I know. I didn't kill Myles Jackman, have you got that? You can try to pin this on me, but I promise you my DNA won't be found anywhere near his body."

Having been grilling him for nearly four hours, Nasreen was tired. A search warrant for his flat had already been issued, and the SOCOs were busy looking for evidence. So far she hadn't heard anything from them. Certain they'd find something on him, she decided to call it a night, looking at her watch.

"You're in for the long haul, Finn," Weekes said. "We can

hold you for twenty-four hours initially and apply for up to four days, so get comfortable, you're going to be here for a while longer yet. Sweet dreams."

Waiting in the corridor, Nasreen closed the door when her partner joined her. "What do you think?"

Weekes was about to answer when Inspector Gupta appeared.

"Sir? I thought you'd gone home?"

"No rest for the wicked," he replied, wearing a serious expression. "I've just got off the phone with Cyber. They've found it. Myles Jackman's video's out there for all to see. Fortunately for us, it's on the dark web, not mainstream. It's had over a thousand views so far."

"Isn't that good?" Weekes looked from Nasreen to Gupta, and back to her. "Cyber can identify where it came from, can't they? They'll trace it to our suspect."

If only it were that simple, thought Nasreen. "I wish. Don't go getting your hopes up, Weekes. It's next to impossible to identify uploaders on the dark web. They'll try, but I'm not expecting miracles."

"I thought you should know," Gupta said. "How's it going with your suspect?"

"It's not him," Weekes replied. "All we have is circumstantial–"

"It's going well, sir," Nasreen interrupted. "I like him for it. The only thing we don't have is the vehicle. If we can put him in a pickup, we'll have him. He has no alibi; he's the right size; he has a history with the victim, even threatened to kill him. SOCOs are scouring his flat, looking for something on him. I haven't heard anything from them as yet."

"You disagree, Weekes?" Gupta asked.

"He has form, sir, sure, but we can't prove he was somewhere he wasn't. As it stands we don't have anything, except the fact he beat up the victim and threatened to kill him. Like Sergeant Maqsood says, we need the pickup, and I don't feel it's him we're looking for. I still like Richard Pryce."

Gupta waited for her response.

"Richard Pryce has a rock-solid alibi," Nasreen replied. "He was working at an animal shelter at the time. We saw him arriving and leaving, sir. He has no priors; he's never been in trouble of any kind. Oh, and did I tell you he loves animals?"

"And doesn't look you in the eye," Weekes added. "He's the right height and build, sir. He was bullied and tormented by the victim for years, even now. People have their breaking point. He was bullied by a lot of his classmates, so if Sergeant Maqsood's theory's correct, and there are more to follow, the photo could be of some of his year group at school. And we saw him arrive and leave, without checking the rest of the footage – he could've left during the night."

"Nas?" Inspector Gupta was waiting.

"It's not him, sir. We have him at the shelter on the night in question. Dr Chilvers is a well-respected veterinarian who volunteers at the shelter, as does Richard Pryce. If she says he was there all night, I believe her. Unless you're suggesting she's in on it as well, Weekes?"

Weekes looked at the floor, then back up at Gupta. "No, of course not."

"That's that, then," Gupta replied. "Focus on this suspect. I'm off home; I'll see you both in the morning." He turned and left.

Nasreen told Weekes to go home, that she would wait for the holding cell officer to arrive. It didn't take long. She walked with Finn as far as she needed, continuing to her desk, where she switched off her PC, picked up her jacket and left.

27

———

Verity Staunton yawned, looking up at the clock on the wall: it was approaching eleven. Alone in the stables office, she decided it was time to go home; she'd finished the weekly accounts, at least. Taking one last glance at the screen-saver on the PC, she clicked on "Shutdown" and waited for the screen to go blank.

Picking up her mobile, she scrolled through her photos, stopping on a picture of her club members. It was a great photo, of her and Myles with the rest of their group. Her long blonde hair was particularly full and attractive in the picture. "I miss you." She sniffed, welling up at the thought of what happened to him. Shaking off her morbid thoughts, sniffing back her tears, she pocketed her phone and packed her handbag.

Taking a last scan of the office, all the electrical appliances were switched off. Happy that she could leave, Verity headed for the front door of the prefab. Taking her keys out of her bag, she walked out into the moonlit car park, turning around and switching off the light, before closing and locking the door.

The hair on the back of her neck stood up; she hated

walking through the isolated car park, knowing her nearest neighbour was a half mile away. It always freaked her out, more so now she knew Myles had been brutally murdered.

In the dim moonlight, she could see her car waiting for her. With the key in hand, nervous, she started walking towards it.

As she approached her beloved red MG Coupe, she heard rustling in a bush in front of her. She stopped immediately. "Hello? Who's there?" She knew how stupid it sounded.

The rustling stopped.

Relieved, feeling ridiculous, she continued walking towards her birthday present from her parents. Almost reaching the driver's door, she pressed the button on her key, as the orange rear lights flashed twice, signalling it was unlocked.

When she was about to open the door, a shadow caught her attention.

Verity screamed when it moved at her at great speed, a gloved hand reaching out and wrapping itself around her mouth.

Before she knew what was happening, she felt a body behind her, a strong body, its hand clamped over her mouth.

Her arms instinctively flailed, trying to find something, anything, to cling to, to claw at. Her heart was beating so fast, she felt faint, except her brain was firing a million thoughts at once, keeping her conscious.

While she fought with Shadow, Verity felt a sharp stabbing pain in her neck, like a needle or something had pierced her skin.

A few seconds later the fight in her seemed to dissipate, replaced with a calm tranquillity she shouldn't be experiencing, not with a huge, strong body behind her.

The panic faded away.

A few seconds later, she was on her back, looking up at a set of angry eyes. Her world was growing fainter, darker, the figure seemed to be getting farther away.

With her thoughts growing quieter, Verity closed her eyes.

DAY 8
FRIDAY, MAY 25TH

28

———————

"Wake up, bitch!"

Her head snapped left sharply, which preceded the stinging she felt in her cheek.

It felt like she'd been hit by a brick.

Verity opened her eyes, only to be blinded by a bright white light.

"There you are," the voice said. "About time."

It took a few seconds for her to realise she was standing involuntarily, strapped to something. It felt like wood. Opening her eyes again, they adjusted, not staring into the white light. Trying to move, she peered down and saw rope around her waist, which also held her arms and legs. Looking up, she saw a tree trunk.

Her brain finally registered that she was tied to a tree, in the middle of some wooded area. In front of her, the bright white light was coming from a camera on a tripod. Shadow walked away from her. "What are you doing?" She needed to pee. "Why am I here?" They were the first two questions to jump out of her mouth. "Please, let me go."

"Sh!" Shadow picked up something she couldn't quite make

out. "All will be explained." Her captor faced her, holding the strange object. "You're here to atone for your actions, like your friend Myles already has."

"Atone for what?" she cried, the lump in her throat strangling her. "I haven't done anything to atone for; I'm a hair stylist." She sobbed. "What could I have done?"

Shadow strode towards her, cutting her off, stopping in front of her and holding up a photograph.

"Please, I wasn't even there. You don't understand, it's nothing to do with me," she begged, the words sounding hollow, false, even to her. "What are you doing?"

Producing a pair of scissors, Verity watched Shadow cut out her head from the photo. Then her captor pulled out some string, pierced a hole in the photo and threaded the string through. It was when Shadow looped the string over her head and left it dangling like a necklace that she knew she was dead. This was Myles' murderer. "Please. Don't do this. I'll give you anything you want, please. Money, I have lots of money."

"You rich people, all the same." Shadow turned and walked back to the camera. "You think you can get away with anything because you have money. You can't buy me off. No, you're going to atone for what you've done. And when you've atoned, the rest of your 'friends' will, too. You all have to pay for what you've done."

Verity sobbed, the tears free flowing. Needing the toilet, her bladder at bursting point, she watched in horror as Shadow picked up the strange object. It was only when her captor's body turned slightly, that the silhouette showed her what she needed to know. Shadow was holding a bow. "No! Please, I'll do anything you want."

Shadow pulled the string back.

And let go.

The pain was all-encompassing.

The arrow shot into the centre of her knee, smashing through bone, cartilage and embedding itself in the tree trunk.

Verity's bladder felt like it exploded, her entire body convulsing.

At the same time, she vomited.

The rope kept her from fitting. It was the most excruciating pain she'd ever felt. Her scream was piercing, blood-curdling, feral.

29

Weekes awoke with a jolt, sweat running down her brow. Her bedsheets were soaking wet, as they were most mornings; sometimes she wondered if she would ever stop dreaming about the missile attack on her aid convoy. Probably not, she thought, attaching her leg.

Three years on and she was still reliving that terrifying moment when her friends were engulfed in flames, their screams etched into her memory forever. Why was alcohol the only remedy? It wasn't fair!

It was four o'clock in the morning. Still angry about her theory being overlooked by Inspector Gupta, she showered and changed into her suit in record time, and instead of going for a run, grabbed her car keys and headed outside. It was still dark out at 04:20. Hopping in her car, she typed in the postcode for Brambles Animal Shelter.

The drive took around an hour and ten minutes, by which time it was light, the sky promising a clear, sunny day. It was warm enough for her to take off her jacket, which she did when she pulled up outside the shelter, having traversed the long, winding Sussex roads.

There were two cars parked outside, one of which was Richard Pryce's and the other a big old Land Rover. It was a typical vet's vehicle, big enough to carry animals and rough enough to get to isolated destinations. It had to be Doctor Chilvers', she guessed. When she stood on the rough tarmac of the car park and closed her door, Weekes thought about calling in where she was. Nasreen had been suspended for investigating a case off duty. If she spoke to Dr Chilvers, she would be doing the same thing as Nasreen. Deciding against calling it in, Weekes walked up to the front door and knocked.

"Detective?" Doctor Chilvers said, once she'd opened up. "It's a bit early for you to be calling, isn't it?" She looked tired, her eyes dark. "What can I do for you?" Her demeanour wasn't rude, more confused.

"I was hoping to have a look around, if that's all right? We didn't get a chance last time we were here. It's just routine, nothing to worry about." She hid her intentions well, knowing she was after something specific. "You don't mind, do you?"

"Anything to help your investigation, of course. Come on through." The veterinarian held the door open for her.

"I was hoping to take a look out back," she said, stepping inside. "I don't mean to interrupt. You can carry on with your duties as normal."

"Follow me," Chilvers replied, taking her through the main building. "Richard's outside feeding the animals. We had a fox and her cubs delivered yesterday. He's in with them now."

Following Chilvers, Weekes was led out of the main building, along a courtyard and into a huge barn-like building, where the injured and displaced wild animals were kept. It was a strange mix of noises in the barn, and smells, too. Not being used to animals, especially wildlife, Weekes wrinkled her nose. "Thank you," she said to Chilvers, who said she had chores to perform before the shelter opened formally.

It wasn't inside the barn she was interested in; it was outside. Hearing Richard nursing and feeding the foxes, she backtracked and let herself outside. The main thing she was interested in was finding out if there was a rear exit to the property, a way of someone, say, driving a pickup on and off the premises without being filmed by the shelter's CCTV.

Creeping along the side of the large wooden building, Weekes found a substantial concreted area at the rear of the barn. It wasn't a car park, yet it was large enough to accommodate eight to ten motor vehicles.

Leading from the concreted area were tyre tracks, and lots of them. They seemed to all point in the same direction, through a field to a row of bushes. The main road she'd travelled down to get here, she thought, hearing cars in the distance. "Uh-huh!" she mumbled to herself, walking towards the bushes.

There was a clearing between bushes.

The tyre tracks were deep, made a while ago while wet. Dry now, she thought any new tyres weren't likely to make an indent on the dry earth. When she reached the clearing, she saw it gave access to the road.

So, Richard could have driven his car here, parked it, walked out the back, got into a pickup and driven away without being seen by the cameras, she calculated. Her theory was taking shape; all she needed now was to find the truck he used.

Nothing had ever seemed clearer to her: Richard Pryce was their suspect. It wasn't that arsehole Finn Palmer, who deserved to be put in prison, but not for Myles Jackman's murder. "I've got your number," she whispered, turning and heading back to the shelter.

After thanking Chilvers for her co-operation, Weekes walked back to her car, Nasreen's comment bugging her. If her theory was correct, how could Richard leave the property without Chilvers knowing? And how could he leave the pickup there beforehand without her knowing? Sat behind the wheel, the cogs in her mind started whirring. It didn't seem likely. Cursing to herself, Weekes started the engine, before driving back along the winding lane towards the main road.

Turning left, she headed in the direction of the clearing. Once she found it, she kept on going, looking for the first camera she could find. Along the way, Weekes came to realise that country roads rarely housed speed cameras. It was frustrating; she drove for a good twenty minutes before she found one. "Shit!" she muttered, knowing there were loads of turnings Pryce could've taken. There was no way she could... Hang on, there was no harm in trying. Making a note of where she was on the GPS, Weekes thought she would contact the relevant council and ask them for their speed camera's footage.

It was approaching seven by the time she headed back to the city. Passing the shelter, she kept an eye out for cameras on the way back, too, finding one after half an hour. It was a long shot, but what did she have to lose?

30

———

Having dropped Mina off at school and given Katerina the morning off, Nasreen arrived at the station to find Weekes busy at her desk. "Morning," she said, settling behind her own desk. Her partner was so engrossed in her work she barely got a "hello" back; it was more of a grunt. It wasn't like she'd expected less. Weekes was probably still smarting after the previous night, she thought, grateful that her partner had to give up her ridiculous suspicions. Deciding to leave Weekes to her own devices for an hour, she turned on her PC.

Determined to find the pickup, or at least give Finn Palmer access to one, she opened up the list of 2005 Ford Rangers registered in the city. She would have to cross-reference the list of owners with Finn's friends and acquaintances. If she could find a name amongst the owners who knew Finn, he would have access to the truck. It was like looking for a particular needle in a stack of needles. Sighing, she pulled up Finn's Facebook account to cross-check his friends. "Here we go," she said under her breath.

"Nas, come check this out," Inspector Gupta said from his desk behind her.

Intrigued, she stood and walked over to Gupta's desk. "What's up?" He was sat in front of his monitor, which had Sky News playing. The headlines at the bottom of the screen read: Woman Murdered in Sussex Woods. Without speaking, she listened to the reporter, a woman with lovely shoulder-length blonde hair. According to her report, the unidentified woman had been found by a dog walker in the early hours of the morning. There was no description of how the woman was killed. "Do we know where this is?"

Before Gupta could reply, the reporter – stood in front of a clearing to the woods, which had been cordoned off – stated that the murder took place in a well-known Sussex park, in woods behind it. It was a popular dog-walking spot, but largely deserted at night.

"Do you want me to give them a call? It could be your suspect," Gupta asked. "The body was left in a public space, a week after your victim was killed, and it's not far from the village. What do you think?" He looked up at her, waiting for a response.

Not wanting her theory to be proved right, and not wanting another victim, she paused for a moment, watching the reporter. "Yeah, if you could, I'd appreciate it. Can you check if they found a photo on or near the body?" she replied, hoping not. "How long do you think it'll take?" There was no way of shaking her fears. Nasreen's gut knew it was her suspect.

"I'm on it now," he replied, picking up his desk phone. "I'll let you know."

Back at her desk, anxiously waiting for confirmation from Gupta, Nasreen couldn't help thinking her current chore – and it was a chore – was futile. If the murder in the woods took place the previous night, and it was their suspect, Finn Palmer was in a holding cell at the time. It couldn't have been him, which meant they were wasting time looking into him.

31

"You have Finn Palmer in custody, Peter," Zack Astor said. "He can't stay inside, I need him. He's one of my biggest earners, do you understand?"

Franks groaned. "What's he been picked up for? I'll see what I can do." This was a headache he didn't need. At home in his study, he got up from his chair and walked over to the door, closing it.

"You'll see what you can do? Do I need to remind you we have a deal? We work for you; you offer us protection. I'm doing my part, now it's time for you to come through for me."

Sitting back down, Franks felt anger bubbling. "What's he done? There are limits to what I can do here, you know! If he's been picked up for something small, I'll be able to help. If he's being questioned for murder, I can't be seen to interfere. Do *you* understand?"

"Great! So, your protection means precisely shit."

"No, it means there are limitations. Tell me what he's in for and I'll look into it for you. I don't need this shit today."

"You know what? I don't give a fuck if you need this," Astor hissed, his tone growing increasingly hostile. "I need him out, now. And I don't have the first fucking clue what he's been arrested for. All I know is every hour he's off the street, he's not earning."

"All right, I'll look into it." He wanted to smash his phone. It wasn't bad enough he had two murder investigations to keep an eye on up north, he had this to deal with as well? "I'm on it. I'll be in touch later." He hung up without giving Astor the opportunity to vent. "Shit!" Franks growled, banging his fist on his desk.

32

————

Nasreen's search for the pickup truck was about as successful as her social life – or what counted as a social life. Nasreen had yet to match any names from both lists. Sighing, she switched to a report compiled by a sergeant in the Sussex Police, who had overseen the interviewing of all owners of 2005 Ford Rangers in the area. Every single truck was accounted for; every owner could verify their whereabouts; and not one truck had been reported stolen.

Peering over her partition, she could see Gupta was on the phone. Not knowing if he was discussing the Skip Body case, or hers, was frustrating. It was almost ten o'clock, which meant that the detectives working the new woods murder would be well under way, the body having been found at around seven in the morning.

Weekes hadn't said a word to her since she'd arrived. Still engrossed in whatever it was she was doing, Nasreen was tempted to find out. Then, she faltered, enjoying the peace and tranquillity; there were no sarcastic remarks, no attitude – it was bliss. A short-lived bliss, she realised, when Gupta ended his call. "And?" she asked, stood watching him over the partition, expecting him to tell her it was a call regarding his case.

Popping her head up, Weekes showed an interest.

"Get yourselves over there," he replied, facing her. "You'll be meeting Inspector Innes and Sergeant Edgeley. There's a photo on the body of the victim, and they found a USB stick on the ground in front of the body."

She slammed her fist on her desk. "Bollocks!" There'd been no doubt in her mind there would be more murders. It'd been her hope that she would prove her gut wrong for once. No such luck. "What was the method used?" she asked.

Gupta paused, looked at the floor, then back up at her. "Bow and arrow."

Weekes gasped audibly.

Who would shoot someone with a bow and arrow in this day and age? "Really?" It was a rhetorical question; she knew Gupta wouldn't joke.

"Five arrows. The victim was tied to a tree. The sick bastard used her as target practise. Weekes, it's a really nasty one. If you feel queasy, make sure you run away from the journos, all right? I don't want front-page pictures of you throwing up again."

Nasreen could tell Weekes didn't like his comment. Her partner's face was a picture, as was the way she slunk into her chair, ignoring the chuckles from their colleagues. It wasn't fair to ridicule her partner; she didn't know any better. The training centre didn't teach much an officer really had to know – it all came from experience. "I don't suppose we know the victim's name, do we?"

"We do, as it happens." Gupta looked down at his notepad. "Her name's Verity Staunton. The poor dog walker who found her identified her. They live in the same village, apparently. She's thirty-three. A hair stylist, according to the witness."

Writing the information down, Nasreen came back up. "And

it looks like he filmed it," she said, to his grim nod. "Can you get Cyber on it, please? We're on our way now."

Picking up her jacket, she met Weekes by her desk and walked out of the office, along the corridor to the stairwell. Racing down the stairs, Weekes close behind, she felt the rush of adrenaline, relishing it. "You drive," she said to her partner in the car park.

33

"You're not upset about last night, are you?" Nasreen glanced sideways at Weekes. "I keep telling you, we can't be right every time."

Focusing on the bendy road ahead, Weekes shrugged. "What? I'm fine," she replied, trying her best not to sound annoyed. "I'm concentrating."

"Good, because you've hardly said a word to me all morning. I thought I'd done something wrong."

There was a signpost coming up for the park they were headed for. A mile to go, or a mile too far, she couldn't decide. "You know, if this turns out to be our guy, Finn Palmer's been in custody all night for nothing, don't you?" she said, wishing the car in front would speed up. Sensing Nasreen's irritation, she added, "I'm just saying."

"You don't think I know that? But Palmer's a more plausible suspect than Pryce."

Desperately wanting to tell her "boss" about her morning's discovery, Weekes nodded, not committing to anything. "Not now, he's not. We pretty much know Finn's out of the equation, don't we? Pryce could still be our man, though."

There was a long silence.

"This is it," she said, driving into the park's car park, where several police cars had been left unattended at odd angles, six in total, she counted, pulling up alongside one in their unmarked white Peugeot.

Switching the engine off and opening her door, Weekes wondered how bad this crime scene would be. Fortunately, she'd eaten breakfast hours ago, so she shouldn't throw it up, she hoped. Hearing Gupta's comment in front of her colleagues embarrassed her more than seeing her photo spread over the tabloids. "After you," she said to Nasreen, as they started walking along the narrow footpath.

It was a pretty park – which was more of a common – surrounding a huge pond in the centre, popular for fishing and feeding the swans and ducks. Weekes followed Nasreen to the top of the hill, taking in the fresh air and natural beauty of the place, with its many types of wildflowers growing in sporadic tufts on either side of the pathways. She imagined it would be busy on Fridays. Not today, though.

When they reached the top of the hill, Weekes saw a uniform up ahead, guarding the clearing which led into the woods behind. "Here we go," she said, as they reached the cordon. Pulling out her ID, she waited for Nasreen to show hers first, then held it up for the uniform to see. He didn't say anything; instead he lifted the crime scene tape for her to walk under.

Tape showed them the way to the crime scene. Walking behind Nasreen, silent, Weekes observed the scenery. It was quite a large wooded area, thick with trees and bushes of varying types and sizes. Weekes recognised oak and sycamore trees, of course. Not being a gardener, it wasn't like she could point out many other species. Bluebells, still out, littered the grass surrounding the paths.

SOCOs in white overalls appeared in front of her. One of them sauntered over to them, handing her and Nasreen their own coveralls. Hat, face mask, foot covers and all-in-one body suits needed to be put on before they could see the body. The SOCO in charge, under instructions by the pathologist, checked they were good to go.

Adrenaline kicking in, Weekes walked slowly towards the body, which was up ahead, obscured by the scenes of crimes officers going about collecting evidence and taking pictures. The SOCO obscuring her view moved.

It was worse than she'd imagined. When Gupta had said five arrows, she'd envisaged five to the chest, not one to each kneecap, one in each shoulder and the fifth through her mouth. She felt queasy. It was awful. And that was from a distance. "Sick bastard," she said to Nasreen, who'd stopped walking towards the dead blonde girl.

Two overalls broke away from the rest and joined them, introducing themselves as Detective Inspector Innes and Detective Sergeant Edgeley, both of whom shook hers and Nasreen's hands. They were in full gear, so she couldn't see their faces, only their eyes. Innes was short and squat, while Edgeley was tall and lean; it was about all she could say to describe them. They were probably thinking the same about her (tall and lean) and Nasreen (short and petite).

"Right, show us the body," Nasreen said.

Taking a deep breath, Weekes walked alongside, Verity Staunton's body growing closer. Her skin had a grey hue to it. Her eyes were open, lifeless. She didn't want to look further down. Verity must've been screaming at the time the suspect shot her in the mouth, although it wasn't a perfect shot, the arrow smashed through her two front upper teeth. The arrow had penetrated the base of her skull and embedded itself in the huge tree she was tied to.

"Here's the USB stick," Inspector Innes said, handing her supervisor a clear plastic evidence bag containing the stick. "We found it between her feet. We've documented everything. There'll be photos of the scene to follow, of course."

Weekes couldn't help but think of the pain the victim must have felt. It made sense to her that the suspect shot her in the mouth last, for where would he derive his satisfaction from in killing her first, only to use her body as target practise? The two arrows in her shoulders wouldn't have killed her outright, and neither would the arrows to her knees. But the pain, it must've been unbearable. Looking closer, Weekes could see dried vomit over the girl's top. And urine covering the poor girl's jeans.

"Tell me what you see," Nasreen said, squatting.

Weekes followed suit, looking at the arrows in Verity's knees. "The suspect enjoyed it," she replied. "He enjoyed inflicting the pain. He knows her; he's angry with her, at least as angry as he was with Myles Jackman, if not more. Look where he shot her, right in the kneecaps. That, there, tells me he enjoyed it. The pain she must've felt – if you want my opinion, this was payback. Revenge for something."

"Good. And look at the accuracy. What does that say?"

"He's a crack shot. It takes practise to get that good with a bow or crossbow. And power; it takes a lot of effort and strength to pull back the string."

"Practise, yeah," Nasreen said, more in musing. "We'll look into places for that. There are probably a few around this neck of the woods. Good job. What else?"

Weekes scanned the surrounding area. She noticed there was a track leading to the tree, going away from the park. "Where does that path lead?" she asked the Sussex detectives. When they said it led to a main road, she stood and studied the earth. There were clear drag marks, and possible footprints. "He wouldn't drag the body from the car park all the way up the hill.

If I had to guess, I'd say that's your entry point. Is there parking on the road?"

"A couple of lay-bys, yeah," the short Innes replied.

"Any cameras nearby?"

"Unfortunately not, no," the taller Edgeley said. "The nearest camera is over two miles away. And there are lots of turn-offs in both directions."

"So, the suspect knows the area," she said, rubbing her chin. "It has to be a local, doesn't it?" She looked down at Nasreen, waiting for her input.

"I'd say so. You don't get knowledge of this area without being local. We'll have to check out the cameras, just to err on the side of caution. But I agree with you. Although, Myles was murdered in our neck of the woods."

"Yeah, but he lived near here," she retorted. "So...?"

"So, I think we need to find out as much as we can about Verity Staunton, don't you? What have you found out about her so far, inspector?"

Weekes waited for Innes to retrieve a notepad. "We know she's thirty-three, but that's all Inspector Gupta gave us."

After flicking through to the correct page, Innes put on his glasses. They started to steam up from the breath coming out beneath his face mask. "According to the witness, like you said she's thirty-three, works as a hair stylist in the city, and works part-time at some stables nearby. Verity Staunton isn't just a hair stylist, apparently; she's *the* hair stylist. She does a lot of rich and famous women's hair, and she's in high demand. Despite her own wealth, she drives back to her childhood stables every Thursday to help with the accounts. The witness uses the stables herself, so she's known Verity a long time. She was very distressed when we spoke to her, as you can imagine."

"We need to speak to her ourselves," Nasreen said. "I think we're all in agreement: this is the same suspect we've been looking for in the Jackman case, yes? With that in mind, Detective Constable Weekes and I will take it from here, if that's okay with you, inspector?"

Stepping closer to the corpse, Weekes studied the small photo hanging from a string necklace, listening to her three superiors discuss the case more. Inspector Innes agreed to assist them in any way he could.

Picking up the necklace photo with her gloved hand, she saw how pretty Verity was, with lovely, long flowing blonde hair and a wide, attractive smile. Her arms were splayed out, like she was hugging the people to her left and right. She could just make out the person next to Verity's side. When they put the two photos together, Weekes was in no doubt they would fit. Having to concur with her supervisor, she turned to her colleagues. "Let's see what's on that USB stick; there might be something we can use."

34

———

Nasreen inserted the USB stick into the computer she'd been given by DI Innes, who was stood with folded arms behind her. The Sussex police station was small and cramped, with computers clumped together. Only partitions separated them. It was noisy, with about a dozen officers, mostly in uniform going about their business. It was a far cry from her station. Weekes sat next to her, while DS Edgeley stood next to Innes and behind her partner. "Let's see what we can see," she said to them all.

The monitor showed the camera being set-up, wobbling, until it was mounted on a tripod. Then it steadied, the light revealing an unconscious Verity Staunton tied to a tree, her head down. It really was like watching a snuff movie, Nasreen thought, as a silhouette walked in front of the camera. It was impossible to make out Shadow's size.

"I'm not sure I want to watch this after all," Weekes whispered.

"None of us want to," she whispered back. "We have to."

There was no sound on the video, which troubled her. Why

go to the effort of filming without sound? The suspect wanted the world to see the murders. Why not tell everyone why? Watching as Shadow stood to Verity's left, Nasreen flinched when the silhouette slapped Verity, hard. Then, the silhouette walked towards the camera, its face hidden, with no way of making out features. The lighting was such that it hid everything. Verity's mouth was moving, not that Nasreen could make out what she was saying. "Can we bring lip readers in on this?" she asked.

"Yeah, that won't be a problem," Innes said.

The silhouette marched in front of the camera, stopping in front of Verity. It pulled something out of its pocket and held it up for her to see. Then, pulled out something else from its pocket. "What's he doing? Is that a–?"

"A pair of scissors," Weekes finished. "He's cutting out her face."

"And there's the string," she added, watching as Silhouette hung the necklace around Verity's neck and walked back towards the camera. Poor Verity Staunton stood petrified, tied to the tree, her eyes wide, begging, her mouth animated, crying out for help.

The first arrow shot out and smashed through Verity's right knee, clearly sending a shock wave of pain through her. Nasreen averted her gaze when Verity's body seemed to spasm. She vomited down her top. "The sick bastard's enjoying this," Nasreen said to her colleagues, noticing how long it was – two and a half minutes – between the first and second arrows being fired.

With her heart rate elevated, she saw the second arrow hit Verity's left shoulder. The poor girl was in so much pain, Nasreen thought it cruel she hadn't fainted. The victim was screaming out, begging for help, while the suspect waited for a full four minutes before an arrow smashed into her other knee. She heard Weekes gasp. Nasreen put her hand on her partner's shoulder and squeezed. "You don't have to stay for this."

Weekes looked down at the floor. "It's okay; I'm fine."

A fourth arrow shot into Verity's other shoulder, the girl's face ghostly white. The camera displayed a dark patch around the victim's groin. "This bastard's going to pay for this," Nasreen said under her breath. It was one of the cruellest murders – if not the most – she'd had to investigate. The suspect really hated Verity, for whatever reason.

It was eight minutes, the suspect relishing the pain he was inflicting, before the final arrow was fired. Verity's mouth was open, screaming, when the arrow ended her life, smashing through the back of her skull and burying itself in the tree.

Silence fell over her group for what felt like an age.

No one wanted to end the respectful moment's silence.

"And after all that, we haven't learnt anything we didn't already know," Weekes said, the first to speak. "We need to catch this bastard, and soon, before he finds his next victim."

"We will. And you're wrong about not knowing more. Look at the time on the monitor. Our guy killed Verity exactly one week after murdering Myles Jackman, to the minute. I checked; he fired his first arrow at precisely 2am. That can't be a coincidence. And we know, without any doubt, that he's a marksman with a bow and arrow. This is all good to know."

"Edgeley and I are going to inform Verity's parents," Innes said. "If you want to speak with the witness, she's in interview room two. All I ask is that you go easy on her; she's fragile. We'll bring the parents back with us, so you can speak to them, too. In the meantime, I've got uniforms at the stables where she worked. We need to find out where she was abducted first of all – that's our priority."

"And we'll need access to her mobile, tablets, laptops, if she has them." Nasreen turned off the PC and pulled out the USB stick, dropping it back in its evidence bag. "Come on, Weekes." Nasreen stood and handed Innes the evidence bag. "Let's go and talk to the witness."

35

"Verity's such a lovely, sweet girl." Mrs Bamford sniffed, a tissue in her hand. "As far as I know, she's never hurt anyone. She wouldn't. I know you must hear this all the time, but Verity wouldn't hurt a fly. She's one of life's good ones. If she sees a worm on the pavement, she'll pick it up and put it on grass or in the earth, you know? She's a child of nature; she loves all living things equally."

Weekes saw the hurt on Bamford's wrinkly face. It was clear she knew the victim well enough to make these judgements about her. "I understand how hard this must be for you, Mrs Bamford, I really do. But we need to ask you these questions. They're going to help us apprehend her killer. Do you understand? He's still out there. He's already murdered two people, and we believe he intends to kill more."

"It sounds like you know Verity quite well, Mrs Bamford," Nasreen said. "Has she had any arguments with anyone recently? Or, say, broken up with a boyfriend? Anything like that? We need help getting to know her."

Bamford, a woman in her late fifties, with dark curly hair with flecks of grey coming through, wiped her nose with the tissue, tears welling up. She shook her head. "No! There's nothing like that; not that I know of anyway. She was delightful, always polite and courteous, always. She had a smile for everyone. It's how she became so successful with the hair styling." Tears rolled down her red cheeks. "I can't think of anyone who would want to hurt her. I met her boyfriend once. He was as lovely as her; they were so together."

Weekes wondered what the two victims had in common. First off, they had Myles, an arrogant, cocky bully, who deserved some form of comeuppance, but didn't deserve to be dragged around a car park naked. Then they had Verity, a kind, polite, animal-loving girl, apparently. The two couldn't be any more different. "Does the name Myles Jackman mean anything to you? He lived locally."

Shaking her head, Bamford answered, "I'm afraid not. Is he your suspect?"

"No, he's the first victim. We found photos of their own faces on the bodies, Mrs Bamford, and it looks like the two photos were part of the same overall picture. It looks to us like a group photograph, and we have no way of knowing how many people are in it." She took out her phone and showed her a picture of him. "This is Myles. Think, Mrs Bamford, have you seen him before?"

"I'm sorry! I haven't, detective."

Thinking they would get more information from family and friends, Weekes glanced at Nasreen and shrugged, letting her know she'd gone as far as she could. "Thank you, you've been a big help." She wanted to show their witness a photograph of Richard Pryce. Deciding against it, she stood.

"Yes, thank you for your co-operation," Nasreen added, joining her in standing. Weekes left her with the witness. "Please take my card. If you think of anything that might be useful or relevant, please don't hesitate in calling me. Any time, day or night."

Outside in the corridor, Weekes waited for Nasreen to come out of the interview room. "Well? What do you think?" she asked, walking towards the small office, where they would find Innes and Edgeley.

"We need to speak to the parents."

Their latest victim's parents were in shock, which was to be expected, having been informed by DI Innes, DS Edgeley and two uniforms of their daughter's untimely death. Nasreen, sat opposite Mrs Staunton, a rotund woman in her late forties, noted her bewildered expression. "You must be in shock, Mrs Staunton, I get it. I really do," she said, reaching across the table separating them and holding her hand, "but I need you to think, really hard, if you've seen this man before. Can you do that for me?"

"She's already told you, detective," Mr Staunton hissed. "We've never seen him before. He's not a part of Verity's life, that's for sure. We know all our daughter's friends. Please, stop pestering us with this nonsense."

"I'm afraid he is part of Verity's life, Mr Staunton," Weekes countered. "We know he is. The person who killed your daughter is the same person responsible for his murder. We know this as fact."

"It doesn't mean Verity knew him," the father growled. "They could be unrelated. It could be some lunatic out there."

Nasreen, hearing the anger in his voice, intervened. "My

partner's right. The suspect likes to leave photos of his victims' faces near the body, sir. This person's cutting out the faces of victims from a group photo. Verity and Myles were in the same photograph together, so, whether you know it, or not, your daughter and Myles did in fact know each other."

Silence.

Nasreen felt the hostility pouring out of him. Having tried the softly-softly approach, she tried a different tactic. "Look, we're not trying to upset you here, okay? The suspect left exactly one week between killing Myles Jackman and Verity, to the minute. If he holds true to form, we have just under a week to find this suspect before he abducts and kills his next victim from the group photo." She saw his expression change. "We'll find this man, sir, I promise you, but we need your help."

"We see her once a week," Mrs Staunton said, her voice fragile.

"Excuse me?" Nasreen tried to engage the wife.

Mrs Staunton glanced at her husband. "We don't know her that well, darling. We only see her once a week for dinner. She could be meeting all sorts of people we don't know about." The wife turned her attention to Nasreen. "Detective, please, ask her friends. They'll know far more about my Verity... her life... than we do. She has a lovely group of friends."

"Yes, please, ask her friends," Mr Staunton concurred. "I give you our permission to use her social media. She was always on Twitter and Instagram. We'll help in any way we can. I wish we knew her passwords."

"That's okay, we have a cyber unit who can access social media accounts," she said, sensing the hostility passing. "Thank you for that. Now, who would you say is closest to Verity? Who's her best friend?"

"That's easy," Mrs Staunton replied. "Tessa."

"Tessa?" Nasreen let it linger.

"Farnsworth," Mr Staunton confirmed. "She lives with Verity in the city. If anyone will know what's going on in our daughter's life, she will."

"That's great, we'll start with her," she replied, about to say "thank you" when her mobile vibrated on the table. It was Inspector Gupta. "If you'll excuse me, I need to take this." Leaving Weekes with the Stauntons, Nasreen walked out of the room and closed the door behind her. "Sir?"

"I thought you should know, I've been ordered to let Finn Palmer go," Gupta replied. "The super didn't give me a choice, I'm sorry. I know you liked him for it."

Cursing under her breath, Nasreen kicked the wall, not hard. "It could still be him, sir. There could be two killers." Even as she said it, she knew how it sounded.

"I instructed him not to go anywhere. Bukhari's playing it safe, watching his back, Nas, that's all. He doesn't want to risk the force being sued. I'd have done the same thing myself. Nothing untoward was found in his flat. We can't tie him to a pickup truck, and this morning's murder kind of proves he wasn't responsible for Jackman, even if he did threaten to kill him. You know we're right, don't you?"

And she did. "Yeah, I know. It just means we're back to square one is all. I was so certain last night. When he tried to run, I thought, 'This is it; this is our guy'. And now we have to start all over again."

"I know how it goes. If it's any consolation, it should be easier to find a connection with two victims. Find out how they knew each other, and you're halfway there, Nas. How bad was it?"

Lowering her voice, she replied, "Bad. Weekes was queasy, but she got through it. We've watched the video of it, too. He enjoys the killing, sir. He left minutes between firing the arrows. A full eight minutes between the first arrow and the kill shot in the mouth. At least we know we have exactly a week between kills."

"Providing he doesn't evolve, yeah. He might be finding his stride. The next one could come sooner, so be ready for it, is all I'm saying."

The thought had occurred to her. "Duly noted." A sudden thought popped in her head. "Sir? What about the assault charge? Palmer attacked Weekes. Couldn't we hold him on that while we look into him?"

"You think I didn't try that on Bukhari myself? It's a no-go, I'm afraid. We need to be looking elsewhere on this one, Nas. Sorry!"

Hanging up, she opened the door, as Weekes whipped her mobile from in front of the Stauntons. It was suspicious, Weekes trying her best to not look guilty. Ignoring it, checking the tape recorder was still on, she took her seat in front of Mrs Staunton. "Have you got anything else for them?" she asked, noting her partner placing her phone inside her suit jacket. "We'll need a list of Verity's friends to contact, Mr Staunton, if you don't mind writing them down?"

After the shocked parents had left the room, and after ordering Weekes to start phoning Verity's friends, Nasreen replayed the interview, fast forwarding until she excused herself and left the room. To her annoyance, her partner had used the alone time to question them about Richard Pryce. Weekes asked questions about him: had they ever seen him?

"That nuisance," Mr Staunton said. "I nearly had to take out an injunction against him, do you know that? Infatuated with her, he was."

"A sweet boy, really," Mrs Staunton said. "And not Verity's type at all. At first he was really shy, but after a while Verity must've got through his defences. He was keen on her. At first we laughed it off; he was just a fifteen-year-old boy, really–"

"I had to resort to going and speaking to his dad," Mr Staunton interrupted. "That put a stop to his stalking. Not a peep from him since."

Nasreen blew out a sigh. Listening to the excitement in Weekes' voice, if she wasn't entirely convinced of Pryce's guilt before, she would be now, Nasreen thought, stopping the recording. The fact that Pryce knew both victims put him higher on her list of suspects. If he didn't have an ironclad alibi, she'd be driving over to pick him up now. "Shit!" She opened the door and marched out to the office, fetched Weekes and marched back inside the interview room. "What the hell were you playing at?"

"What? What are you talking about?"

"Richard bloody Pryce is what I'm talking about. What's your bloody obsession with him, huh? Isn't it bad enough he gets bullied everywhere he goes, now he's being bullied by you? Leave the poor guy alone!" Her hands were shaking.

"He's still a suspect," Weekes replied, her voice growing in volume. "Just because you've discounted him, doesn't mean I have. Did you listen to the playback? He knows both victims!"

"Yes, I heard the tape, thanks, but it doesn't matter. He has an alibi, in case you'd forgotten. He was at the shelter at the time of Myles' murder. Shit, we even have video footage of him arriving and leaving. And I bet we'd find he was there this morning, too. What don't you understand about alibis? You've only been here five minutes and you think you know better than more experienced officers. Why is that?" There was a red haze in her peripheral vision.

"Because I'm right, that's why," Weekes replied. "You were wrong with Palmer, weren't you? Admit it, to my face. Admit you were wrong!"

Nasreen glared at her irritating partner. "I'm not admitting anything. It could still be Palmer. There might be two killers."

"Oh, I've heard it all now. You're so arrogant, you can't admit it, can you? You believe your own hype. The newspapers and news channels think you're special, so now you believe them. Well, you're not always right. It was Pryce, I'm telling you."

"What the hell's going on in here?" bellowed the stocky Inspector Innes, flying inside, as the door escaped his grip and banged against the wall. "This is a police station. We can hear you all the way down in the office, you know." His face was red with anger. "Whatever you're rowing about, it stops right now, or shall I give Inspector Gupta a call? Hmm? Shall I? Or are you going to shake on it and move on? It's your call."

Nasreen found herself staring at the floor. "I'm sorry, sir," she said, chided like a naughty schoolgirl. "It won't happen again." When she rose her gaze, Weekes was still staring at her. "It was very unprofessional of me. I apologise."

"Detective Constable Weekes?" Innes said, expectantly.

To Nasreen's joy, Weekes dropped her glare and apologised. Nasreen walked past her partner and DI Innes and into the hallway, where the officers were stood staring at her. They'd heard everything.

37

Weekes went to her refrigerator and took out her third can of cider. Still stewing after her argument with Nasreen, she grumbled to herself, opening the ring pull to the familiar hiss, sipping the bubbles overflowing. "You want another beer?" she shouted to Brian, who confirmed he did. Taking out a can of Fosters, she walked through to her tiny lounge, where he was sat on her sofa. There was some crappy show on her television, not that she was watching.

Lying back, getting comfortable, the can of cider in hand, she took a big mouthful. "She thinks she's this big shot because she caught Cara Mooney."

"Why does that name ring a bell? Cara Mooney," Brian asked, opening his can.

"She was that psycho woman. You remember, a month or so ago, she killed about eight people. It ended up in Scotland on a cliff. It was on the news for days after." Having to recount the story annoyed her.

"Oh, that sexy blonde. Oh shit, Nasreen caught her? Wow!"

Annoyed, Weekes turned and stared at him. "Hey! Whose side are you on?" He raised his eyebrows, his eyes wide, before he apologised, and she settled back in. "And now she thinks she's this expert detective. But she's not."

"Sod her, she's not worth it," he said, changing his tune. "I'd put my money on you any day. If you think it's this young fella, I believe you."

This was why she'd invited him over, she thought. And because it kept her away from the pub. It was Friday night and she didn't want a repeat of the previous week. This way, she'd control her drinking. If she had two or three cans of cider, she'd have enough to fall into a dreamless sleep, and not have a hangover in the morning. It was a tried and tested trick. She'd gone overboard the previous Friday, and it wouldn't happen again. "I knew there was a reason I let you come over."

Brian leaned in and kissed her.

Life sucked! It really did. Before her leg had been blown off, she'd had a career, husband, daughter... A family. A brilliant life, that's what she'd had. A beautiful home. Everything in the world to look forward to. What did she have now? A prosthetic leg; a shitty flat that she hated; a second-choice job with a crappy supervisor who didn't know what she was doing. She only got to see her Hazel on the weekends. The only thing she had was this builder she was sharing her Friday night with, who wasn't even her boyfriend.

"This is boring," Brian said. "Do you fancy going out for dinner? That new Mexican place has just opened. I can ring and see if they've got a spare table."

Weekes leaned forwards, letting him sit up. She studied him. "What, you mean, like a date? A sit down at a table and eat and chat date?" Perturbed, she didn't know what to say. Since losing her leg, she'd been on three terrible dates, the last one ending abruptly when she'd told him about her leg. "I don't know," she said, resting her can on the coffee table.

"Come on, it'll be great. Let me treat you to a meal for once.

I'll buy us a nice bottle of wine. You can order whatever you want from the menu. And you can tell me all about this nasty Nasreen. What do you say?"

"You know what? You're on." She stood and smiled down at him. "It's been ages since I got dressed up. Give me half an hour to get ready." Walking to the hall, she said, "Help yourself to another beer if you want one." Yeah, going out for once was just what she needed.

DAY 11
MONDAY, MAY 28TH

38

―――――――

Fiona Armstrong loved running. She loved a lot of things: riding horses, swimming, aerobics, to name a few. Her biggest love, though, was running cross-country. It was the adrenaline rush she felt after a run that she enjoyed the most. Behind her house that she shared with her beautiful boyfriend, Kieran, were acres of fields and a lovely thick area of woods which was perfect for her daily runs.

Every morning she donned her favourite Nike trainers, jog bottoms and tight-fitting vest and ran over the fields and into the woods. She hadn't missed a cross-country run in over a year. At thirty-four, none of her friends were as active as she was. If truth be known, she loved the comments she received from her friends about how fit she was, loved the attention Kieran gave her taut body. He was always touching her, squeezing her. It was addictive, being sexy. But most of all, she loved the attention it brought from strangers.

It was her long blonde hair and startlingly clear blue eyes that drove guys mental, she knew, except on top of that, she had the perfect hour-glass figure, which took hours of exercise and a healthy diet to achieve. No one honed a body as glorious as hers without it. And it was glorious. Fiona could spend hours getting ready for a night out, not that it took that long; she enjoyed admiring herself in the mirror, posing, pouting, taking selfies. Was she vain? Hell, yeah, she was. The way she looked at it, anybody with looks as stunning as hers would be. Kieran loved the way she looked; that was all that mattered. The strangers glancing at her from afar was an added bonus.

This morning's run was extra special. She was starting her new position as Senior Client Advisor at McGill, Farnham and Hill, her hedge fund company. And she deserved it, having missed three promotion opportunities to guys over the last five years. Now was her time to shine, and she knew she would. She would shine as bright professionally as she did in front of the mirror, for Fiona was ambitious, in addition to being fabulously fit and healthy.

It was a couple minutes past five o'clock when she entered the woods, having run three miles through the fields behind her house. The sun was up, and it promised to be a belter, with temperatures predicted to be as high as twenty-six. While running, she thought about what to wear to work to celebrate her new position, her new authority. Thinking of her staff, the thought of being their boss turning her on as she ran, she heard the faint sound of barking. Thinking nothing of it, she continued dreaming of the power she now yielded. Oh yes, life had been kind to her.

Running past big old oaks and younger sycamores, ash trees and numerous bushes she couldn't identify, she felt the earth under her feet as she flew along at a good pace, her lungs burning. Focusing on her breathing, she heard the barking again, this time louder. There were two, no three sets of barking. Looking behind her, slowing her pace, she couldn't see anything. Picking up speed, she ploughed ahead, smiling at visions of her small team of underlings beavering away at her behest.

The best part of working for MFH was being one of only five women in a company of over thirty. It gave her the pick of the bunch, which was how she'd met Kieran. He was the best-looking guy there, so obviously she'd had to go for him, after playing hard to get for a few months. She wasn't easy, not in the slightest. Fiona made him wait until their eighth date for him to get what he wanted. And it had been worth it, she thought, narrowly missing a bush that appeared out of nowhere. She needed to concentrate, instead of daydreaming.

From behind her came a loud growling.

A scream escaped her when she turned her head and saw a muscular dog chasing her. It wasn't a staffy, she realised, its snout was too long. Panicking, she ran, picking up speed, everything blurred, while she ran for her life.

Desperate to find the dog's owner, scanning for a person, she screamed when she felt a nip at her ankle. Its growl, when she managed to free herself, told her it was after blood. And it kept coming. "Help!" she shouted, wanting the owner to call off his dog. "Help!" Her cries more desperate.

Still running, the dog attempting to grab her every couple of seconds, Fiona knew she couldn't continue like this. The dog would bite her eventually; it was a matter of when, not if. She needed a way out, and soon.

Up ahead, there was a big old oak tree. Up was the only way to avoid being mauled by the brutish mutt chomping on her heels. There was a branch low enough to grab if she ran up the trunk a little way. It was her only hope, she realised, feeling the dog's breath on the back of her leg. It was now or never.

Reaching the tree, Fiona lunged at it, her left foot finding the tree's bark.

As she was about to launch herself up, she felt the pain of teeth puncturing her Achilles tendon. Pain soared through her.

She screamed as the dog yanked her backwards, making her fall flat on her face.

It tore into her leg, munching on it, like it were a treat.

Clawing at the earth, screaming, Fiona tried to crawl towards the oak, its size and height her only safety. It was futile, the dog was gnawing on her leg, occasionally pulling her back, growling while he tore into her flesh.

She saw another lump bounding towards her. It growled, too. Clawing harder didn't help. Teeth tore into her back, sinking in. Warm blood soaked into her vest. She was dying.

If she wasn't to be torn to pieces, her only hope was turning onto her back and trying to grapple with the dogs. Their front legs were their weak point. If she could pull them apart, they'd die of a heart attack.

A third muscular dog barked from behind her.

Hope faded fast.

The dogs, growling at one another, fighting over her, rolled her onto her back.

They were too strong for her. She had one on each leg and the third ran in and grabbed her breast. The pain was overwhelming. Fiona tried grabbing at the dog chewing her breast; she managed to find one of its ears and tugged at it as hard as she could, hearing it whimper, then let go of her.

Her victory was short-lived, as it recovered and came back angrier than before, sinking its teeth into her breast again. Screaming, a feral scream, she saw yet another dog running towards her. It wasn't fair! She couldn't fight off three mutts, much less four.

It came in fast, bypassing the others, straight for her throat.

She felt it clamp its jaws into her neck, tearing at her, snarling, feeding off her life force. She conceded, feeling every bite, every gnaw from the four dogs.

Blood poured down her from the torn flesh in her neck.

Her screaming turned to gargling,

She heard a whistle.

All four dogs stopped feeding off her and ran away, leaving her lying on the blood-soaked earth beneath, the earth she'd once cherished pounding on. Everything went dark.

The last thing she saw was a masked figure stood over her.

39

Nasreen had calmed down after Friday's row with Weekes. It took a full weekend of interviews with Verity's friends and relatives to do so. While Weekes was off, looking after her daughter, Nasreen had visited numerous witnesses, all of whom seemed to agree that Verity was a largely loved, vibrant, happy-go-lucky girl. She had a good social life, a hectic professional life, and indulged in several hobbies, her favourite being horse riding.

Hearing a couple of her colleagues saying hello to Weekes, she knew her partner was in. Without looking up, she clicked on a website for the stables Verity worked at. It advertised special deals for joining the riding club, discounts for children and students. There were photos under the gallery section, showing off the grounds and surrounding countryside. Not that she knew why, Nasreen had a gut feeling that there was a link at the stables.

"Morning," Weekes said, smiling.

"Morning," Nasreen replied, getting back to it, leaving Weekes to her own devices for a while. She had shown a photograph of Myles Jackman to every friend of Verity's she'd interviewed and not one of them recognised him, which she found odd. They knew Verity and Myles were acquainted – more than acquainted, they were filmed in the same photo, next to one another beaming about something. Her friends not recognising Myles posed a problem. The family hadn't proved helpful, either.

There was one friend she hadn't managed to interview yet, Verity's housemate, Tessa Farnsworth. Nasreen had knocked on Verity's door expecting to meet Tessa. Instead, she'd walked away with nothing. After phoning Tessa's mobile and listening to a voicemail, she then knew Tessa was away for the weekend, from Thursday night until Monday morning. She had hoped that Tessa might know more than Verity's other friends, who'd all wanted to help, but couldn't.

Verity's car had been found in the stables' car park, so Nasreen knew that the suspect had abducted her from there. The crime scene was a good three miles away from the abduction site, which meant Verity had to have been driven by the suspect to the crime scene. Nasreen hadn't had the chance to speak with anyone at the stables, which she hoped to remedy today. "How was your weekend?" she asked Weekes, not averting her gaze from the monitor.

"Great, thanks," Weekes' cheerful voice replied from behind the partition. "Yours?"

"I managed to interview a lot of Verity's friends. They all agree she was a lovely person. None of them recognise Myles Jackman, although they're all from around here. We still need to interview her oldest friends from the village, but they're all dotted around the country. Most of them left the village and made lives for themselves elsewhere."

Weekes stood and peered over the partition. "We'll have to phone them, I guess. If you give me the list, I can make a start now, if you want?" Her face was fresh, and she looked happy, for once. "Hey, I just wanted to apologise for Friday," she whispered. "I had no right to shout at you like that."

Sitting back in her chair, Nasreen was so taken aback she thought she might fall off it. An apology was the last thing she'd expected. After a long pause, she replied, "Yeah, same here. It got out of hand. I'm sorry, too." When Weekes smiled at her, she saw how pretty her partner really was. The animosity between them had hidden it from her. "Are we good?" she asked, hoping their argument had broken the thick ice.

"Yeah, we're good."

With a smile, Nasreen got back to work. They had a long day ahead of them, which would've been made longer had Weekes been sulking. Nasreen picked up her landline phone and dialled Tessa Farnsworth's number. It was the worst phone call she'd ever had to make. The girl could barely speak she was so upset.

During the five-minute call, Nasreen managed to glean that Tessa had found out about Verity's death in Manchester, where she was visiting her parents. Instead of travelling back to her shared house with Verity, she'd taken comfort with her family, who'd rallied around her. Tessa was home, just, and invited her to come over.

"We've got our first interview of the day." Nasreen grabbed her jacket. "This isn't going to be an easy one, either."

40

Weekes felt better than she had in a long time. Friday night's dinner with Brian was just what she'd needed. He bought her food and drinks, and he'd been quite charming, complimenting her on her black dress when she appeared in the living room, saying how beautiful she looked. The food and company had been more than welcome. And in the early hours of the morning, she'd asked him to leave her bed, which he obeyed, kissing her goodbye. For the first time in their union, she thought she might see a future with him? She didn't know.

And her weekend with Hazel couldn't have been better, either. Nevan dropped her off nice and early on Saturday morning. After watching silly children's TV, she took Hazel to the park before lunch, then on to a museum in the afternoon. McDonald's for dinner, followed by the cinema in the evening. It was the perfect day.

Sunday was quieter, which was always the case, the highlight being Sunday roast over at her parents' house. Hazel loved her grandparents; they made such a fuss. Movie night on the sofa went down well, even if they did watch the same Disney films. Weekes didn't mind; she was happy to be with her daughter.

"You're on good form this morning," Nasreen remarked.

There was no denying it, she was. "Yeah, I had a great weekend with Hazel," she replied, as Nasreen brought the car to a stop outside a semi-detached house. "Is this it?" she enquired, observing the unkempt lawn and battered picket fence. "They aren't gardeners, that's for sure. Looks like it hasn't been mown in weeks."

"Come on, let's see what Tessa has to say."

Weekes knocked on the door. It was answered by a tall woman in her early thirties, who Weekes took to be Tessa Farnsworth. With long ginger hair, a pale complexion and freckles, Tessa was pretty, in an unconventional way. Their host invited them inside, hiding most of her face with her hair. She'd been crying, Weekes noted. "We're sorry for your loss, Miss Farnsworth," she said, being led into the lounge, where she sat on a comfortable black leather sofa. Weekes waited for Nasreen to make the introductions.

"We need to know more about Verity," Nasreen said, producing the photo of Myles. "Can you tell me, did she know this man?"

Weekes watched, hopeful. "Have you seen him before?"

"Myles, yeah, I've met him," Tessa replied, holding the picture. "Verity was devastated when she heard about what happened to him." She paused, holding a tissue. "Wait! You don't think they're connected, do you?"

"We know they are," Weekes confessed, glancing at Nasreen. "I'm sorry to say they were killed by the same person, of that we're certain. What we need to know is why? If we know how Verity and Myles met, we might get closer to finding the suspect."

"Do you know how they knew each other?" Nasreen asked.

Tessa handed the photograph back to Nasreen. "I only met

him a couple of times. All I can tell you is they both lived in villages in Sussex. As far as I know they met here, in the city, though. She brought him home one Sunday lunchtime, and he spent the best part of the afternoon crying about how his girl-friend was cheating on him. That must've been three, maybe four weeks ago now. He seemed like a decent enough bloke, though."

"Is there anything else you can think of?" Nasreen asked. "Did they have anything in common? Apart from living in Sussex, I mean."

"I think they both liked horse riding," Tessa replied. "I don't get it myself; I don't see what all the fuss is about. But I remember Verity telling me she went for a ride with him one Sunday. She always went riding on Sundays. Every week, without fail."

"From the stables she worked at, is that what you mean?"

"Yeah, she drives there every Thursday to help with the accounting, and then goes there every Sunday morning, early... Or rather did." She brought the tissue up to her eyes. "I'm so sorry! I said I wasn't going to cry... I just want... I want her back."

Glad that Nasreen was more empathetic than she was, Weekes watched her comfort their distraught interviewee. It had something to do with the stables. That was the link. But what? Both Myles and Verity visited the stables and rode together, on at least one occasion.

Eager to get going, Weekes stood. "We don't want to take up any more of your time, Miss Farnsworth," she said, seeing the nod of approval from Nasreen. "You've been a huge help, and we assure you, we're going to bring Verity's killer to justice, okay?"

Nasreen took another few minutes comforting Tessa, while Weekes saw herself out and waited in the car. Weekes was excited to see what secrets the stables held – there had to be something there. "Get in! Get in!" she ordered Nasreen. "We've got to get over there."

"You are keen," Nasreen replied, sitting in the passenger seat, fastening her belt. She glanced over at Weekes, a smile forming. "I'd call that a breakthrough, wouldn't you?"

41

Pulling up in the stables car park, Nasreen was excited to see what secrets it held. Tessa Farnsworth's linking Verity and Myles was a huge breakthrough for them. It was about time they had some luck on this case, she thought, getting out of their car, closing the door. So far they had two murders and were no nearer finding a suspect than they were when they'd received the case. "There's someone," she said to Weekes, spying a woman wearing jodhpurs, black boots, a khaki green jacket and black hat. She put the woman in her mid to late fifties. "Excuse me!" She waved.

The slim lady stopped. Taking her identification out, Nasreen explained who she and Weekes were and why they were there. Identifying herself as the stables and riding school's manager, Olive Kramer welcomed them, inviting them into the office, where Verity worked, she added. Nasreen liked Olive; she had a pleasant manner about her, an affable demeanour.

Sinking into her leather swivel chair, Olive's face crumpled. "I still can't believe it," she said, fighting back the tears. "She was such a lovely girl. And to think she was abducted just outside in the car park sends shivers down my spine." Dabbing her eyes with a tissue, she said, "I only wish I'd argued harder about getting cameras fitted."

"You don't have any cameras at all?" Weekes asked, surprised.

"No! We've never needed any before. Well, not until someone broke in and slashed one of the horses. I argued with the owner about installing CCTV, but she disagreed. The police found out it was the boyfriend of one of the horse owners. He was jealous of how much time his girlfriend spent here, apparently."

"That's awful." Changing the subject, Weekes asked, "Who was the last person to see Verity on Thursday evening?"

"Me. I left her at her desk at around half six. Verity stays late updating the accounts." Olive dabbed her eyes again. "I'm sorry! I told myself I wasn't going to cry. I haven't known her that long, but she was such a lovely girl."

"Oh? Can I ask how long you've known her for?" Weekes asked.

"I started working here a little over two months ago."

"And your predecessor? How long was she here for?"

"A long time, apparently. I was told I had large boots to fill by Winifred, the owner."

Knowing what Weekes was driving at, Nasreen asked, "And Winifred, where is she? The reason we're asking is that we need to know the history of this place." She saw the understanding appear.

"She's on holiday, I'm afraid. She's due back next week. I've left a voicemail for her to inform her of Verity's... But she's on a cruise. I don't know how often she'll check her phone, though."

Bloody cruises! While hunting for Cara Mooney, Lucy's parents had been on a cruise. "Not to worry. What about your predecessor? Do you have a number for her?" They needed a break. She wanted to speak to someone with knowledge of the stables. "What is it, Ms Kramer?" Their interviewee was wearing a worried expression.

"She died, I'm afraid."

Weekes glanced at her. "How?"

With a sudden pang of excitement, Nasreen waited for Olive to respond. When the manager explained that her predecessor died of cancer a month earlier, the excitement disappeared. Hoping for an unexplained death, those hopes were dashed. Although nothing seemed untoward, so far, she had a gut feeling the stables were at the centre of the investigation. It was their only link to date. "Is there anyone here we could talk to about Verity? Who knew her best, in your opinion?"

"I'd say Claire," Olive replied. "She's clearing out a stable. I can go and get her."

"Please, don't get up, Ms Kramer," Nasreen ordered, making her sit back down. "We'll chat to her in due course. What we really need is a list of employees and customers to cover, say, the last fifteen years. Would you be able to get that for us?"

"Absolutely." Olive pulled her chair forwards, turning her attention to the PC in front of her. "I have full access to the database. It shouldn't take long to find that for you."

"I'll be outside," Weekes said, getting up.

Behind Olive, hanging up on the wall were photographs in frames of people. There were lots of them, some taken years ago, while others were more recent. A lot of them had children smiling next to horses, wearing their riding gear. Some were of groups of youngsters. "May I?" Nasreen asked Olive, who nodded, telling her that the owner liked to show these photos to her future customers. Nasreen hadn't noticed, but there were a lot more out in the front office, where Verity had worked.

One photo took her by surprise. It was Irwin Landers, the gay student Myles had tormented at Beacon Downs. The picture was old, but she was certain it was him. Having interviewed him very briefly, she'd been satisfied with his alibi for the night of Myles' murder. Now, she was sensing a rat. According to Landers, he'd been at a party with his partner. She'd verified it with the homeowner of the party. He and Warrick, his partner, had left at half nine and spent the rest of the night at home – Warrick was unwell. Now, seeing the photo, she'd just put Landers at the top of her list. "You don't mind if I take this, do you?"

"Help yourself," Olive replied, off printing her list. "Here it is. Employees, current and past, and all customers for the past fifteen years. I hope it helps. The thought of this person being out there fills me with dread. I hate leaving here alone now."

"Thanks," she said, gesturing to the picture of Landers. "And I wouldn't go worrying too much, Ms Kramer, it appears the suspect knows who they're after. He's not an opportunist; he has a list of victims. That being said, I really need to speak with Claire."

"I'll introduce you now." Olive got up and made her follow her through the office outside, where Weekes was looking at the photographs on the wall.

"Weekes," she said, quietly, handing her partner the picture in the frame. Why hadn't she dug in deeper with Landers? Was it because he was gay? Did she not think a gay guy capable? "Check it out," she whispered to Weekes, while following Olive out into the courtyard.

"Where is she?" Olive asked, walking up to an empty stable. Grabbing a fellow stable worker's attention, she brought the girl over. "Have you seen Claire?"

"She was here a minute ago." The stable hand turned fully around. "She can't be far."

"Please, forgive me, detective." Olive looked around the courtyard. "Her car's still here. She must be around somewhere. Let me go find her for you."

Nasreen's suspicions were aroused when she heard Olive in the distance. "This is it, Weekes. This is the place, I know it," she said to a nod from her partner. "What's wrong, Ms Kramer?" she asked Olive, who was running towards her, flustered. "What is it?"

"I can't find her," the panicked manager replied. "I've looked everywhere. She wouldn't leave here without her car. It's her pride and joy."

"You're absolutely certain she's not on the premises?" Nasreen asked, needing to double-check, just in case.

Olive nodded, saying it wasn't like her to just up and disappear.

"In that case, it's a good job we're here."

42

———

"She can't be far," Weekes said, driving slowly along a country road with fields either side. "If she left minutes before we spoke to that stable hand on foot, she won't be this far out. We should head back to the stable."

"Let's go." Nasreen sighed, holding her mobile.

After finding a suitable place to turn round, Weekes drove back in the direction of the stables when Nasreen's phone rang. It was DI Innes. Listening to the conversation on speaker phone, Innes informed them that Claire Padnall, the stable hand they were looking for had no history on the PNC; she was an unknown entity. All they had were her address, vehicle registration, and next of kin. Focusing on the road, Weekes glanced at Nasreen writing the addresses down. Nasreen thanked Innes and ended the call.

"Do you want to try her house?" Weekes asked, pulling the visor down against the sun and feeling grateful that the car came with air con.

"If we're quick, we might beat her there. If that's where she's heading. Something tells me it's not, though. I think she has something to do with it."

"I'm inclined to agree with you. Even if she's not directly involved, she knows something. It's a bit suspect for her to take off like that, especially without her car." Typing the postcode into the dashboard GPS, while concentrating on the road, Weekes couldn't help but feel the excitement. They were getting closer, she could feel it in her gut. They had the link they were looking for. While driving, she wondered how Richard Pryce fitted into it. Maybe Claire was on her way to him now?

Nasreen's phone rang again.

"Go ahead, sir, you're on speaker!" Nasreen shouted over the noise of the car.

"We've just been called out to a dog attack," Innes replied. "A colleague was called this morning. When his partner found the photo, he immediately called me. You'd best get over there. I'll give you the postcode, hold on."

Weekes groaned, waiting for it. She listened, tight-lipped, as Nasreen and Innes spoke and Nasreen typed in the postcode. The identity of the woman found was unknown. It looked like she was out running when she was attacked by a number of dogs.

Hungry, but not wanting to eat before viewing a bloody body, Weekes turned the car round as soon as Innes rang off. "So much for our theory of having a week to find him."

"Shit!" was all Nasreen said.

Following the bends across the Sussex countryside, Weekes wasn't looking forward to reaching the crime scene. Yet as much as she was dreading it, she was excited. She'd been working with Nasreen for over a week, and although she'd hoped to be partnered with someone else, she was enjoying the case. If she and Nasreen successfully brought this case to a conclusion and found out who the suspect was, she'd be a step closer to making sergeant. While driving towards the crime scene, Weekes decided not to badger Superintendent Bukhari, to leave it until after they'd brought the suspect to justice.

43

"Nasreen, is this murder linked to the dragging and bow and arrow murders?" a reporter shouted above the throng of voices trying to be heard. "Do you have any suspects yet?"

"When we have anything to announce, you'll be the first to know," Nasreen replied.

Weekes followed, stooping to walk under the cordon the uniform was holding up for them. It was another wooded area situated among acres of fields. She thought it would make the perfect cross-country run, had it not been so secluded. Behind her, about three miles away was a housing estate, which was probably where the victim lived. A SOCO, dressed in a white protective suit, handed her one.

It was becoming routine for her to crawl into the forensic overalls. Covering her mouth and nose with a mask, Weekes was ready to venture into the crime scene, which wasn't dissimilar to their last. Nervous, she followed Nasreen through the woods. Up ahead, she could see at least half a dozen SOCOs carrying out their duties. The area was heavily wooded, meaning she had to weave in and out of trees and bushes, much like the victim must have, she thought, except the victim would've been running for her life.

Inspector Innes and Sergeant Edgeley, one short, the other tall, walked up to them. Weekes could see the body, but from a distance she couldn't see much. Innes was carrying a polythene bag. In it, she could see a tiny photo. Nasreen took it, studied it, and handed it to her. It was a picture of a really pretty blonde girl beaming. "Two women and a man," she said, more to herself than anyone else.

"And just the stables in common with two of them, so far," Nasreen replied, taking the bag back.

"This one's brutal, so prepare yourselves," Innes said, taking the bag from Nasreen and leading them to the body. "We have an ID now. Her name's Fiona Armstrong. She had her mobile on her arm in one of those pouches for when she runs. My colleague called her boyfriend's number and left a message to meet with us. She has no priors, never been in trouble. All we have is her usual address and car reg details."

There was so much blood, on the body and seeping into the mud beneath her. Weekes saw the gashes, the torn flesh from where the dogs had mauled her legs, breasts and neck. Fiona Armstrong was staring skyward, permanently fixed in a state of terror. Her vest top was red, with patches of its original white. The dogs had torn through the breast area; she could see where chunks of flesh had been ripped away. "Oh my God! They're getting worse," Weekes said, feeling nauseous.

The victim's throat injuries were by far the most extensive. Her neck was gone, flesh torn, veins and arteries severed. And she was so pretty, with her whole life in front of her, she thought, sorrowful at the needless loss of life. Sorrow passed over for anger. "Damn it! We're supposed to be stopping this," she cried, noting Innes's stare. "What? We are. This is our job, and we failed."

"Weekes, unfortunately this takes time," Nasreen replied, trying to calm her. "I wish we could conjure up our bad guy, but we can't. We need help with this. Sir, we need to find Claire Padnall, like now."

"I've got my best team on it. They're looking all over for her. If she's still around the area, they'll find her. Don't worry."

Listening to her three colleagues converse, Weekes bent down and studied the body closely. It wasn't that she wanted to; she had to. "Dogs," she said to her superiors. "You can't just order a dog to attack someone. These have to be fighting dogs, or specially trained, or something. Even a pack of dogs won't kill someone if ordered, unless they've been trained. We need to compile a list of dangerous dog owners in the area."

"That's a good idea," Nasreen said.

"Consider it done. I'll call the office and get it for you," Edgeley said.

"But the kind of dogs these are, the owners won't be on a register. They'll be hidden." Innes stared down at her with apologetic eyes.

"Shit!" Weekes was still studying the neck wound; it was so deep and bloody. Looking up at Nasreen, she had it. "Extend the list to include noise complaints from angry neighbours. These kinds of dogs will be noisy."

"Done." Edgeley wrote it down on his notepad.

"And if this is our guy, he'll be driving a 2005 Ford Ranger," Nasreen said. "We'll need to go door to door, asking people if they've seen one in the area."

After the inspector left to speak with the boyfriend at the station, Weekes studied the surrounding area. The earth was softer under the trees, boggier, than it had been at Verity's crime scene. She could make out scratch marks from where Fiona had tried to claw her way to safety. Back towards the reporters, Weekes identified separate, large foot indentations. The SOCOs

– the consummate professionals that they were – had seen them and marked them with flags. They would take impressions of them as evidence. They were big feet, too.

"I'm going to ask Inspector Gupta to ask Cyber to look into all three victims on social media," Nasreen said, her mobile to her ear. "They all knew each other, so there has to be a social trail we can follow."

"I'll go through their tablets and laptops, if you want? I know what I'm doing. Only if you want?" Weekes' nice act seemed to be paying off. Nasreen agreed without comment. She and Brian had agreed her strategy on Friday, at the restaurant. Weekes had put in a request for the speed camera footage near Brambles Animal Shelter and was waiting for a reply. Until she'd seen the video, she would play good cop, until it was time to play bad cop. Nasreen walked away, pulled her mask down to speak to Gupta. Nasreen and the inspector were talking about Irwin Landers. "Well?" Weekes asked.

"Cyber are on it," Nasreen replied. "And uniforms are going to bring in Landers for us. Sergeant Edgeley, you're good finishing up here, right? We've got to head back to our station."

Sergeant Edgeley said it was fine. They had uniforms out looking for Claire Padnall, too. Weekes would start getting dizzy with all the trips back and forth. All she wanted was to find the killer before he struck again. She didn't even care if it was Richard Pryce, or not.

44

───────

"You're going to need a better story than that, Irwin," Nasreen said, not buying it. "As it stands, we have three murders and you don't have an alibi for any of them. Take Myles Jackman's murder, for example. You were at a party with your partner until half nine, right?" She waited for him to nod. "Then, you say you put him to bed and let him drift off, meaning you could easily have left the flat, driven to the car park and abducted Myles."

"What? That's crazy talk, detective," Irwin scoffed, a tall, broad-shouldered man with bleached white hair, receding on top. He was wearing a Guns N' Roses T-shirt and blue jeans. "I didn't like the bloke, sure, that's no secret, but I didn't kill him. And I know you can't prove I did because I know I didn't."

"Please watch your tone, Detective Maqsood," Irwin's solicitor said. "He's co-operating. The second I think you're badgering him, we're out of here."

"Okay, Irwin, tell us again where you were last Thursday night from midnight until six o'clock Friday morning. For the record. We know where you said you were at the time of Myles' murder. What about Verity's?" Weekes said.

183

"At home alone. I just broke up with Warrick on Thursday morning, so I rang in sick to work. I stayed in all day, drinking myself into a stupor, until I fell asleep and woke up with the daddy of all hangovers on Friday morning about eight."

"And you didn't see anyone all day?" Nasreen asked. "Not one person? You'd just broken up with the love of your life and you didn't seek solace in any friends or family members? You didn't invite anyone over? You didn't drive to a friend's house?" All she got was a shake of his head. "And this morning, where were you at around four?"

"Asleep, at home. I haven't been in the mood for going out since Warrick left. I was in bed when you guys came knocking on my door. You know you can't bully me into a confession, don't you? I'm a single guy, living alone in a flat. I know it doesn't sit well with you, but I haven't done anything wrong. I certainly didn't kill those people, although part of me feels like shaking the hand of the guy who killed Myles; he was a special kind of prick, that guy. You've probably done your own research on him, you know what I'm saying."

"Irwin, that's enough," his solicitor said. "Answer the questions they ask, and don't give them any more than they need."

Nasreen needed that stupid truck. Without it, they had very little, certainly not enough to charge him. He was right: even without an alibi for each murder, it wasn't enough. "And you didn't go out to a shop, or off-licence, nothing like that? We're trying to eliminate you from our enquiries, you know, and you're not helping us here."

"It's not my client's job to help you, Detective Maqsood," the solicitor said. "The onus is on you to prove my client's guilt. And so far, you haven't provided one shred of proof that Irwin murdered those poor people. Now, I'm going to have to ask you to save your questions for another time; I'm needed elsewhere, I'm afraid."

"Excuse me?" Her temper was beginning to boil. "I don't really care what you have planned this evening, Mr Yates. We're not finished and given that your client knows two out of three of the victims, I'd say we're going to be here a while, so buckle up."

"And given that your client was bullied relentlessly by the first victim, I'd say that alone is motive to murder, Mr Yates, wouldn't you?" Weekes added.

There was a palpable silence.

Passing the photo of Irwin she took from the stables, Nasreen waited for Irwin's reaction. Raised eyebrows. "I found that at the stables where Verity worked," she said, studying him for any tells. "You say you don't know her, but we know you do. So, my question is, why lie about it, hmm? What good can come from lying to us?"

Irwin glanced over at Mr Yates. "All right, I know her. I don't know why I said I didn't. Probably because I thought it'd make me look guilty."

"How well did you know her?" Weekes asked.

"Not that well. We rode together, okay? I joined the riding school around the same time she did, maybe fifteen years ago. I went there twice a week to learn to ride, so did she. One afternoon after a lesson we got talking and hit it off. She knew I was gay; I think she liked the idea of having a gay friend. After that we were inseparable for a couple of years, until she started hanging out with a group of idiots. We had a huge row one day, and the next day, a couple of those idiots beat me up on my way home from the riding school. We didn't talk again."

"So, you had a grudge against Myles and Verity," Nasreen said, catching a knowing look from Weekes. She was almost certain he was their guy – he was the right size for the dragging killer; he'd been beaten up by Verity's friends and bullied by Myles. It was the third victim, Fiona, that they had to tie him to. "I have to say, Irwin, it's not looking good for you right now. You have motive for both murders. Why not come clean and tell us what happened?"

"What is this, amateur hour?" Yates said. "All you have is circumstantial. My client admits knowing two of the victims, even having run-ins with them, but you and I both know the CPS will throw this out in a heartbeat. You're going to need a lot more than this before you ask for a confession."

"Oh, we will. We haven't even started your client's background check yet. I'm betting we find a link to Fiona Armstrong, and when we do... Let's just say charges will be brought against him." She turned her attention to Irwin. "Do yourself a favour and come clean now, Irwin; it'll be better for you in the long run."

"That's it! Enough. Get up, Irwin, we're leaving."

There was nothing she could do to stop the solicitor leaving with his client. She'd stepped too far, too fast. It *was* all circumstantial. Still, her gut told her it was him. Standing up and meeting Irwin's stare, she said, "Don't go leaving town. I'm certain we're going to have more questions for you."

The interview room door opened, and Inspector Gupta poked his head inside. "Nas, Weekes, can I see you, please?"

"Sure," Nasreen replied, getting up. "Mr Yates and Irwin are just leaving."

"Um, no they're not," Gupta corrected.

"Excuse me, inspector?" Yates said, stopping at the door.

Gupta blocked their way. "Some new information's come to light, I'm afraid, Mr Yates. Take a seat, please. We'll be right back." His tone was forceful, official.

The way Gupta was talking excited Nasreen, who watched Yates and Irwin reluctantly take their former seats. He had something good, something they could use, she was sure of it. "Coming, sir," she said, Weekes following her.

Out in the corridor, Gupta walked back to the office, Nasreen and Weekes following, wondering what the new information could be. At his desk, she stood by his side as he sat in his seat. Weekes stood the other side. When he pressed his mouse button, the screen showed Verity Staunton's Facebook account. "So, Cyber's been over Myles, Fiona and Verity's social media accounts with a fine toothcomb. They put a team of six on it. It's pretty clean, actually, except this." He clicked on a thread. "Over two hundred and fifty comments on one of Verity's posts."

Nasreen read the post. It was a newspaper article in favour of animal culling – more particularly the culling of badgers and foxes for the good of other groups of wild animals in the UK. Gupta scrolled through the comments slowly enough for them to get the gist of the argument. "That doesn't sit with what the dog walker said about her, does it?" Nasreen said. "She's supposed to be a nature lover. Picks up worms off the pavement, apparently. Now she's in favour of culling animals?"

"Now she's in favour of fox hunting," Weekes said, ahead of Nasreen in the comments.

"What? That can't be," Nasreen said, reading the row between users. "How can anyone be in favour of fox hunting in this day and age? It's barbaric!"

"She grew up on a farm in rural Sussex remember," Weekes reminded her. "Maybe growing up there gives them a different take on it. Hey, I'm just saying."

"The topic isn't the interesting thing." Gupta scrolled further and pointed at a name on the conversation feed. "Look who it is," he added, excited. "He knows all three victims."

"And threatened them, too," Nasreen added, reading Irwin's comment about how *they* all needed culling, not the innocent wildlife. It was a nasty argument, with Verity saying how foxes were vermin, scavengers, murderers. Irwin went on to say that humans are the real vermin, not foxes. Further down, after the comments had turned to lots of capitals, Myles, Verity and Fiona ganged up on Irwin. In fact, a lot of Verity's friends seemed to be pro culling and pro fox hunting. "Oh my God! He did threaten to kill them," she said, taking control of Gupta's mouse. "I hope you burn in hell," she said, reading Irwin's words out loud. "We've got you now, Irwin."

"Steady on, Nas," Gupta said, bringing her back down to Earth. "We're getting there, at least. That's two lies we've got him on now. We've got him knowing all three victims with no alibis for any of them. What we don't have is real, solid proof. If we could tie him to a truck, that would be something."

"Give us another crack at him, please," she begged. His nod gave her hope. Excited, she said, "Yes!" And high-fived Weekes, who was smiling that pretty, genuine smile again. "You won't regret this, sir. And if we're unsuccessful, we've got enough on him to keep him in for questioning, haven't we?"

"I'll put a request in for another twenty-four hours in the morning," he replied. "I'll keep Cyber on it, and if we don't have enough this time tomorrow, I'll ask for another extension. And I'm going to ask a magistrate for a property search warrant for his flat. Now get going, detectives, we're going to need a confession on this one."

45

"Sorry for the delay." Nasreen closed the door, stepped up to the table and switched the tape recorder on, getting back to it. Irwin looked worried, biting his bottom lip, his leg bobbing up and down. It was how she wanted him. Facing him, with Weekes next to her facing Yates, she leaned on the table. "Didn't know Fiona Armstrong, huh?" She couldn't help adding a sly smile. "That's Verity and Fiona you say you don't know. We know the first one's a lie, Irwin. Now we know you lied about not knowing Fiona, too."

"What?" He looked like a deer caught in car headlights. "I don't know her; I don't know what you're talking about." He glanced to Yates for reassurance. "I don't."

"Yeah, quite the row you had with her, as it goes," Weekes added, her arms folded.

"You're off your rockers, both of you. I don't fucking know her, okay? I've never met anyone called Fiona."

"Quite the temper you've got there," Nasreen said in the calmest voice. "Things get to you, don't they? Being in here, talking to us, culling, fox hunting."

Irwin tipped his head back and rubbed his eyes. Nasreen

could practically hear him moaning, "Oh no!" It was almost comical watching him squirm.

"Do you want to tell us what happened?"

"I knew that fucking threat would come back to haunt me," he said, his hands on top of his head. "It was nothing, a disagreement, that's all. It got out of hand, but it doesn't mean anything."

"I disagree. It means a lot, Irwin. Now we know you lied to us, twice. And if you can lie like that to us about something as simple as knowing Verity and Fiona, what else are you lying about, hmm? You're going to be held overnight for questioning, and tomorrow we're searching your flat, so you'd better start praying we don't find anything incriminating."

"You won't, because I didn't do it."

"How's your archery?" she asked, out of nowhere.

"Better than average, why?"

She couldn't believe it worked – he could use a bow and arrow. "Above average, you say. Are we going to find you're a member of a club?"

"What? No!" His voice betrayed him.

"Right, you've said enough, Irwin," Yates said, glaring up at her. "From now on, you speak through me. It'll give you time to think before you open your trap."

"I think you're right, Mr Yates," Nasreen said, adrenaline spiking. Any doubts she had that Irwin was their guy had been squashed. Knowing that he knew his way around a bow could be a game changer, she thought. It was still circumstantial, but the more they had, the more likely the CPS would take it on. There were too many coincidences in her view. "I'll get an officer to take him down to a holding cell until the morning. As soon as we've done the property search, I'll call you."

When she received no argument from Yates, Nasreen excused herself, leaving the solicitor and his client in the interview room. Outside, Weekes walked along the corridor with her.

"Do you really think it's him?" Weekes asked.

"Absolutely! You heard the evidence. We're going to his flat tomorrow with the search team. I'm positive we'll find something. Right now, though, we're going to go through the victims' laptops."

DAY 12
TUESDAY, MAY 29TH

46

Weekes rubbed her eyes. Watching the footage from the council was laborious, boring and put strain on her eyes. And having to conceal it from Nasreen proved problematic. Every time Nasreen walked past her desk, Weekes had to click out of it and pull up her "real" assignment, which was looking up businesses that taught archery. So far, no sign of a pickup truck driving past the cameras on the night Verity was abducted.

"How far have you got?" Nasreen asked, poking her head over the partition.

"I've contacted five places in Sussex and asked them to send over their client lists. Most have complied; two are giving me the warrant crap. I've asked Inspector Gupta to contact them." She pulled up the screen with her list of leisure facilities. "I've got another twelve to go, unless you want me to widen my search?"

"Really? There are seventeen in Sussex? How many locally? We could look closer to home. Irwin lives here now."

"Twenty-one. I can start on them, too."

"On second thoughts, let's just stick to Sussex, for now."

Going back to her footage, Weekes was beginning to think she was wasting her time. They may very well have their suspect in a holding cell; it was possible that Irwin Landers was their man. Deciding to leave searching for the pickup, she switched to her true assignment, pulled up the contact details of the next archery training facility and picked up her landline phone. After identifying herself, explaining the reason for her call, she spoke to the manager of Oakfield Leisure. Her conversation lasted five minutes.

"I tell you what," the manager said, "instead of wasting time, why don't you tell me the name of the person you want me to look up, and I'll tell you right now if he's a member. It'll save us both time."

He sounded genuine. "Fine. Could you look up Irwin Landers, please?" It didn't take long for him to come back on the line; she heard him typing on his computer. It would be easier if they all went about their business this way, she thought.

"Irwin Landers. Yep. Been a member since 2002. He hasn't visited for a couple of years, but prior to that, he was a regular visitor, coming here once a month without fail. Does that help?"

With excitement, Weekes stood, waved at Nasreen and beckoned her over. "2002, you say? So, he was a regular with Oakfield for sixteen years, give or take?" She could see the excitement in Nasreen, too. "Could you send me all the information you have on him, please. Here, take my email address."

Rattling off her email, Weekes thanked the manager, so excited in fact, that she'd sounded giddy, which she was. It was yet another breakthrough. Irwin now had no alibis for any of the three murders, had lied about knowing the victims, had been bullied by Myles; had had a run in with Verity and some of her friends; not to mention the row over culling with Verity and Fiona. And now, was a member of an archery club. It was looking more and more likely he was their man. "And that's how you do it," she said to Nasreen, replacing the phone, grinning. "I'd like to see him talk his way out of this one."

"Well done, Weekes." Nasreen squeezed her shoulder. "Now all we need is to find something at his flat. We still need to tie him to the truck somehow, and the dogs. Here's where we fall short. We need that truck."

Feeling like she could take on the world single-handed, she offered to look into the pickups again; more importantly, widening their previous search and cross-referencing owners with Irwin's Facebook friends. And including trucks reported stolen. It was a needle and haystack situation again, but she didn't mind. If anyone was going to find a link, she would; she was great with number crunching and data analysis.

Back on her PC, Weekes heard Nasreen swear under her breath. Concerned it was work related and something she needed to know, she stood up and asked her what was wrong.

"Sorry! It's nothing," Nasreen replied. "My sparring partner ruptured a ligament at practise last week. She says she'll be out of action for weeks."

Feeling charitable, Weekes said, "I'll do it. I'll be your sparring partner. It's been a while since I was in a ring, but I guess it's like riding a bike."

"Wait! You and Weekes are getting in a ring together?" Terrence said behind her, his voice excited. "Now this I've got to see. Hey, sir, Nas and Weekes are stepping in the ring together. Fancy a flutter?"

"Put me down for twenty," Gupta replied.

"Who's your money on?"

"Twenty on Nas. No offence, Weekes. I've seen how mean she is in the ring." Gupta turned back to his computer.

Weekes saw the reaction on Nasreen's face; her partner was mortified. Maybe she shouldn't have said it so loud. She'd been half joking. "Sorry! I didn't mean for that to happen. It was just a thought, really. I can do with the practise." To her amazement, Nasreen agreed.

"No, it's fine. But we aren't doing anything until we've closed this investigation, agreed? Oh, and guys, if you're fluttering, all proceeds are going to a charity of our choice, yeah?"

Looking around the office at the interested faces of her colleagues, Weekes almost laughed when she heard a chorus of disappointed groans. "Come on, it's for a good cause. Not that we know which one, but it'll be a good one, we promise." After they'd gone back to solving crimes, she smiled down at Nasreen. "And don't worry, I'll take it easy on you."

Getting back to her work, Weekes started looking for stolen pickup trucks. It was another arduous task, but her confidence was sky high.

Fifteen minutes later, Gupta stepped up to her desk, catching her attention. "Everything okay, sir?"

"The magistrate's given the all-clear to search Irwin Landers' flat. Get yourselves over there now. SOCOs are on their way. Good job on finding his archery club, Weekes, but we need more before we hand it over to the CPS."

Grabbing her suit jacket from the back of her chair, Weekes said, "We're on it."

Meeting Nasreen, there was an air of excitement between them, as they walked into the corridor towards the lift.

"I want this house turned over again," Nasreen said. "It's not good enough. There has to be something here, has to be. We're not leaving until we have something we can use, do you understand?" The frustration at having ripped apart the house was giving her hot flushes beneath the white coveralls and face mask. Weekes and the six white-clad SOCOs stood there. "What are you waiting for? Go!"

"We've turned this place inside out, and upside down," Weekes said, to nods from the crime scene officers. "There's nothing here."

"There's something here, I know it."

Weekes stepped up to her, wading through Irwin Landers' belongings strewn on the living room floor. "We're wasting our time," she said, her voice quiet, calm. "Remember what you told me about Richard Pryce? You want it to be Landers so much, it's clouding your vision."

"Oh please. You can't even compare them. Pryce was never our guy. His only link was Jackman. Landers had dealings with all three. He's threatened them all, for crying out loud." Nasreen saw the uncertainty in Weekes' eyes, the only part of her face she could see. "Let's give it one more go, please?"

With a big sigh, Weekes turned to the SOCOs. "Okay, one more try."

When they all went back to tearing the flat apart, Nasreen relaxed a little. Her first port of call was walking into the bedroom, where all drawers and the wardrobe had been opened and the contents thrown on the threadbare carpet. "What a shit-hole," she murmured. There was nothing they could use against him here. Nasreen picked up a pile of papers, bills and banking slips. Stood at the foot of the bed, exhausted from the heat inside the coveralls, she glanced up at the ceiling. "Guys? Come here."

Weekes was the first to join her in the small bedroom, followed by the six SOCOs, who stood waiting for her to speak. Nasreen looked up at the ceiling. "Has anyone been up there?" Heads shook. "Please tell me we haven't missed the attic." One of the SOCOs spoke up, telling her they must have missed it. "Quick, look around, see if you can find the pole."

It didn't take long to find the metal pole with the plastic end that fitted the lock on the loft door. Taking it from Weekes, she unlocked the attic door, letting it fall down. There was a ladder lying inside the loft. With the help of the SOCOs, Nasreen moved the bed over enough to let the ladder drop to the floor. As she climbed the metal rungs, excitement took over. If Landers was going to hide something, it would be here.

Switching on the loft light, Nasreen hoisted herself inside the small space, looking around at the junk. It was just like every other attic in the country, full of odds and sods. Standing up, she cast her eyes over everything. Not spying anything of interest, she moved things about until she came to a wooden chest.

Hope hung in her breath, until she opened it. "Jackpot!" she shouted down to her colleagues. She heard footsteps on the ladder and Weekes poked her head up.

"What is it?" Weekes asked.

Reaching inside, Nasreen pulled out a heavy bow. "Possible murder weapon," she replied, holding it with her gloved hand. Handing it to Weekes, she pulled out a dozen arrows. "I don't suppose you recall the make of the arrows, do you?"

"Not off the top of my head, no. Sorry."

"It doesn't matter." Nasreen smiled beneath the mask. "We've got him!" The rush of adrenaline was overpowering to the point that her hands were shaking. Three murders and they had him, before he could strike for a fourth time. With the bow and arrows, she was sure they had enough to charge him with three counts of premeditated murder.

Satisfied they had enough, Nasreen climbed down, thanked the SOCOs for their time and let them go. Securing the bow and arrows, she and Weekes changed out of their protective gear and prepared to leave Landers' flat. "I can't wait to tell Inspector Gupta," Nasreen said to Weekes when her mobile rang. "Sergeant Edgeley, you're on speakerphone. Any luck finding Claire Padnall?"

"Unfortunately not, no," Edgeley replied. "But that's not why I'm calling."

"Why are you whispering?"

"I can't go into it here, but I need your assistance. We've been looking into dangerous dogs, both on the register and noise complaints. I think I've found something." He sounded excited, and shifty, a strange combination.

"That's great news, sergeant, but we can't come your way. We've got our guy in holding. We have a murder weapon and enough circumstantial to charge him. You go ahead and look into the dog angle."

"Come on, Nas, let's go," Weekes interrupted. "This is only a possible murder weapon. What harm can looking at the dog angle do? Sergeant Edgeley is asking us for help."

"But we don't need the 'dog angle'," she replied, noting that Weekes had called her Nas for the first time. Was she warming to her? It was possible; her partner was in a far-improved mood of late. "We need to question Landers some more, hit him with this."

"Every angle needs looking into. You taught me that."

Now she was conceding that she'd learnt something from her? It was surreal. "You really want to go all the way down there?" It was the pleading in Weekes' eyes she couldn't ignore. With a sigh, she relented. "All right, Sergeant Edgeley, we're on our way."

48

―――

Franks closed Suzanne Embry's office door and walked over to her desk, where she was sat waiting for him, wearing a smart grey suit and white blouse. He'd called her on her burner phone to request the meeting; it was the first time he'd met her without Harry being present. "Thanks for agreeing to meet me, ma'am," he said, formality a must.

"It's highly irregular, Peter, but given your dedication to the project, I felt inclined to agree to it." She invited him to take a seat. "What can I do for you?"

All morning he'd rehearsed what he was going to say. After his last meeting with Harry, he had no choice but to inform her. He sat down, choosing his words carefully. "It's Harry... Harold, ma'am. I need to discuss something with you."

Embry leaned back in her comfortable chair and regarded him. "Oh? And what's that? I trust everything's going smoothly."

"As it can, yes. My only concern is Harold."

"Go on."

"He's having second thoughts, ma'am," he said, noting her raised eyebrows.

"It's a bit late for those, don't you think? The project's already underway." She didn't look all that concerned, he noticed. "Has he told you this himself? He's told you he wants out?"

"Yes, but I've managed to talk him round, for now," he answered, feeling sweaty under his armpits, hoping it didn't show. "If you want my opinion, he's falling apart. I've never seen him like this before."

There was a long silence. Embry studied him.

"And you've come to me with this, why?" Her question didn't require an answer, yet. "What do you expect me to do, hmm? If he's having second thoughts, what can I do about it? I'm not here to hold his hand or reassure him."

"No, ma'am, and neither am I. I'm supposed to be his right-hand man, but I find myself taking control of the project. He's an empty shirt, ma'am. He might as well not be here for all the good he does. I need you to know what's going on, that's all."

She sighed, tapping her fingers on her desk. "Thank you for bringing this to my attention, Peter," she said finally. "I've pencilled in a meeting with Harold for next week; I'll see how he is then and reaffirm his commitment."

Rising from his chair, Franks thanked her for her time. Deep down, he wanted to tell her about Harry and Amelie Desmarais, about how he'd fallen in love with Lennox Garvey's mistress. But then he'd have to explain what happened to her. The project may have been Suzanne Embry's brainchild, but he doubted she'd want to hear of more players dying in its name. Project Cleansweep was supposed to save lives, not end them.

No, he'd have to find another solution for his Harry problem... And he had an idea how.

49

———

"Explain again why Inspector Innes isn't coming with us," Weekes asked, sat in the back of Sergeant Edgeley's white Peugeot. "It doesn't feel right. We need his permission."

"We won't get it," Edgeley replied, driving. "I respect the inspector, don't get me wrong, but he can be so blinkered sometimes. If I'd gone to him with this, he'd have shut it down immediately, okay? Where we're going, these ex-travellers, he's spent years cultivating a good working relationship with them, and he won't want us going in and upsetting the apple cart. Which isn't my intention, by the way."

"So, why are we going there?" she asked, noticing Edgeley watching her in the rear-view mirror. It wasn't that she minded; it was unsafe to do so on such bendy roads.

"Because, their neighbours have complained numerous times about dogs barking all day, and Innes is too chicken to do anything about it. The guy I'm interested in has a long history with us, okay? Call it a hunch, but I'm interested in checking out his dogs." He was still watching her.

"Weekes, don't worry about any comeback on this." Nasreen turned to her in the front passenger seat. "I'll take the heat."

"I just don't want a reprimand on my record, that's all," she replied, sitting back. "It's all right for you two, you have history in your departments; I've only been here five minutes." It was just like Nasreen to agree to go behind the inspector's back like this, she thought.

"We're just taking a look around," Edgeley said. "If you want, you can stay in the car while Nas and I take a look. We'll keep you out of it, right, Nas?"

That was all she needed, Nasreen and Edgeley to take the praise if this guy turned out to be their suspect. With a sigh, Weekes agreed to come along. "Where are they from? Are they Irish, what? And how do you mean ex-travellers? They're either travellers or not."

"You'll see when we get there," Edgeley replied. "They live in a gated community in static caravans. They're ex-Romany gypsies. They settled here over thirty years ago on a plot of land the council sold them, so the majority of them are British citizens. They've integrated with the rest of the community, so the kids go to school locally and the adults work. The women work mainly in schools and offices, the men in all sorts. And in fifteen years we haven't had trouble of any kind from them. Except one guy, Emilian Keeble; he's who I'm interested in speaking to."

"And what's he into?" Nasreen asked.

"All sorts. He was sent down for aggravated burglary twenty-three years ago, and even before that he was a tearaway. So, when I said we haven't had any trouble from them in fifteen years, it's not entirely true. He burgled a number of homes around here, but the rest of the family are good as gold, which is why the inspector wouldn't want us here. Plus, I heard through the grapevine that Emilian's involved in dog fighting. Those kinds of dogs could be the ones that mauled Fiona Armstrong."

It made sense, thought Weekes. Up ahead there was a

double wrought-iron gate on the left. She felt the car slowing down. "We're here," she heard Edgeley say.

Their car stopped outside the gate. The sergeant honked the horn and a large guy stepped up to the gate. Edgeley waved and the big guy opened it for them. Once parked, Edgeley led the way by opening his door. "Let me do the talking."

The compound was huge, with static caravans on each side of the stony man-made road leading through the mini-village. Weekes got out and surveyed the land. They were expensive caravans, most of which had satellite dishes, awnings and tables and chairs outside. A group of locals walked up to them.

"Morning, Otis," Edgeley said to the obvious head of the family.

"Richard," the elder said in greeting. "What brings you here?"

It was all very congenial, thought Weekes, watching them shake hands. The children surrounding Otis were well turned out, mostly wearing labelled clothing. The women were well manicured, too. Weekes was learning a lesson about gypsy life, or rather ex-gypsy life.

"We're here to speak with Emilian, if he's here?"

"What's he being blamed for now?" Otis asked. "Whatever you think he's done, he didn't do it. He hasn't been out of the compound in weeks."

"We've got some routine questions for him, that's all. Nothing to concern yourself about, I promise. Is he here?"

Weekes smiled at the children of varying ages, following Nasreen and Edgeley through the complex. They were all polite. The children and elders left them to walk along the makeshift road by themselves, Edgeley clearly having been here before. Her estimation of the area being huge was an understatement; it was vast. How they'd bought the land from the council, she had no idea.

"There's his caravan," Edgeley said. "The one at the back. And they must be the kennels over there." He pointed in their direction. "Keep your eyes open, okay? He can be a handful, this one."

When she reached the caravan with Nasreen and Sergeant Edgeley, Weekes noticed how luxurious it was. It looked brand new and big enough to sleep ten. Edgeley called out for Emilian, three times. There was no answer. Weekes saw what looked like a stone-built garage right at the far end of the compound, its door closed.

"It looks like he's not home," Nasreen said.

Weekes heard dogs barking. She started walking towards the makeshift kennels, Nasreen and Edgeley following her. The barking grew louder. Thinking about how dogs had savaged Fiona Armstrong, Weekes grew nervous. The dogs were visible through the wire. "It could be them," she said, to agreement from Nasreen and Edgeley. "They're pit bulls, aren't they? I thought they're banned in this country."

"They are." Edgeley pulled his mobile out of his jacket.

With Nasreen and Edgeley staring at the dogs, Weekes turned and looked back at Emilian's caravan. She gasped when she saw a man stood on top of it. He was holding something in his hand. With one hand stretching back, it dawned on her he was holding a bow. "Look out!" she said, leaping in front of her colleagues.

The arrow would have sent her prosthetic leg flying, had she not been wearing trousers. The power dislodged it, breaking the suction. Weekes fell to the floor, the arrow wedged in her artificial leg. "Don't worry about me," she said, watching Emilian disappear behind his caravan. "Go after him!"

50

Following Weekes' order, Nasreen took off with Edgeley by her side. Reaching the caravan, she continued on, spotting the bow on the ground. Slowing to a stop, she couldn't see Emilian anywhere. "Where'd he go?"

It didn't take long for her question to be answered. She heard revving coming from the stone building. There was a colossal bang as the door was battered and a pickup truck came roaring towards them. It was heading directly for them.

Nasreen didn't have time to think. She pushed Edgeley out of the way before diving in the opposite direction, narrowly missing the truck. On her front, she picked herself up and watched the pickup accelerate away. "Let's go!" She grabbed Edgeley and ran after the truck, towards the gate.

With Edgeley running beside her, she watched the truck smash through the front gate and turn left onto the road they'd just been on. "Give me the keys," she demanded, to Edgeley's insistence he was driving. No time for argument, she got in the car and strapped herself in, the car reversing onto the road. "Let's get this bastard."

Edgeley floored it, Nasreen pinned to the passenger seat,

feeling the adrenaline coursing through her. They had their suspect. Emilian was driving the pickup they'd been searching for, and he'd shot Weekes with an arrow. The clincher: he owned dangerous dogs.

With Emilian's truck in front, Nasreen could only admire Edgeley's driving. It was like he'd done this before. The road they were on was too bendy to drive fast, not that it stopped Emilian or Edgeley. "Careful," she said, their car missing a civilian by mere centimetres.

"I can do without a back seat driver, Nas," Edgeley said, taking another bend at fifty.

There was another steep bend approaching, she noted, spying the road sign. Her colleague would have to slow down considerably, except Emilian didn't. "Oh shit!" she shouted, seeing a lorry coming towards Emilian's truck.

Emilian was driving too fast to slow down enough.

Nasreen watched in horror as the smaller truck collided with the lorry in slow motion. It didn't stand a chance. The pickup's impact was severe, the vehicle's length reduced markedly before it shot off to the left.

After Edgeley slowed to a stop, Nasreen shot out and ran over to the lorry driver, who looked shaken but unharmed. "Are you okay, sir?" she asked, the guy shaking his head in the lorry's cab. "We'll get paramedics to take a look at you."

The steaming wreck of Emilian's truck was in the middle of the road. She heard Edgeley on the phone to HQ asking for all the emergency services. Walking slowly to the driver's side of what counted for the truck, Nasreen saw blood, so much blood...

Weekes heard the sirens, instinctively knowing something had happened. With her prosthesis in her hand, the arrow still wedged in it, she used Otis and another male local as crutches. She asked them to take her to Emilian's caravan, which they obliged. They were supportive and helpful, even apologising for their family member.

Being helped to Emilian's caravan, the elders placed her down on a chair beneath its awning. As it was a crime scene, she didn't want to contaminate it by going inside. "Thanks," she said, accepting their offer of a cup of tea. Bringing her mobile out of her jacket, Weekes phoned her partner, who picked up after only three rings. "What going on?"

"He crashed into a lorry," Nasreen replied. "It's a proper mess here."

A pickup crashing into a lorry, Weekes thought, no point asking if he survived. "How's the lorry driver?" It didn't matter to her how Emilian was.

"As far as I can tell, fine. Whiplash for sure, but otherwise minor cuts and bruising. Emilian's dead. Are you okay?"

"Having tea with these lovely people. I'll wait here for you."

Weekes' tea arrived and the two elders joined her. Surprised that they weren't angry with her, she asked them why. Otis, the alpha, explained that Emilian was always a lone wolf, a pain in their arse. Otis had the faintest accent, yet his English was immaculate. He explained that his second cousin had always been trouble, an embarrassment to their way of life. A throwback to the old ways, he said.

Something puzzled her. "You said earlier that he hadn't left the compound for weeks. Are you sure about that? Do you mind me asking where he was yesterday morning?"

"In his caravan, I'm guessing, although he could've left early. It's not like we keep tabs on him, or anything. Thinking about it, I do recall hearing his truck in the early hours. I didn't look at the time, though."

"And what about last Friday morning, at about 2am?"

"Oh, he was definitely here then," Otis replied, his expression one of disdain. "I had to have words with him about the music. That was about two in the morning. He had friends staying over. We got into a bit of a fight." Otis pointed at the remnants of his black eye.

"You're sure about that? It was definitely last Friday?"

"I'm certain. The whole community was woken up by that. We'll all testify to it, I'm sure. We had words Friday afternoon, too."

They had the wrong guy! Weekes sat there, puzzling over why he'd attacked them with a bow and arrow? Everything seemed to fit Emilian as their suspect, the truck, bow and arrow and dogs. They couldn't have it wrong. "Thanks, Otis, you've been a big help," she said, Nasreen walking towards her with Edgeley. Looking at her watch, their conversation had taken an hour and a half. "Are you done?" she asked.

Nasreen sat down next to Weekes, Edgeley the other side. Otis and his cousin excused themselves. Picking up her prosthetic leg, Nasreen apologised to her. "Hey, it wasn't your fault," she said, taking her leg back.

"What's that?" Nasreen asked, pointing at her leg.

"That?" She opened the hatch. "Oh nothing, just my storage compartment."

Nasreen's interest was funny to her. Her partner was acting like she'd never seen an artificial leg before. In honesty, no one had seen a prosthetic leg like hers before; it was custom built. "I didn't want a peg leg, so my dad paid for this. It has two recesses built in, so I store things in it. This side has my butterfly knife, and the other a compass and mace. Everything a growing girl needs."

"I think that's the coolest thing I've ever seen," Nasreen said, taking it off her again. "It's like having a Robocop leg, or something. And you keep it in this hatch?"

"Yeah, sure, when there's not an arrow stuck in it." She smiled. "It's lucky I have a spare at home. My dad's going to be pissed, though. This is going to increase his premiums."

"Your leg's insured?" Nasreen's face was a picture. "That's crazy."

"It's not when you know how much it cost."

Edgeley was interested in it, too.

Weekes continued. "That's custom made, with a titanium central column surrounded by a carbon outer shell. I wanted it to look and feel like a leg. It cost a fortune, so much so Dad paid to have it microchipped." That nugget made Nasreen smile, before she handed it back.

After five more minutes chatting, Edgeley and Nasreen helped her to the car. She asked Nasreen if she'd drive to her flat so she could get her replacement leg. In the rear seat, she waited until they were well on their way back to Edgeley's station before she said, "It wasn't Emilian." Nasreen turned her head and stared blankly at Weekes. "It wasn't him," Weekes insisted.

"What the hell are you talking about?" Edgeley asked, staring ahead. "Of course it was. Everything's there, the truck, the bow and the dogs. It was him!"

"Otis says Emilian was at the compound causing trouble last Friday morning. He and Otis got into it. Otis's still got a shiner. Our guy's still out there."

"That's crap, Weekes," Nasreen added. "It was him; I have no doubt."

"Like you had no doubts about Irwin Landers only this morning?" she countered, noting her partner's annoyance. "I'm telling you, it wasn't Emilian."

"And we're telling you it was," Edgeley said, as annoyed as Nasreen. "Otis is embarrassed about it; he'll say anything to make us believe Emilian's innocent. Everything matches. And when we seize his caravan and belongings, I guarantee we'll find more evidence to support his guilt. We'll get the dog's teeth checked with Fiona Armstrong's bite marks before the dogs are destroyed. It's over, Weekes, give it up."

"If you say so," she replied, making sure she got the last word. The rest of the journey back to the station was silent. She didn't want to be the negative ion. But Otis had no reason to lie, or to be embarrassed. If her superiors were so adamant of Emilian's guilt, there was nothing she could do about it.

51

It was mid-afternoon by the time Nasreen returned to the station with Weekes on two legs. A chorus of clapping and cheering stopped her. News of their morning's discovery had taken hold. Why were they cheering? She and Edgeley had chased Emilian into a lorry and killed him. They didn't have a suspect in custody; he was on his way to the morgue. Playing to the crowd, she bowed, forcing her partner to join her. "I've no idea what that's about," she whispered.

"Good job, detectives!" Gupta shouted, clapping. "That's another one wiped off the board. Great stuff." He continued clapping.

"Yeah, when's your sparring session?" Terrence joked.

"So, that's why they're cheering," Weekes whispered. "Looks like we have an audience to keep happy. We don't want to disappoint them, do we?"

"I guess not," she replied, the clapping petering out.

When her colleagues had tired of praising them, Nasreen strolled to her desk. The case was far from over. They had a ton of paperwork to fill out, plus they still had a missing person to find: Claire Padnall. Although they'd identified and stopped their suspect, they had to figure out why he'd murdered Myles Jackman, Verity Staunton and Fiona Armstrong, and how he knew them. Motive was the key, and so far they couldn't find one. Identifying him had been a fluke. "We need to find out as much as we can about Emilian Keeble. Weekes, you're good with the data crunching, can you look into that for me, please?"

"Sure. What are you going to be doing?"

"Trying to figure out how he knew the victims."

"Now we have our guy, what are we going to do with Landers? He's still in holding, isn't he?"

"Oh, bollocks!" She searched for Gupta. "Sir? Where are we at with Landers? Is he still in holding?" It was embarrassing having to ask. With all the excitement, he was the last person on her mind, which was odd given that he'd been her prime suspect only a few hours ago.

"We released him when we heard about your suspect," Gupta replied. "I told him not to leave the city, that we might have questions for him."

Relieved, she thanked Gupta and sat down, turning on her PC. Something Weekes said in the car troubled her. What if Emilian wasn't their man? Shaking away the thought, she tried to bury her qualms in her work. The evidence against him was overwhelming.

"He wasn't a great archer," Weekes said from behind the partition.

Here we go, thought Nasreen, standing up and regarding her partner. "All right, Weekes, I'll bite."

"Our suspect's a professional archer, right? We saw that in the video of Verity's murder," Weekes said, looking up at her. "Emilian shot me in the leg. Not that I'm complaining, but from the distance he was away from us, if he were a marksman, a professional archer, he'd have easily shot me in my back. I'm just saying."

It was puzzling. "Yeah, but he was using Verity Staunton as target practise," she retorted. "It's different with a moving target. The pressure of knowing we were onto him must've spooked him. It's the same with firearms. While under fire, nerves kick in, so–"

"And that's it? You're giving up on Landers?"

Exasperated, annoyed, Nasreen regarded her partner. "Emilian Keeble's our guy, Weekes. That's what our reports are going to say, okay? Please don't argue any more. The evidence is overwhelming."

Weekes sighed. "All right."

"Let's just get on with clearing this investigation up, shall we? We've still got a few loose ends to tie up." She was thinking about Emilian's archery skills, if she could call them that. Weekes was right, though, any decent archer would've hit their target higher, in the back, not in the leg. Desperately burying her negative thoughts, Nasreen clicked on her mouse.

52

Claire Padnall heard the rustling of trees and felt the warm night breeze over her face before she opened her eyes. It was dark, save for the patches of dark blue sky peeking in through the trees. She was lying on her back, fully clothed, her wrists tied together beneath her. Trying to wriggle free, she realised they were fastened tight. Her legs were tied together as well. Gagged, she tried screaming for help. It was no use, it only made her cough.

A twig snapped to her left, followed by rustling.

Crying into her gag, she watched as a shadow emerged, darker than everything else around her. It grew larger, until it loomed over her. Claire could make out the lighter colour of flesh and a pair of eyes. She begged to be let go.

"Good, you're awake," Shadow said.

She tried talking to Shadow, asking to be freed. In response, Shadow chuckled, crouching down, checking her restraints were bound tight. Tears rolled down her cheeks. It wasn't fair! Why was she here? She wasn't *one of them*.

Shadow stopped tugging at the rope, regarding her. "I know what you're thinking," said the voice. "I'm not supposed to be here. I had nothing to do with it." The voice was mocking her. "You were always on my list, Claire. You started this whole thing off. If you hadn't shown me the photo, you wouldn't be here, and your *friends* would still be alive. And had you been stronger, she wouldn't have died in the first place."

Shaking her head, not able to argue her case, she tried freeing her hands beneath her back. The rope was so tight, it almost restricted blood flow. "Please, I tried helping you," she shouted into the old rag wedged in her mouth – it sounded nothing like it.

"What was that? I wasn't even there? No, you weren't in the photo because you took it, didn't you? That's why you're the biggest disappointment. If you'd been stronger willed, less star-struck by that bitch Reagan, she'd be alive today. No, I've saved something extra special for you, Claire." Shadow stood, glaring down at her. "Your atonement's going to hurt more than the rest, but not to worry; I've heard it only hurts for a couple of minutes." Shadow walked away, into the dark.

Claire shouted into the night sky.

When Shadow returned, carrying a plastic container, there was a strong smell of petrol. Desperate to live, she shouted, "No!" into her gag.

Without warning, Shadow unscrewed the cap and lifted the plastic container over Claire's head. She felt the liquid seep into her hair; it stung her eyes. She screamed louder, not words, a long feral scream. The petrol seeped into her vest top, soaking her bare arms. Shadow continued pouring until her entire body was soaked through.

"Please! I don't deserve this," she cried, the words so muffled, even she couldn't understand them. In desperation, her bladder gave way, warming her crotch. It was only when Shadow stopped pouring and threw the container into the bush that it felt like her heart started beating again, so fast it might've well been one long beat. "No wait!"

Claire watched in horror as Shadow pulled out a Zippo lighter, the only way she knew was by the iconic metallic clicking sound. A single orange flame appeared in the darkness, taunting her, telling her it wanted to dance. "Please! I don't want to die! I want my mummy!"

"You brought this on yourself," Shadow said, dropping the lighter on the ground at her feet.

DAY 14
THURSDAY, MAY 31ST

53

─────────

"You look really good on TV, sir," one of Nasreen's colleagues joked, stood watching the press conference. "You missed your calling. You should've been a journalist."

"Wash your mouth out with soap and water," Inspector Gupta replied. "Well, it's out now, Nas. It's over. All I need to do is sign off on your investigation and you and Weekes can move on to a new case. When will I have it?"

Nasreen, stood behind Gupta and next to Weekes, glanced sideways at her partner. "When we've found Claire Padnall, sir. We're still going through Emilian Keeble's belongings. There seems to be no motive, not that we can find anyway."

"It happens like that sometimes. The dog bites match Keeble's dogs. That coupled with him firing at you with the same brand of arrow as the ones used to kill Verity Staunton pretty much nails it, not to mention finding the pickup truck used to drag Myles Jackman. It's done, Nas. But you keep looking for Claire Padnall; just not for too long, yeah? We need you two back in-house."

"Yes, sir," she replied, watching Gupta on the television. He did look good on-screen, it had to be said. "I'll get our paperwork to you as soon as I can."

"What time's your 'sparring session' tomorrow?" Terrence asked.

"Eight o'clock," Weekes replied. "So be sure to bring your money. It's for a really good cause. No shirking, any of you." Her tone was jovial.

"And why did you say, 'sparring session' like that?" Nasreen asked. "It's not a fight, Terrence. You're not going to see me and Weekes belting each other. If that's what you're hoping for, you'll be sorely disappointed, right, Weekes?" Her partner nodded, non-too- convincingly. "Right, Weekes?"

"Right." Her partner smiled. "It's a nice, gentle sparring session."

"Okay, everyone, back to work," Gupta ordered. "Playtime's over."

Damn Weekes, thought Nasreen, sitting down at her desk. They'd identified and stopped Emilian Keeble, murderer of three innocent victims, and her partner had her questioning herself, doubting he was their suspect. Weekes probably still thought it was Richard Pryce. "How are you getting on with Keeble's belongings?"

"There's nothing here," replied Weekes, her voice carrying over the partition. "I'm looking through photos found in his trailer. I haven't found anything yet."

"Right, well, keep on it. He's our guy. There has to be something here." Quashing her doubts rested on finding more evidence in support of Keeble being their culprit. "I haven't found anything linking the victims with Keeble, either."

"No fucking way!" Weekes stood up holding a photo, her hands shaking.

Concerned, Nasreen stood. "What? What is it?"

With speed, her partner strode around to her desk, holding the picture out. It was a printed photograph of Emilian Keeble with a young lad, his arm around the boy's shoulder. The lad looked maybe fifteen, or sixteen. "Is that–?"

"Richard Pryce." Weekes nodded, her hands still shaking.

"What is it, Nas?" Inspector Gupta walked over to her desk, followed by Terrence. "I'll be." He paused, taking the photograph from Weekes. "Of all the coincidences." He showed the photo to Terrence. "I guess it really is a small world."

"A small world? Is that all you're going to say?" Weekes asked.

"What else is there to say?" Gupta retorted. "It's a coincidence, Weekes, nothing more. You've already identified your suspect. And he's no longer with us."

"But, sir, surely we should bring Pryce in, question him."

"Absolutely not! This investigation is over, do you understand me? I want to sign it off. I'm only giving you time to tie up loose ends because you have a missing player. And once Claire Padnall is found, I want the paperwork on my desk. Honestly, what is it with you and Richard Pryce? You're like a dog with a bone, Weekes."

Nasreen felt embarrassed for her partner. "It's a coincidence, Weekes. Don't dwell on it. They don't live that far from one another. The compound's a quarter of an hour's drive from Pryce's farm, tops."

Once Gupta had gone, Nasreen sat down in front of her PC. There was a distinct air of resentment between them now, but she was ready for it. The past few days had been enjoyable, with a far more affable and friendly Weekes as her partner. Before she could click on her mouse, her mobile rang. "Inspector Innes, this is a surprise."

"I wish it were a nice surprise. We're still no nearer finding

Claire Padnall." He gave a long pause. "And I'm sorry to say we've found a body."

"Please, no," she said, closing her eyes. "Another photo?"

"Relax, Sergeant Maqsood, we haven't found a photo; you're in the clear. Your suspect hasn't risen from his grave. I'm calling because the body's badly burnt, found in woods not far from where Verity Staunton was murdered." He paused briefly. "I'm calling to let you know I'm ordering a comparison between the body's and Claire Padnall's dental records. Until we find her, I'm not ruling anything out."

"How long do you think that'll take?"

"I've requested it be expedited. But you know as well as I do what forensics are like. Could be twenty-four hours, could be days. As soon as I know, I'll call you. Unless you're planning on coming back down this way. We could use the help."

Nasreen looked at Inspector Gupta, who had his back to her on his computer. "I would, but I'm not sure my inspector will go for it. He didn't like us being there all day yesterday. I've still got a mountain of paperwork to fill out," she said, quietly. "I'll see what he says, but I wouldn't go getting my hopes up."

"I understand, sergeant. I'll keep you posted on the results."

Hanging up, she found Weekes watching her, expectantly. Filling in her partner, she attracted Gupta's attention and explained the situation to him at the same time. When she asked if they could join the Sussex Police in their search, he overruled it, saying they had more than enough to do. "Right you are, sir," she said, sitting back down.

She and Weekes spent hours with Innes and Edgeley yesterday searching for Claire Padnall, along with a number of uniforms, going from one of Claire's friends to another. Not one had seen or heard from her since she'd fled the stable. Nasreen wanted to interview Winifred, the owner of the stable. Unfortunately, she wasn't back from her cruise until Wednesday of the following week. Sighing, Nasreen got back to work, looking through Claire Padnall's social media accounts. Just like a lot of girls her age, Claire was heavy on Instagram and Twitter. Looking at the clock on her monitor, it was already half past five.

54

Franks sat down on a bench, waiting for Zack Astor to join him. Already ten minutes late, it was just like Astor to be tardy; it was probably payback for Finn Palmer being picked up. "Come on, where are you?" he asked his watch, tapping it. He'd thought about his Harry dilemma for days. Finally, the previous night, he'd decided enough was enough. He had to act. He wasn't about to let the Project collapse because Harry was having second thoughts.

It was a warm evening. He could feel perspiration soaking into his shirt. He spotted Astor approaching, unaccompanied as requested. A trickle of sweat rolled down Franks' temple. He wiped it away as Astor arrived, wearing blue jeans and a plain white T-shirt. He shook hands. "Shall we walk and talk?"

"In this heat?" Astor sat on the bench.

"All right." The reason he chose the park was its seclusion. It may have been situated in a big council estate, but no one used it. He'd been waiting for ten minutes and hadn't seen anyone. "Are you going to thank me for getting Palmer out?" Astor glared at him. "Obviously not. In that case I'll get straight to the point.

We've got a problem with Harry. He's having second thoughts about our little arrangement."

"A bit late for that, isn't it?" Astor leaned back like he was sunbathing.

"That's what Suzanne Embry said. Be that as it may, he's coming apart at the seams. He's been unravelling for a while now, since Amelie Desmarais."

"That bitch again." Astor groaned. "And what do you expect me to do about it?"

Franks said nothing; he let the question hang in the warm breeze, lingering.

"Oh, wait a minute, you nutcase." Astor broke away from his bathing and leaned forward. "No fucking way! You can forget about that right now."

"Forget what? I didn't say anything," he replied, knowing Astor understood.

"If you think for a second… No way am I going to be a part of that." Astor stood, turned and looked down at him. "Offing Amelie was one thing. This is something else. He's the highest ranking police officer in the country, for fuck's sake."

"It needs doing, Zack. If he unravels, we all go down, do you understand? That's you, me, Embry, everyone involved."

"Why me? Why do my guys have to do it? I've already helped you out of a tight spot, Peter. It's about time someone else contributed, don't you think? Try Foster, or Walker. They might go for it, but you can count me out."

Before Franks could argue, Astor made his way back the way he'd come. Shit! he thought, watching his colleague leave. "It has to happen, Zack! Think about it." But Astor was right; it didn't have to be him, or his guys. Sitting back down, Franks contemplated asking Foster. Foster was a new breed of criminal, though. He didn't seek the limelight; if anything, he shied away from it, actively avoiding it, hiding behind the air of respectability he'd spent his life building. No, Foster wouldn't go for it.

What about Walker? He ran the south-west region, but Franks didn't know all that much about him. He could approach him, at the very least. Astor was his go-to man. Damn it! Why did he have to be so stubborn? Harry had to go, there was no getting away from it, and he couldn't disgrace his boss. Harry knew what was going on. Before he approached Walker, he decided he would go back to Suzanne Embry and get her take on the Harry situation.

55

Weekes was bored of waiting. It was a long shot, parking in a lay-by near the back entrance of Brambles Animal Shelter. But, having seen Richard Pryce in Emilian Keeble's company rung alarm bells for her; she knew he was their suspect, even if Nasreen, Gupta and Terrence thought she was wrong. "I'll show you who's wrong," she muttered, opening her car door and getting out.

It was five past eleven and dark outside. There were no street lamps along the road, no houses nearby. Without a flashlight, she couldn't see her hand in front of her face. Switching hers on, she shone it down the road. Following it, she walked two hundred metres, listening for approaching cars, until she reached the opening.

Sticking to the edge of a bush, Weekes peered up at the animal barn, or more specifically the concreted area she'd found behind it. "Bugger!" she said, disheartened. There was nothing there; no cars, trucks, empty. She'd been sat in her car since eight o'clock, which was the same time Richard Pryce started his shift. "I can't have missed him," she said to herself, stamping her foot in frustration. No cars had left from this exit.

She'd been so certain she would see a vehicle leaving the shelter. With her plan shattered, Weekes started walking back to her car. Could she be wrong about Pryce? Maybe Emilian was their guy; maybe Otis was trying to save face, just like Edgeley said. Was she a terrible detective? Doubting herself, she opened her car door and got in, depression taking hold. "Damn you, Nasreen!" Weekes said, bitterness smothering every word.

Had she somehow missed Pryce leaving the shelter? Had she fallen asleep for the briefest of moments? There was no way of knowing. One thing she felt in her gut was that Emilian Keeble wasn't their guy, despite sufficient evidence to the contrary. "Come on, Pryce, show yourself," she whispered.

Sitting in the dark, she felt stupid. Willing him to appear wasn't going to make it happen, she thought, debating whether or not to call it a night. Just because Pryce wasn't here, didn't mean he wasn't their suspect. And that doubt crept back into her head again. Emilian could be their guy. But Otis told her Emilian was at the compound on one of the nights in question. Deciding to give up, conceding defeat, Weekes started the engine and drove away.

56

Exhausted, after a full day in the office, followed by a night on the town with his colleagues, Leighton Oldridge slugged the last of his whisky down, already feeling the effects of copious amounts of doubles at the bar. He placed the tumbler in his kitchen sink, debating whether to rinse it out or not. Sod it, he thought, leaving it for the morning.

Having seen the news that the killer had been caught – his friends' killer – Leighton felt relief for the first time in a good couple of weeks, knowing he would sleep well tonight. When he'd heard about Myles Jackman, he'd chalked it up to bad luck, misfortune. He'd never really liked Myles anyway; he was a twat, and a bully – not that Myles had ever bullied him. Hearing how his group member died had made him wince. The pain he must've felt.

A week later, he'd heard that Verity had been murdered. Two group members killed in as many weeks had freaked him out. While concealing his panic from colleagues, he'd phoned Fiona, who'd met up with him that evening. They'd talked about Myles and Verity like they'd died of natural causes, toasting them with drinks. She'd made him feel silly for believing someone was after them; it was the way with Fiona, though.

It wasn't until he'd found out that Fiona had been mauled to death by dogs that he'd thought about going to the police. He'd been on his way out of the office to drive to the nearest police station when Reagan had greeted him, unplanned, as though she'd known what was going on inside his head. Reagan invited him back to hers, which he'd accepted.

Knowing what was going to happen, he'd ended up in bed with her, enjoying her body. It sure beat working in the office, dealing with customers. After a vigorous session with the delightful Reagan, his first love, they lay together beneath the bed sheets, his arms around her soft, supple body. That was when she'd begged him not to go to the police, that they'd be in so much trouble if he did. And she begged him while grinding her body on his, promising more action later if he agreed. Of course, he'd agreed.

"It's over," he said, blowing out a big lungful of grateful air. It was too bad for Myles, Verity and Fiona. Yeah, too bad for them, great for him (and Reagan). The killer had been found and stopped; it said so on the news. Now, he could get on with the rest of his life with Reagan, or at least that was what she'd texted him earlier.

Stumbling out of the kitchen, into the hallway of his large, detached home, he noticed the front door was open. "Odd," he said, stumbling towards it. "I could've sworn I closed it." With a shrug, he closed and locked it.

He found the banister and hoisted himself upstairs. Two flights later, he was on the landing, the room around him spinning. He asked himself if he should bother brushing his teeth, or just flop on his bed? Choosing the former, he staggered into the bathroom and cleaned his teeth, not to his usual standards, the minty paste reacting with the whisky. Feeling queasy, he stooped over the toilet and vomited, the room steadying itself.

In his dark bedroom, the curtains drawn, he stumbled out of his work trousers, unbuttoned his shirt and collapsed on his bed in only his pants and socks. It wasn't a great look. Lying on his back, his limbs relaxing, he closed his eyes, drifting off.

Panic gripped him when he felt a hand cover his mouth.

A shadow loomed above him, its whole body on top of his.

"Help!" he cried into the gloved hand, his voice muted by the leather. It was like a bad dream, or the most vivid nightmare.

Shadow's other hand moved towards his neck. Leighton felt a stinging sensation, like he'd been stung, or stabbed with a needle. Shadow's eyes bored into him, accusatory, angry. It took only a minute for Leighton to start feeling drowsy, or was it the alcohol? Either way, his surroundings turned darker with each passing second.

DAY 15
FRIDAY, JUNE 1ST

57

Leighton Oldridge felt rope around his wrists. It was so tight, it pinched his skin. The last thing he recalled was lying on his bed after returning home from the bar. And then... That wasn't the last thing he remembered: someone was in his room. Shadow had drugged him, stuck him with a needle. He could feel the warm breeze on his face, legs, arms and stomach.

Lying on his back, the moisture of the grass soaking into his skin, the sky above him was clear; dark but clear. Behind him was a tree, he noted, trying his hardest to tilt his head back. His wrists were tied to the fat oak tree by a length of rope. "Help!" he shouted, suddenly bathed in bright white light. It was from a camera mounted on the back of a Jeep.

Feeling cold, petrified, he noticed he was wearing only his pants and socks – he'd been dragged out of his house without his clothes. Panicking, he jostled with the rope around his wrists, praying it would break. It was no use; he was helpless.

"Call for help if you want, Leighton," Shadow said from beside the Jeep. "It won't do you any good. We're miles from the nearest village."

Whoever it was, they knew him, knew his name. "Who are

you? Why are you doing this?" he asked, hoping he might be able to talk Shadow into letting him go. "I haven't done anything wrong. If you get to know me, you'll find I'm a good guy."

Shadow stepped out from the side of the Jeep carrying what looked like a length of rope. Leighton's fears were confirmed when Shadow stopped behind the Jeep and squatted, his arms moving.

"What are you doing?" His voice was desperate, higher than normal. "Please, you don't have to do this. You can let me go; I won't press charges, I don't even know who you are, what you look like."

Finishing, Shadow stood and walked towards him, still carrying the rope. "I could let you go, you're right." Shadow knelt down next to him. "But, I'm not going to. It's judgement day for you." Shadow held the end of the rope and showed it to him. "Specially made for you. It took me a long time to bury the blades in here."

Gasping, Leighton saw the razor blades embedded in the rope. "What are they for?" he asked, despite not wanting to know. His question was answered when Shadow reached beneath him and threaded the rope under his back and wound it around his waist, the blades slicing into his abdomen, back and sides as Shadow tied it in a slip knot. "Help!" He screamed, seeing the other end tied to the rear bumper of the Jeep. "Help!" His cry was more desperate.

"You asked earlier why I'm doing this." Shadow stood and reaching into a pocket, pulled out a photo. "I'll show you why."

Leighton knew he was going to die when he saw the photograph. "That had nothing to do with me, you have to believe me," he said, beseeching his captor to see reason. "I wasn't even there when it happened. Fiona, Myles. They're responsible for it."

"Don't lie to me!" Shadow put the photo away and pulled out

another. It was a group photo with three heads cut out. "But you talked her into it, didn't you? Huh? Tell me you didn't talk her into this. Look at it!"

Lying wasn't going to help him here. He desperately looked around for help, knowing in his gut it was wishful thinking. "No! I didn't have to talk her into it," he said, Shadow's glare growing more severe. "She invited me along... Please, you have to believe me."

"Liar!" hissed Shadow, taking out a pair of scissors and cutting out Leighton's head. "Just for that I'm going to do this slower; I'm going to savour every second of your pain."

"Whoa! Wait!" He was trying to free his wrists. "We can talk about this, like adults, can't we?" he pleaded. "I've done something to piss you off, I get that... I piss a few people off... But, please, can't we come to some sort of arrangement here? Isn't there room to negotiate?" He noticed Shadow stop.

"Are you talking about money?"

"It doesn't have to be," he replied, feeling blood dribble down his waist. "It can be whatever you want it to be. And whatever you want, I can afford, so."

Shadow turned in the bright white light, becoming a silhouette again. "I'm already getting what I want." Shadow crouched, taking the string necklace and hooking it over his head, leaving it sat on his chest. "You're getting what you deserve. You're atoning."

When his captor stood and walked towards the Jeep, he tried to stop it from leaving, begging Shadow not to go, to stay and talk this through. It was no use. Leighton watched as Shadow closed the Jeep door and started the engine.

Panic set in; he knew he didn't have long – a couple of minutes max – before he was dead, pulled apart, ripped in two by the rope tied around his waist.

Think, damn it, think! he kept telling himself, scanning the field for a way out.

There was nothing.

He felt the rope attached to the Jeep and his waist move with the vehicle. It was getting tauter. Shadow was toying with him, making the Jeep go forwards by mere centimetres. "Please! It's not too late," he cried, tears rolling freely.

The rope stretched as far as it would go.

Leighton felt the razor blades slice into his skin.

The Jeep went forwards and kept going. His wrists and arms were stretched to their limit. Then, he felt his body being lifted off the ground, the rope around his waist slicing deeper into his flesh. When he felt his flesh tearing, he screamed again.

Surprised at how many of her colleagues had turned up, Weekes walked out of the changing room wearing a white vest top and a pair of light grey jogging bottoms. Her false foot looked realistic enough to pass as real from a distance. Had she not had one of her legs blown off, she'd be wearing shorts. It was wise not to shock people with the way she was now, especially colleagues. "I thought only a handful would turn up," she said to Nasreen, walking towards the professional-sized boxing ring.

"Hey, you bigged it up. This is your fault. I only wanted a new sparring partner, not this. Whatever this is."

Correct, as usual, she thought, lifting the ropes for her shorter partner to get through. Once through the ropes and on the canvas, Weekes waited for Terrence to help her tape up for the "sparring session", not that she thought she needed it. Even if she were up against Nasreen with one hand tied behind her back, Weekes knew she would have her on the floor inside two rounds; it was inevitable. The size difference alone dictated so. "Why are you getting so into this?" she asked Terrence, who was busy wrapping her hands.

"You're kidding, right?" He didn't look up. "How often do you think I get to have a wager with you lot? That's right, never. Now stay still while I finish off."

"Is she as good as people say?" she asked, observing Nasreen, in her grey vest and black joggers. If she didn't know better, she'd think Nasreen was confident, judging by the long, unblinking stare. But not only was Nasreen short, she was also petite too; there was nothing of her. Maybe she needed to rethink coming out all guns blazing. Weekes didn't want to hurt her.

"Better. Watch out for her right hook and jab; they're lethal. And I speak from personal experience."

"I hear she almost took out Cara."

"Had Cara not gone after Lucy, Nas would've annihilated her," Terrence replied, finishing up. "You wouldn't think it to look at her, but Nas is tough. Don't underestimate her, or go soft on her, either. She won't go easy on you."

It was noisy in the gymnasium with her colleagues – some from her department, mostly from other departments – stood around the ring. When she did a three-sixty on the spot, Weekes saw they were surrounded by suits and uniforms. 'Come on, Nas,' she heard someone shout. 'Come on, Weekes,' she heard another cry.

With gloves on, Weekes approached Nasreen and Inspector Gupta in the centre. 'I want a nice, clean fight, ladies,' Gupta said, holding her glove and her opponent's. He added a couple of rules. She wasn't listening. The inspector called it a fight once more.

"How many more times? It's a sparring session," Nasreen moaned. "Right?"

Wishing she could agree, Weekes nodded. And when told to go back to their corners, she turned and winked at Terrence, who gave her a water bottle to drink from. "Don't underestimate her," she said to herself.

The bell marked the start of their first round.

Out of her corner in record time, she met Nasreen in the middle of the canvas, giving it a left, right, left, right, like a professional boxer, straight off the ropes. Taking Nasreen by surprise, Weekes felt the second right impact her opponent's lip. The first draw of blood. She hadn't felt this alive in years, not since back at barracks, before she'd moved into private security. She missed the army, missed her friends. The crowd was behind her.

Nasreen wiped her lip with the back of her wrist; she wasn't happy, Weekes noticed, too far away for her supervisor to retaliate. Instead of going in for a second battle, she hung back expecting something from her sparring partner.

With Gupta in the ring, too, Weekes had to take a couple of steps back when Nasreen retaliated with a stunning combination of punches and kicks, most of which she countered. The last kick caught her in the ribs, which stung. "Hope you enjoyed it, that's your one and only free kick." Anger biting away at her, she waded into her shorter, more petite partner, throwing punch after punch at her, Nasreen backing onto the ropes, mostly defending them.

Cheers rang out from the crowd. Weekes kept pummelling Nasreen, until her partner grew tired of the ropes, and the punishment. One heavy right, followed by a nasty left jab left Weekes stunned. It wasn't expected. Tiny people like Nasreen couldn't have that much power. It was absurd. Fortunately, the bell rang.

59

───────

Nasreen couldn't get away from the ropes; she was hemmed in by her physically superior partner. This wasn't a sparring session, she thought, resentment pouring out of every punch she planted on Weekes' kidneys. Her partner was out for blood. After the bell rang and Weekes let her go back to her corner, she sat down on a small wooden stool.

"What are you doing out there, Nas?" Gupta handed her a water bottle. "I've got twenty quid on you, remember? You're better than this."

It was true. She was better than this. "I can't get through her reach," she said, out of breath, sweat streaming down her face. Grey wasn't the most flattering colour to wear, seeing how dark her vest was. "Every time I try, she flits me away like I'm some annoying fly. I need a way in."

Why was she behaving like this was a fight? It wasn't. If it were, she'd have Weekes on her back on the canvas by now. Fighting for real was different from sparring. Waiting for the bell, she glanced over at Weekes, who spat water into a bucket. Her partner was out of breath, too, her chest rising and falling quickly.

The third round bell rang.

Gupta raised his arm, pausing the fight, when his mobile rang.

Judging by the expression on Gupta's face, it wasn't good news. "I see. I'll let them know." Nasreen stood in front of him, expectantly. "Sir? Are we good to go?"

"I'm afraid we're going to have to postpone the fight... I mean, sparring session," shouted Gupta to all the officers watching. He turned to her. "Innes has been called to another murder scene. It's our guy, Nas."

Anger built up in her gut. When was this case going to be over? She ran up to the plastic water bottle sat on the canvas and kicked it, launching it halfway across the gymnasium. "Shit! Is there a photo?"

"On a necklace, yeah. Get changed and get over there. I'll text you the address. Weekes, are you good? You're with this?"

"Hell yeah." Weekes took off her gloves. "I knew it wasn't over."

"But we got the right guy," Nasreen countered.

"Relax, Nas, no one's saying we got the wrong guy. Just that there's still one more to catch. It's not unheard of for killers to work in pairs."

"Bollocks!" she shouted, following Weekes to the changing rooms.

60

"Nasreen, will you comment? Is this one linked to the others?" a journalist asked from behind the police cordon. "Inspector Gupta informed us you caught the man responsible. Is that not true? Is there a killer still out there?"

Holding up her hands, Nasreen approached the media filled cordon. There were cameras and journalists with microphones everywhere; she couldn't get through there were so many. Instead of talking to them, she attempted to creep through them. "Look, until we get to the crime scene and see what's what, you're not getting a statement from me, do you understand? Let me through, please." Her tone wasn't hostile; it was serious. A gap opened up, and seizing her chance, she crept through it and under the cordon that a uniform lifted up for her. "I promise, as soon as I know something, I'll let you all know, okay?"

Turning away from the throng of reporters and towards the crime scene, Nasreen noticed there were two tents. One tent was long and up the top of the field, a good five hundred metres away, while a second tent had been set up nearer them. She saw two SOCOs lingering by the smaller, nearer tent. "Here we go again," she said to Weekes, who was walking by her side. "I hate these overalls."

"Me too," Weekes replied, picking up a set of coveralls from inside the tent and putting them on. Nasreen followed suit, covering her shoes, hair and mouth. By the time she and Weekes left the tent, they were as nondescript as the SOCOs, Innes and Edgeley. The only way she could tell the detectives apart from the crime scene investigators was by their manner and stance; they were in control of the crime scene.

"One photo necklace," Innes said, handing her a plastic bag. "Oh, and we already know who he–"

"Leighton Oldridge," Edgeley interrupted, handing her a driver's license in a bag. "Cyber are looking into him as we speak. We've asked them to look into linking him with Myles Jackman, Verity Staunton and Fiona Armstrong. He has to know them somehow."

"And Claire Padnall?" she asked Edgeley. "She's part of whatever this is, too. Have we heard anything back about the burnt remains yet?"

"Nothing, I'm afraid," Innes responded.

Paying the body the attention it deserved, Nasreen surveyed the scene. Leighton Oldridge's wrists were tied to a fat tree trunk with rope. His upper body was lying on its back, his eyes staring blankly up at the blue sky. It was a scene of such evil chaos, she wanted to vomit. His intestines were sprawled out on the once green grass, which was now red.

The victim's legs and the rest of his waist was detached and lying on the grass twenty feet from the upper body. There was a rope on the ground near the legs. Bending down, inspecting the rope, she could make out razor blades inside the slip knot. "This was specially made." She pointed at the silver blades. "It must've taken the suspect ages to get those in there like that. He went to great lengths to cut the rope and make the holes for the blades. He's patient, I'll give him that."

"And the slip knot made sure that it kept slicing into him," Weekes mused. "Tyre tracks. Fat, they look like SUV tyres. What do you think, Jeep or Range Rover?"

"We know it's not a pickup," Nasreen replied. "This suspect is something else, though. Look at the level of hatred he has. The pain this poor guy must've felt as the blades cut him in half." She shuddered.

"I've got my guys looking at cameras nearby, to see if we can identify the off-roader used," Innes said. "My guess is, the suspect knows his way around and would've avoided all roads with cameras. You never know, though, we might get lucky."

"I doubt it," Nasreen replied. "I think we'll have more luck looking into his background. The more people we have on this the better, sir. I'll call Inspector Gupta and ask for extra resources, if that's okay with you?" When he nodded, she called Gupta and he gave the green light for more manpower.

"We can start by chatting to Richard Pryce," Weekes said.

"Please don't start, Weekes. We need to move forwards, not backwards."

"He knew Emilian Keeble. I found a photo of them together," Weekes insisted. "That's got to at least make him worthy of interviewing, surely?"

"Forget it, he has an alibi," Innes said. "We need solid leads, not vendettas, Weekes."

Nasreen insisted that she and Weekes go back to the local station and work from there.

61

"Come here, Bev, let's take an early morning selfie," Reagan insisted. "You look all sleepy, wearing that T-shirt, and I look – well, sexy as fuck. Everyone'll know what we were up to last night."

Beverly Livingston placed the remote control on the coffee table and joined Reagan in front of the staircase, putting her arm around her host's shoulder. She half pouted, half smiled for the smartphone camera Reagan was holding. Her best friend was wearing a slinky negligee, and looked good enough to eat. "Come on, let's go upstairs."

"What did you come down here for anyway?" Reagan took her hand and led her up the stairs. "I was nice and relaxed just now, then you disappeared. You're not still worried about it, are you? He's been caught, babe. It's over."

Feeling Reagan's soft, warm skin, Beverly relaxed a little when she lay on top of the duvet. Sometimes, she wondered how she'd managed to attract Reagan. Her best friend and lover was so glamorous, so fine, it hurt to look at her. With long, soft dark hair, tanned skin and high cheekbones, Reagan was known everywhere she went. Her friend had over two million followers on Instagram and a million and a half on Twitter; she made money just by waking up in the morning. It seemed everyone wanted to advertise with her. "I know it's over," she replied, Reagan straddling her. "But Myles, Verity and Fiona. I can't believe they're gone. It's so sad."

"Better them than us." Reagan pulled the negligee over her head and threw it on the floor. "We can get on with our lives, yeah? I'll start looking for new members this weekend."

"Don't you feel even a little bit bad for our friends?" she asked, taking in Reagan's naked splendour. If she weren't so in love with her, Beverly might think Reagan was a cold fish. "They were murdered, babe."

"I know what happened." Reagan pulled Beverly's T-shirt up and off, dropping it on the floor. "But I try not to think about it. The police did their job and caught the guy, right? So, it's over. There's no point crying over it, is there?"

Beverly accepted Reagan's long kiss, revelling in it. With her lover still on top, she looked up at her stunning face. "I guess, since you put it that way," she said, placing her hand on the back of Reagan's head and pulling her in for another kiss. While enjoying the throes of passion on the outside, she was squirming on the inside, thinking about Leighton's lack of reply. "Wait! Wait!" she said, pushing Reagan off her and sitting up.

"What?" Reagan whined. "What's wrong with you? Do you know how many guys would drop everything to be in bed with me? Hell, how many girls for that matter?"

Bev wasn't listening. There was something niggling at her, which was why she'd gone downstairs in the first place. Picking up her phone, Beverly looked at the screen. "Leighton's not replied. He always replies."

Getting off the bed, Reagan walked over to her. "It's early. He's probably still in bed, which is where we should be right now." She grabbed Beverly's hands and pulled her along. "Let's get all cosy under the covers, yeah?"

"Maybe," she said, uncertain. Her gut told her something was wrong, even though the police had stated the case was closed. Trying to shake off the negative thoughts, she regarded Reagan's fine body, deciding to join her for some fun. It might take her mind off the whole miserable affair.

62

"Sir, that's brilliant! Please thank Cyber for us." Nasreen hung up. "They've found a photo in Oldridge's social media. All three victims, plus Oldridge. And get this, a fifth person, female. She could be our guy's next intended victim. I'm waiting on the photo to come through any second."

"Finally, something we can work with," Weekes replied, feeling the excitement. The station office was buzzing, a hive of activity. There were suits and uniforms working together to help them find their suspect. In addition to the extra Sussex police, Inspector Gupta had freed up additional manpower in the city, as he said he would. "Is that it?"

With urgency, Nasreen pulled the picture up and showed it to her.

"There it is, all four victims together," she said, regarding Myles Jackman, Verity Staunton and Fiona Armstrong on the top line, with Leighton Oldridge and an unidentified female kneeling next to him, in front of the others. Behind them were five horses in the distance. It looked like they were in a field somewhere. "We're getting so close."

"All we need now is to identity her," Nasreen said. "The

inspector said Cyber are putting her picture through facial recognition software, but doesn't know how long it'll take. Let's drive over to the stables, see if anyone knows her."

Anything was better than sitting around in front of a computer, Weekes thought, taking the keys from Nasreen. "I'll drive," she said, knowing it would only take twenty minutes or so to get to the stables. Picking up her jacket, Weekes walked with her supervisor out of the office and into the staff car park.

It only took fifteen minutes of silence to reach the stables. At one point, she thought about trying to clear the air with Nasreen, but thought better of it, deciding it wasn't her fault her superiors were too blinkered to see her suspicion of Richard Pryce. Their best lead was free to come and go as he pleased, because they didn't want a rookie to make fools of them. That's what it was really about.

When they arrived in the stables offices, the manager, Olive Kramer, was sat at her desk, buried neck deep in paperwork, or so she said in greeting. "What can I do for you, detectives? I heard they caught the man responsible. Have you found Claire? Or is this just a follow-up visit?"

"I'm afraid not," Nasreen replied. "We're still looking for Claire. And while we caught one suspect, we now believe it may be a pair of suspects. We found a photo with all the victims in, plus a girl we've yet to identify. Do you know her?"

Weekes observed the manager's reaction, the photo stuffed under her nose. It didn't look like the manager knew the answer by the way she shook her head. "Take your time, Ms Kramer. I know you haven't been here long. If you haven't seen her, is there someone else here we can talk to who has?"

"I'm sorry! I haven't met her before. But I can ask Ingrid to come in; she's worked here forever. If anyone will know who she is, Ingrid will." She picked up the landline phone and dialled. "Ingrid, can you come into the office, please."

While they were waiting, Weekes studied the pictures hanging on the wall. There were so many, too many to look at in one go. She grabbed a framed picture and pulled it off the wall. "Nasreen, take a look at this," she said, showing the group photo of six riders to her supervisor. "All four victims, plus two."

"Four victims? I thought there were only three," Olive said, concern in her voice.

"A fourth was killed in the early hours of this morning," Nasreen replied, vaguely glancing at the framed picture. "Which is why it's imperative we find this girl; she could be his next intended victim."

The office door opened and a tall, slender woman in boots, jodhpurs and a body warmer entered. "You wanted to see me, Olive?" She looked her and Nasreen up and down.

"Yeah, do you recognise this woman?" Nasreen held up the photo.

"Sure! That's Beverly Livingston," Ingrid replied, handing back the photo. "She's a regular rider here. Oh, and she used to go out with Verity and her friends every Sunday. I often saw them heading off in the morning."

Writing the name in her notepad, Weekes showed Ingrid the framed photo in her hand. "And this woman? Do you recognise her?" Excited at getting an answer on the first photo, she felt she might be on a roll. The excitement faded when Ingrid shook her head. "Ah, well, thanks for your help anyway." By the time she'd dismissed the stables employee, her supervisor was on the phone to Gupta.

"We need contact details for a Beverly Livingston," Nasreen said.

"You don't happen to have her address on your system, do you?" Weekes asked Olive.

Olive Kramer sat down and turned to her monitor. Within a minute, she had the address. "It's old, but whoever's there now might have a forwarding address. She hasn't renewed her membership in a few years, I'm afraid."

It was a start, she thought, writing the address down. When she stood, Nasreen was still on the phone with Inspector Gupta. The door was open, so she wandered into the other office, to where Verity used to work. It was an empty desk, her belongings in police custody, at least until the case was solved.

A picture hung on the wall next to the door leading to the courtyard outside grabbed her attention. Above it, in good looking italic writing, were the words "In Memoriam". Slowly walking up to the picture, a pretty face formed. Louise Thatcher. "Ingrid!" Weekes shouted. The tall woman joined her. "Who's this?"

"Ah, poor Louise." Ingrid removed the frame from the wall. "She was a wonderful young woman. A real rider; she lived for horse riding. Well, for these stables, really. Such a terrible tragedy."

"Why? What happened?" Weekes couldn't help but feel excited.

"The horse bucked. It sent her flying. The poor girl landed on her neck. Verity called an ambulance. By the time they arrived, she was dead. It's probably for the best, though. Had she survived, she'd never walk again, which for someone like Louise, would be worse than dying."

"You say she was friends with Verity?"

When Ingrid nodded, Weekes asked, "And what about these people? Did you ever see Louise riding with them?" She handed Ingrid the picture of the six she'd found in Olive's office.

"All of them. Except her; I don't know her. They all went out riding together. Every Sunday, Verity led their way, being the most seasoned rider. I still can't believe they're all gone. Do you even know why he did it?"

Making sure Nasreen was still inside the office, out of

earshot, Weekes pulled up a photo of Richard Pryce. "Him." She showed Ingrid the photo. "Do you know him?"

"Of course, detective. That's Richard Pryce. Everyone around here knows Richard. His father owns the Labrador breeding farm, and Richard volunteers at Brambles. Lovely young man, he is. So courteous, polite. And he just adores animals."

"And what about Louise? Did she know Richard?"

"It'd be pretty hard for her not to. She worked at the shelter, too. They were close, she and Richard. Why are you asking?"

It was all coming together. The case revolved around Louise Thatcher and the stables. Louise died in a horse riding accident a year earlier, and now all bar two of the people there were dead, brutally murdered. Could Richard Pryce have been in a relationship with the so very pretty Louise? Did he blame her co-riders for the accident?

"Weekes, we've got to go," Nasreen said, striding out of Olive's office. "That was the receptionist from Brambles. Doctor Chilvers is missing. We're meeting Yasmin outside the vet's house. She has a spare key."

Wanting to show Nasreen her findings, her partner was too tense to listen, so Weekes thanked Ingrid, took a quick photo of Louise Thatcher's memorial picture and ran after Nasreen. It was Richard Pryce! She'd called it on first meeting him, but no one would listen. Doctor Chilvers was missing, presumed dead, probably because she'd found out about his murderous extra-curricular activities.

"I'll drive," she said, excited about what they might find at Chilvers' home.

"I'm going to take a shower," Reagan said, kissing her. "Are you joining me?"

Beverly lay under the covers, receiving her host's kisses. "I'm comfortable here," she said, her skin tingling with excitement. "You go. I'll have one later." The covers came up and Reagan's face peered out. Beverly laughed. "Go on! I might be in to join you in a minute."

Taking her leave, Reagan walked out of the bedroom naked, her hips swaying hypnotically. Beverly could watch her for hours, literally. Her girlfriend was the most dazzling woman she'd ever seen, and her followers seemed to agree. Whenever Reagan uploaded a photo on Instagram, there was always a mad flurry of likes and comments, mostly from guys looking to hook up with her. And Reagan had chosen to share her time – and bed – with her. Honoured didn't do justice to how Beverly felt.

Reaching over to the bedside chest of drawers, she picked up the remote control and switched on the television. Sky News. As she was about to change channels, Beverly saw the headline: Fourth Sussex Murder. She gasped. "Oh my God! Please, not Leighton!"

Turning up the volume, she listened to the reporter talk about how a dog walker had found the body in the field behind him, which was cordoned off by police. Then the reporter spoke about how the murder was most probably linked to the three previous murders that police said were solved. Beverly called Leighton on her mobile. There was no answer and after four rings went to voicemail. "It's me! Please call me when you get this," she said, her hand shaking. "I'm heading over to the police station now."

Switching off the television and throwing the remote on Reagan's bed, she found the previous day's clothes, throwing them on, all the while listening to her girlfriend singing in the shower, which wasn't pleasant; it was one thing Reagan wasn't great at. Creeping past the bathroom, down the spiral staircase to the ground floor, she hunted the huge house for her bag. It was behind the couch.

Thinking about calling out to Reagan that she was leaving, Beverly decided against it, opting to leave the house before her host talked her out of going to the police, just as she had after Fiona had been murdered. Reagan's most annoying trait was her ability to persuade people out of doing what they wanted.

Outside, on the driveway, Beverly climbed into her little red Fiesta, relieved that Reagan had left the gate open. Reagan's parents' summer house was made mostly of glass, so wherever guests were, they could see the beautiful surrounding views. Reagan had chosen to come here to get away from the trappings of city life. Beverly felt the house could be a trap, especially given that the killer was still out there, and judging by the photo she had in her bag, if the order of deaths was anything to go by, she was next.

Flooring the accelerator, Beverly shot out of the driveway, onto the road. The clock on her dash said it was almost ten. The journey to Sussex would take roughly three hours, but once she was on the road, she felt safer than being stuck in the glass house, a half mile away from the nearest neighbour and two miles away from civilisation.

64

———

"You stay here, and don't touch anything." Nasreen took the key from Yasmin and opened the door with her gloved hand. "It could be a crime scene." Upon arrival, she'd seen the vet's Range Rover in the driveway, which wasn't a good sign. There was no indication of forced entry, at least not from the front of the detached home. Instinctively, she pulled out her cosh, held it in her hand, ready to extend it at any given moment.

"Doctor Chilvers?" Weekes stepped inside the hallway behind her. "Shout out if you can hear us. It's Detective Maqsood and Detective Weekes."

There was silence; all she could hear was the scuffling of her own feet, as she went from room to room. The lounge showed no sign of life: the television was switched off. The dining room looked untouched. It was only when she entered the kitchen that she saw the mess; there was blood on the lino, a lot of blood. The back door was wide open and there were two broken chairs strewn across the floor. Chilvers had put up a fight. Nasreen was careful not to tread in any evidence. "Weekes, call this in, will you? I'm going to grab our evidence kit from the boot," Nasreen said, walking towards the front door.

It was only a couple of minutes before she was back in the kitchen, wearing a face mask, hair net, gloves and shoe covers. Looking at the blood, it looked like the vet had been cut, then dragged to the back door. Nasreen followed the blood trail to the side of the house, where it led her to the double garage.

"Now will you hear me out about Richard Pryce?" Weekes asked, distracting her.

"He didn't come into the shelter yesterday either," Yasmin said, who was looking down at the floor, knowing she shouldn't be there.

Nasreen felt anger rising. "Did he call in sick, or what?" This was all she needed, Weekes getting back on her Pryce theory. "Relax, Weekes, it doesn't mean anything."

"He's never rung in sick," Yasmin replied. "Not once. And he's never missed a shift at the shelter."

A SOCO appeared in the doorway. Nasreen waved him through, letting him know to commence proceedings. "Shit!" She had no choice but to look for him. "So, we have three missing players now." Turning her back on Weekes and Yasmin, Nasreen studied the blood trail.

"Are we looking for Pryce?" Weekes asked.

There was nothing for it; she had no choice but to let the investigation take her where it wanted to go. Deep down, she didn't believe Pryce had it in him to kill people. No, it wasn't him. But, then again, she could be wrong. "I'll call it in to Innes and Edgeley," she replied, taking out her mobile. "I'll ask them to pick him up. We've got too much to be getting on with here."

65

Reagan couldn't believe Beverly had deserted her. It was so rude, to just take off without so much as a goodbye. To think she'd thought they might have had something. Huffing in front of the mirror, she glanced at the clock on her phone: 11:46. The sun was beaming down on the patio outside, her sun chair waiting for her. Picking up her mobile, she tried Beverly once more, hoping to serve her "friend" a mouthful of venom pie. "Bitch!" she hissed, stabbing at the screen with her finger. "It's your loss. Look what you're missing out on."

Putting finishing touches to her soft and shiny dark hair, she smiled in the mirror, knowing how great she looked in the light blue bikini she was wearing. It was time to show Beverly what she was missing. Reagan took a selfie.

There was a crash downstairs.

Reagan screamed. What the hell was that? Scared, she made her way out of the bedroom and down the spiral staircase slowly, trying to be as quiet as she could. It was funny how holding her phone made her feel less scared, a lifeline somehow.

Every footstep made a noise. Reagan peered into the kitchen, scanning the room for broken glass: nothing. Everything was as it was supposed to be. Then, she backed up and checked the lounge: nothing. It had to be in the dining room, she thought. Bingo! She stood, looking at the broken patio door, which was once a solid sheet of glass. It was there, trembling, that she felt she wasn't alone.

Reagan froze, knowing someone was behind her. It wasn't fair! This kind of thing was only supposed to happen in movies, at night, in the States, in some small town. It wasn't supposed to happen in the United Kingdom, in the south-west.

She screamed into a gloved hand that covered her mouth.

Every fibre, every atom that she was comprised of fought the attacker, not that it did any good. The figure whose body she could feel behind her was at least five feet eleven, to her five six. And its arms were strong, powerful; they gathered her up easily. She screamed, feeling something in her neck, a needle, if the stinging pain was any indicator.

The intruder let go of her. Reagan turned and faced the masked figure, who was wearing a scarf, crowned by a hood. Feeling woozy, faint, she tried fleeing. As she fell, the intruder's strong arms caught her, breaking her fall. "What do you want with me?"

"You'll find out soon enough," the voice replied.

While lying on the expensive carpet, Reagan wanted her mum. She even called out for her, tears welling. Everything was blurry, and getting darker by the second. Trying to fight it, she looked up at the intruder one last time, before she fell into a dreamless sleep.

66

"And you're determined for it not to be Richard Pryce, aren't you?" Weekes said, trying to keep her voice calm, even. "It doesn't matter what I say, you'll still veto any notion he might be our suspect. Why can't you see it?"

A SOCO appeared in the doorway and she asked him to give them a minute. He put his hands up and left. "He was bullied by Myles Jackman for most of his life, and he was friends with Emilian Keeble, who you still think killed them all, except now there's another dead body, isn't there?" She wanted to hit Nasreen with the knowledge of Louise Thatcher, but held on to it. "Maybe Pryce is the second suspect we're looking for. Maybe the good doctor found out and he's killed her. There's enough blood in there to support the theory."

"And it's a great theory," Nasreen replied. "Except it isn't Pryce; I can tell you that right now. You know what your problem is, Weekes? You think you know everything, but you don't. I've interviewed hundreds of suspects and witnesses in my time, and I'm willing to bet big money on the fact that Richard Pryce isn't our guy. In fact, I've never been more sure of anything in my life."

It was time to hit her with it. Weekes pulled her phone out. "Oh really? Explain this, then. Here." She showed Nasreen the photo. "Louise Thatcher died in a tragic horse riding accident a year ago. She was with all four of our victims when her horse bucked her off, killing her. And guess where Louise volunteered? Go on, guess!"

"Brambles Animal Shelter," Nasreen said, her expression grim.

Weekes made a bell sound. "Correct! And she was very close to him, too, by all accounts. Do you still doubt he may be involved?" Her speech was making an impact; she could see Nasreen turning. "Can we finish up here and go look for him, please?" When Nasreen nodded, she felt a rush of excitement.

"I'll call Innes." Nasreen tapped her phone's screen. "See if he's picked Pryce up yet. I'm still not convinced, but if you're right, we can't have him on the streets."

Listening to her partner on the phone, Weekes put her mobile in her pocket, looking at the house where the SOCOs were still beavering away, cataloguing the crime scene. Nasreen shook her head. It seemed Pryce really was missing. It wasn't a good sign. "He's in the wind?"

"Apparently he didn't come home last night. His dad said he left the house yesterday at about five in the evening and hasn't been seen since. We already know he didn't go to the shelter. He's gone to ground."

"So, what do we do now?" she asked, unsure of protocol.

As Nasreen was about to answer her question, the mobile rang. "I'm putting it on speaker, sir," Nasreen said. "You're on with me and Weekes. Go ahead!"

"I've just had a call from the station," Innes said. "There's someone there you'll want to talk to. Her name's Beverly Livingston; she has information pertaining to our case, apparently. It could be just the break we're looking for. Get yourselves over there asap."

"On our way, sir," Nasreen replied, hanging up.

Driving to the station, Weekes was buzzing. They were so close to solving the case, she could almost taste it. Being ninety-nine per cent certain she had the correct suspect made her quietly confident. It was always the quiet ones, she thought, turning into the station car park after a half hour drive along the narrow Sussex country lanes.

After following Nasreen through the police station reception, she found herself outside interview room two, the desk sergeant having told them where their interviewee was being kept. "Are you ready?" she asked, her hand on the door handle.

Opening the door, she was greeted by a nervous girl in her early thirties, pretty, blonde, athletic. Their interviewee was biting her nails. "Beverly Livingston?" The girl nodded. "I'm Detective Constable Weekes, and this is my partner, Detective Sergeant Maqsood."

"Please, you have to protect me," Beverly cried. "I'm next; I just know it."

"Whoa! Slow down, Beverly," Nasreen said calmly. "What do you mean you're next? You're talking about the recent murders, aren't you? How do you know you're next?"

Weekes sat down, her knee jigging up and down with all the excitement. It peaked when Beverly pulled out her mobile and started thumbing through photographs. "What've you got there?" she asked, trying to hurry her.

Beverly turned the phone around for them to see the picture. "You see?" Beverly pointed at Myles Jackman. "Myles was first, then Verity, then Fiona." Her finger jumped to each person in turn on the top row. It dropped down to the bottom row. "And now Leighton's dead."

"Leighton?" Nasreen asked.

"Leighton Oldridge," Weekes replied, surprised that her superior didn't understand it. "But how do you know it's Leighton? That information hasn't been declared yet, Beverly. How did you know it was him?"

"I didn't but I do now. And he wasn't responding to my messages. You have to protect me, please. I know he's coming after me next. Look!" She pointed at her picture. "I have a clearer one."

Weekes waited, her leg still jigging up and down beneath the table. She heard Nasreen gasp when Beverly showed them the clearer picture. "You're fucking kidding me!" She sat back in amazement, anger boiling up. "It all makes sense now. That's why he's after you." Next to her, Nasreen got up and rushed to the door, calling for Innes.

"Shit!" Nasreen cursed. "If the reporters get wind of this, we're in trouble."

"Why? What do you mean?" Beverly asked.

"When they find out why he's been killing your club members, they're going to make him a vigilante, not the murderer he is, do you understand?" Nasreen replied. "I don't believe this! How could you? It's barbaric."

"You wanted to see me?" Innes closed the door behind him.

"We know what this is all about now, sir." Weekes showed him the photo of the six club members smiling above a mauled fox. There were four English foxhounds in the picture, with their horses in the background. Each club member, including Beverly, were wearing satisfied smiles.

"Oh dear God!" Innes said. "The bloody press'll have a field day. He'll be a hero before the week's out, you mark my words. Until this is over, not a word of this leaves this room, right?" He rubbed his hair in frustration. "And you, young lady, you're in protective custody until we've apprehended the suspect."

"But you don't understand," Beverly said. "If I'm in here, he's going to go after Reagan next. You have to fetch her from the house, please. She's all alone there." She grabbed the phone and pointed to the sixth person in the photo. "That's Reagan, my girlfriend. You have to rescue her before he finds out I'm here, please."

Nasreen stared at the photo. "Why does she look familiar?"

"It's Reagan," Beverly repeated, like they should recognise her. "Reagan Embry?"

"Embry," Weekes said. "Embry?"

"Not Suzanne Embry's daughter?" Nasreen asked, a frown forming. "Oh bollocks! He's going after the home secretary's daughter, of course. If you're an animal rights activist, who better, or bigger than the daughter of the person you're trying to persuade. Quick! Where is she, Beverly? I'll have a car over there in a matter of minutes."

There was nothing Weekes could do. Instead of getting in the way, she watched as Nasreen tried calling the house Reagan was staying at, which was situated in the middle of nowhere, down in the south-west. She wasn't surprised when Nasreen shook her head, no answer. Then, her supervisor was on the phone, ordering a squad car to speed over to the property and collect the home secretary's daughter.

It was the longest fifteen minutes in history. No one in the room spoke, for fear of jinxing the situation. Weekes noticed tears welling up in Beverly's eyes. She reached into her pocket and brought out a tissue. "I'm sure she's fine," she said, trying to comfort the girl. "Why didn't you bring her with you?"

Beverly's mouth crumpled. "I couldn't tell her I was coming here. She'd have talked me out of it, just like she did after Fiona was murdered. The thing about Reagan is, you don't go against her, ever. Both me and Leighton wanted to come here after we heard Fiona had been killed, but she wouldn't let us... She said we'll be in so much trouble if anyone found out what we do.

And then, of course, you lot said it was over, that you'd caught the guy responsible."

Nasreen's mobile rang. "I see. Thanks for trying."

Weekes could tell it was bad news by the way Nasreen held her head down. "And?" It was infuriating not being the person in control.

"They're treating it as a crime scene," Nasreen replied. "The patio door's been smashed and there's signs of a struggle inside. I'm so sorry, Beverly."

"Tell me, Superintendent Bukhari, how many officers do we currently have looking for my daughter?" Suzanne Embry stood and glared at him. "Why don't I see helicopters in the sky, hmm? This isn't some runaway we're dealing with here, this is Reagan. This is *my daughter*."

Franks wanted to intervene, but he didn't want to deflect her anger onto him either. Poor Bukhari was taking the grilling like the consummate professional he was. None of the fifteen other officers in the room uttered a word, or even cleared their throats. Embry had that effect on people. "I believe we have thirty down this way and another twenty-five in the city, uniforms that is," Franks said, finally. "Not to mention the fifteen detectives we have across both regions, ma'am."

"We're going to find your daughter, ma'am," Bukhari added.

When Franks received the call from Bukhari informing him of the situation, he'd organised the meeting in the Sussex police station. Everyone involved in the case believed the suspect would bring Reagan Embry back to Sussex, even though she was abducted in the south-west, where the home secretary had her holiday home. "That we are," he agreed. "I promise you, we'll find her before anything happens to her."

"Don't make promises you can't keep, Peter," she said, her voice calm, tempered. "Because if anything happens to her, I swear your head will be the first on a pike on my front lawn, do you understand? Followed closely by yours, Superintendent Bukhari, and yours, Detectives Maqsood and Weekes."

A chill went down Franks' spine. He believed she'd do it. "We all know what's at stake, ma'am," he said, placating her. "Let's recap where we're at. Inspector Gupta, do you mind showing the home secretary what we know." He watched as Gupta stood and walked over to the conference room's whiteboard.

"These are the four victims," Gupta said. "The first was Myles Jackman; he was abducted, tied up and dragged naked around a car park, ma'am. It was through investigating Jackman that we found out he knew the second victim, Verity Staunton, who, as you know, was tied to a tree and shot with arrows. She was a friend of Reagan's, we believe? Did you ever meet Verity?"

"I think we've ascertained she's never met any of the victims, inspector," Franks interrupted, moving things along. He didn't want Embry questioned. "Continue."

"A few days after Verity's body was found, Fiona Armstrong was attacked by four dogs and killed in woods near her home. It was at this point that Inspector Innes, Sergeant Edgeley, Sergeant Maqsood and Constable Weekes thought to look at owners of dangerous dogs, and more specifically neighbour noise complaints. Sergeant Edgeley, who has local knowledge, knew of dogs at a static caravan site nearby. During a routine search, Sergeants Edgeley and Maqsood, and Constable Weekes were shot at by Emilian Keeble with a bow and arrow. A high speed pursuit ensued between Keeble and Edgeley and Maqsood, whereupon Keeble's pickup truck, which was used to kill Jackman, hit an oncoming lorry, killing him instantly. Keeble's dogs' teeth were checked against the marks on Armstrong's body and found to be an exact match. There's no doubt that Emilian Keeble was responsible for Armstrong's murder, maybe all three, we don't know."

"Well, it can't have only been Keeble, can it, inspector?" Embry continued. "A fourth body was found, wasn't it?"

"Right, Leighton Oldridge," Gupta said. "His hands were tied to a tree, and his waist to a car with razors embedded in the rope. He was split in two from the waist down. And since that macabre discovery, Detectives Maqsood and Weekes have found out that a former suspect, Richard Pryce – previously thought to be cleared – was in fact friends with Emilian Keeble. And in addition to that, they've learnt that all four victims attended a local horse riding school, where a Louise Thatcher died a year ago when she was thrown from her horse. Thatcher volunteered at Brambles Animal Shelter, the very same shelter that Pryce volunteers at; they were firm friends, apparently."

"And you think this Pryce is the suspect? You think he has Reagan?" Embry asked, interested, the hostility waning.

"Yes, ma'am, but not just because of that." He nodded at Bukhari, who handed Embry a photograph. "Pryce is missing, and the vet who volunteers at the Shelter, Doctor Chilvers, is also missing, presumed dead. Blood was found in her home. It's believed she found out about Pryce murdering our victims. Pryce is an animal lover, you see, ma'am. We believe he blames the fox hunting club for getting Louise involved, and subsequently killed. I'm sorry to be the one to show you that; I know it must come as a shock to know Reagan was a part of it."

Surprised at Embry's lack of emotion, Franks winked at Gupta, telling him to stop for a moment, to let it sink in. "Ma'am? Would you like a glass of water?"

"What for?" she answered. "For this? It really isn't a big deal, you funny lot. But I told her to use the bird of prey, not the dogs." She looked back up. "What? They're vermin. They need culling, why shouldn't we get some enjoyment out of it? Oh please, don't give me those looks. Fox hunting's been around for centuries, and it'll be around long after we're gone, I assure you. So, is this your best guess? You believe this Richard Pryce is our guy?"

"We do, ma'am," Gupta replied.

"Very well, let's get out there and find my Reagan." Embry stood. "Oh, and Peter, I meant what I said earlier. If anything happens to my daughter, you can all look for new jobs. Am I clear?"

"Crystal." Franks watched her walk out of the room, her bodyguard closing the door behind him. "Right, that could've gone better." Everyone let out a big lungful of air in relief. "I want everyone out there, knocking on doors, understood? Detectives Maqsood and Weekes, I want you looking into this death at the stable, Louise whatsherface. If your theory's correct, there must be something there."

Every officer in the conference room piled out, except Franks. He walked over to the door and closed it, taking his burner phone out of his uniform jacket pocket. "Yeah, it's me," he said to Astor. "Let's meet at the park, usual place, say eight?" With his meeting planned, he sat back in his chair with a grin. With Harry out of the way, he'd be the acting commissioner, at least until the election... If they found Reagan Embry alive.

68

Franks was expecting to have to wait for Astor, but not for twenty minutes. The last time they'd met there only a couple of days earlier, Astor had made him wait for long enough; this was ridiculous, bordering on insulting. When he was about to give up and start walking back to his car, he saw Astor heading towards him along a path. "I was about to give up on you and go back to the station! You're twenty minutes late."

"Hey, if you want to do this yourself, be my guest," Astor replied, no apology. "The way I figure it, you need me, late or not. So shut the fuck up and get to the point. When do you need this done by? And how do you want it done? You mentioned gas before. Is that how you want to play it?"

"It can't be suspicious. If he gets shot, it's no good for us. It has to be written off as accidental. Fires start sometimes, even on boats. Harry has at least three canisters of gas on board at any given time; it's perfect. You get your guys to cut the gas line, leave it a couple of minutes and kaboom."

"Do you think it'll be that easy? They've got to gain access to *The Albatross* first; how are they going to do that, huh? Harry's not going to let a couple of my guys on board, is he? Once on, there's no problem. They can finish the job."

Franks leaned forwards, checking there was no one about. "We need to put it on hold for now, until I get confirmation from the home secretary."

"How's she coping? I heard her daughter's been kidnapped. Tough break, that. For what it's worth, I hope she's found safe."

"We're out en masse trying to find Reagan. All this might be moot if anything happens to her daughter. Embry's already threatened me with the sack if we don't find Reagan in time. So, leave it until this has all blown over, okay? When the time comes, I'll contact you with more details."

"It's fine with me." Astor stood. "I thought you wanted this done yesterday. I can't say I'm disappointed; this is a bad move, I can feel it."

Franks stood and met Astor's stare. "If your guys don't fuck it up, everyone'll think it was a tragic accident. A gas leak on a boat isn't exactly unheard of, is it? Anyway, let me talk to the home secretary first." He shook hands with Astor, then walked with him back to his car, where he got in and drove back to the station in Sussex, a good hour's drive.

69

Nasreen glanced nervously at her watch: 23:46. After the meeting in the conference room, Inspectors Gupta and Innes, Sergeant Edgeley, Weekes and she had agreed that the suspect was probably going to wait until two o'clock in the morning, which held significance to Pryce, for whatever reason. "We're running out of time," she said to Weekes, who was deep in concentration.

"I've just spoken to Jenny, she's Louise's best friend. If anyone's going to know if there was anything going on between her and Pryce, I imagine she will. I've told her we're on our way." Weekes stood and picked up her jacket.

Mirroring her partner, Nasreen put on her jacket and joined Weekes in walking towards the staircase. "After you," she said, at the top stair. "We should be out there looking for her, not chatting to one of Louise's friends."

"I know, but we don't know where to look," Weekes replied, reaching the bottom step. "Maybe Jenny might know where we should start."

"I guess." But Nasreen was not convinced. The station was deserted, with every officer, uniformed and plain-clothed out looking for Reagan Embry and Richard Pryce. Inspector Innes had appeared on the News at Six on the BBC and Sky, asking for witnesses to come forward, and asking the public to be vigilant, that Richard Pryce was considered armed and dangerous.

She opened the driver's door and got in, fastening her seat belt and starting the engine. Driving out of the station car park, her thoughts turned to Reagan Embry. The poor girl would be scared stiff. Whatever Pryce had in store for Reagan, she knew it wasn't anything good; on the contrary, Pryce would be saving something savage for the most famous member of the club, and the home secretary's daughter.

Weekes was deep in thought as well, she noticed, glancing over at her partner. It made her sad to think that Weekes was right all along, and she'd flatly refused to back her up. Telling herself that she'd make it up to Weekes, the radio crackled to life. The Ditchling Beacon patrol checked in, informing everyone that they'd not found anything yet.

"It's such a big place." Weekes was staring out of her window. "Sussex, I mean. And Pryce might not be in Sussex, anyway."

"Now's not the time to start doubting ourselves. We all agreed, he's going to wait until two o'clock, right?"

"Yeah, and he might've expedited it. With this much attention, do you think he'd wait for his perfect time? I wouldn't; I'd get it over and done with." Weekes looked over at her. "That's just me, though."

Trying not to think about it, Nasreen ignored the last comment. No, Reagan Embry was still alive; she had to be. They were going to chat to Jenny, and she was going to give them an idea of where to look. Needing to believe it, she indicated right when the GPS told her the turning was approaching.

DAY 16
SATURDAY, JUNE 2ND

70

———

"What a complete waste of time," Nasreen said, opening the driver's door. "She didn't know anything." She glanced at her watch. It was half past midnight. They only had an hour and a half until the deadline, she hoped; in truth, Reagan could be dead already for all they knew. A niggling feeling she had told her the home secretary's daughter was still alive, though. And she'd learnt to trust her gut. Nasreen sat down heavily and slid the key in the ignition.

"I know." Weekes closed the passenger door and fastened her seat belt. "Maybe the others have had more luck." She turned on the police radio.

Driving back towards the Sussex station, Nasreen listened to the radio chatter. There were over twenty patrols out looking for Reagan Embry and Richard Pryce, and as yet no sign of them. She heard Gupta commenting. He was out with Terrence, walking along Ditchling Beacon. Sussex was a huge area to cover, with acres and acres of fields and woods to get lost in. "He's going to make this one bold," she said to Weekes, who nodded and said she was listening. "Well, he's pissed about Louise, right?"

"If we're right, yeah."

"So, he'll try to make a statement," Nasreen continued, focusing on the road, while thinking at the same time. "He'll kill her somewhere with meaning. It'll be somewhere linked to Louise somehow."

"Okay, I'm with you. It could be a place that was special to them."

"Right." She put the headlights on full beam through the winding country road. "It could be where they first met, had their first kiss. Either way, it's going to have meaning to Pryce. He blames Reagan for Louise's death. That's it! All we need to do is find that place, in," she looked at the dash clock, "an hour and twenty-four minutes."

"Is that all?" Weekes asked. "No pressure then."

They were no nearer finding Reagan now than earlier in the conference room. It was hard, but she didn't want to start thinking negatively. Positivity was the key. However, with time ticking along, her positivity was waning. "Maybe we'll find something on her social media," she suggested, thinking out loud. "Let's look into places she's been."

Weekes sighed. "So, back to the drawing board, then?"

It was how Nasreen felt, too. There was more chatter coming through on the radio. Four groups checked in, reporting nothing of interest; they hadn't found Pryce or Reagan. The group covering Devil's Dyke were still out en masse, with nothing interesting to report. Innes and Edgeley were out with uniforms, and they'd found nothing of interest either. Nasreen wanted to check in. Without anything to say, she decided against it.

It was ten to one by the time she pulled into the police station car park. There was only one squad car in the staff parking area. It was like a ghost town. The reception clerk was manning the doors. Nasreen waited for the buzz before going inside, Weekes behind her.

Taking the stairs two at a time, Nasreen found herself at her temporary desk within two minutes, her partner next to her. "Let's do this!" she said, encouraging Weekes, who was getting more discouraged with every passing minute.

71

Reagan awoke in a panic. Her eyes were wide open, yet it was dark. Instinctively, she tried to rub her eyes. It was then that she realised her hands were tied behind her back, restrained by something thin and tough; it wasn't rope, or chains. Thin. Cable ties! She heard a click when she wriggled.

Trying to move her legs, they could only move so far. There were ties around her ankles as well as her wrists. She was still wearing her bikini, she noticed, shivering inside this... She didn't know what it was. It surrounded her, like a bag of some sort.

She prayed she wasn't inside a... body bag? Panic took hold; she tried screaming into the sock or rag or whatever was stuffed in her mouth. Her scream came out muffled. "Help!" She yelled. "Help me!" Although it was unrecognisable. The scariest thing was the lack of sight. Screaming, tears running down her cheek, she tried wrestling with the bag, trying desperately to break her restraints, which were digging into her skin.

Above her, she heard a noise. A click followed. It was still dark inside the bag. Praying for someone to find her, Reagan heard movement above her. She stopped breathing, listening to the sounds.

"Good, you're awake. It's nearly time."

The voice was low, muffled. Reagan screamed when she felt a hand pull at the bag above her head. Her whole body moved, the arm was so strong. Then she felt another arm grab her waist and pull her up further. With her head lifted, Reagan realised she was in the boot of a car, being dragged out.

When she landed on her back, it winded her briefly. Then, she felt the strong arms dragging her. There was nothing she could do to prevent it. The ground was bumpy, and it felt like she was being dragged up hill.

When the arms stopped dragging her, Reagan lay waiting for the voice to say something. Instead, she heard the zip opening. Shadow pulled the bag away from her face, and glaring down at her were two angry eyes. "What do you want from me?" she asked, the words muffled, nonsense. "Fuck you!" she spat, into the rag.

"You sure are feisty, I'll give you that," Shadow said.

Reagan could barely see through the tears. Blinking hard twice, she then watched Shadow pick up a shovel and jump down into a great, big hole. It was a grave! It would be her grave, she realised, suddenly panicking at the thought of being buried alive. For fuck's sake, she was already in a body bag. "Help!" she screamed, as loud as she could.

"Keep it up, Reagan," Shadow said, still digging. "There's no one here."

She looked around. Behind her was a huge water tower, its concrete frame looming over her, eerie in its elegance and practicality. Reagan knew where she was; she knew the relevance of this place. For how could she forget what happened here? She'd spent the last year trying to forget it. "I'm sorry!" she yelled, hoping Shadow might forgive her.

Shadow stopped digging and climbed out of the hole, throwing the spade down. "Was that 'I'm sorry' I just heard?" Shadow asked, bending down and taking the rag out of her mouth. "If you want to repent, now's the time. Confess your sin to me here, in this special place. Meet your fate with a clear conscience, Reagan, I urge you."

"I'm sorry about Louise," she cried, tears clouding her vision. "We never meant for it to happen. Her horse bucked." Shadow was listening. "You have to believe me, it was an accident... A tragic accident. No one was sorrier than me."

Shadow squatted, pulling a photo out of a pocket. "This is why she died, Reagan. It was karma. And now I'm giving karma a helping hand by punishing you for inviting her into your little club. You might not have killed her yourself, but by bringing her along on your hunt, you got her killed, didn't you?"

"It was an accident," she repeated. "It wasn't anyone's fault. Louise asked to join the club. I didn't need to invite her." She knew she'd said the wrong thing when Shadow shouted, "Liar!"

Her captor bent down and shoved the rag back in her mouth, before picking up the spade and jumping in the grave.

72

"We're getting nowhere!" Nasreen said, nerves getting the best of her.

Weekes looked up from her monitor. "Nowhere sticks out. The only place I can think of that might hold some relevance is where she died." She noticed the pained expression on Nasreen's face change visibly. "What?"

"That's it! Why didn't we think of it sooner? Of course it's where she died. And where is that?"

Turning back to her monitor, Weekes pulled up newspaper articles from local Sussex newspapers about the horse riding accident. "I don't know. The articles are vague on location. None of them specify. Even the police report's vague; I can tell you it happened in a field near here, but I couldn't tell you where."

Nasreen pulled out her mobile phone, then stood.

"What is it?" Weekes asked, still sat down. "Where are you going?"

"The police report might be useless, but we know someone who knows where it happened," Nasreen replied, encouraging Weekes to accompany her. "And she's downstairs as we speak. She'll be able to point it out to us on Google Maps."

"We need to be quick." Weekes grabbed her jacket and followed Nasreen. "It's already twenty to two." Following the desk sergeant's directions, she walked with Nasreen to the basement, where the holding cells were located. "We'd better pray she knows," she said to Nasreen, as they arrived at the cell door.

Nasreen used the desk sergeant's key to unlock the door and opened it.

To her surprise, Beverly Livingston was asleep on the makeshift bed, which was the only piece of furniture in the depressing cell, bar the toilet and tiny sink. When Nasreen stepped inside, Beverly awoke with a jump. "It's okay, you're safe. It's only us," she said.

"We don't have much time, Beverly," Nasreen said, on one knee, her phone in hand. "I need you to show us where Louise was thrown off her horse. We think Reagan's there. Please show us."

To Weekes' relief, Beverly took the phone from Nasreen and played with Google Maps until she had the destination in the centre of the screen. She took Nasreen's phone from Beverly. "It's by a water tower?"

"Yeah. We think it spooked the horse somehow. Please find Reagan. Please, I beg you. I love her!"

Handing back Nasreen's phone, Weekes said, "We're on our way. If she's there, we won't let anything happen to her, you have my word." She followed Nasreen out of the cell, locking it before heading up the stairs to where the desk sergeant was waiting for the key. "Let's go!" she said to Nasreen, who had the car key in hand.

73

"It's time!" Shadow put the spade down and towered over her.

"Please! No!" Reagan screamed into the rag. When Shadow bent down, she tensed every muscle she could, trying her best to prevent Shadow from pushing her over the edge of the grave. It was no use. She felt her body roll twice, with Shadow's strong arms pushing her, until she fell over the edge, landing on the soft earth, which knocked the wind out of her for the second time. Her face was in the dirt, when she heard Shadow jump into the five feet deep hole with her. Shadow rolled her onto her back. "Please, don't do this," she mumbled.

"Look at you, so pretty in your bikini," said Shadow, looking at her body. "You won't be so pretty when they finally dig you up and the worms have had a feast."

"No! Please, I don't want to die." Tears of desperation were wetting her cheeks.

"You won't die straight away." Shadow zipped up the bag. "No, you'll have whatever oxygen's left in the bag, until you start choking, clawing at the bag for air. I've heard it's quite calming, dying of asphyxiation. But you'll find out soon enough."

Back in the dark, Reagan couldn't stop crying. She wanted

her mum. It wasn't fair! She had so much to live for, so much to see and do. This should be happening to someone else, not her. "Let me out!" she cried, coughing into the rag.

Something hit her from above. Then it happened again. It had weight to it.

When she realised Shadow was filling in the grave, she screamed. It was the earth hitting the body bag, covering it, covering her. In a few minutes, she would be buried below several feet of soil, hidden from everyone, forever. She desperately tried to break the cable ties. They were too strong, slicing into her flesh.

74

———

"It's just past these trees," Nasreen said, looking at her mobile, while trying to navigate their way through the woods. She'd almost fallen over on three separate occasions. The time on her mobile said it was 02:10. If Pryce was as obsessed with time as she thought he was, they were too late. The problem was parking. They'd had to leave the car outside the opening to the woods, which was five minutes away.

"There it is," Weekes said, stopping at the edge of the woods. "The water tower."

It was dark without torches, which she'd decided to leave in the car. If they'd shone flashlights and Pryce *was* up there, it would have given them away and given Pryce a chance to run. Scanning the field for Pryce, a shadow caught her attention; it was the way it moved. The soft moonlight gave the figure away. "There he is!" she yelled to Weekes.

Shadow was holding something long, and the movement suggested it was a... "Spade!" she yelled, running towards the figure. "He's burying her alive!" She ran at full pace, Weekes matching her. Her plan had been to sneak up on him, but knowing Reagan was below ground meant she was the priority, not apprehending Pryce. "Richard Pryce, it's the police!" she yelled. Her cosh was in her hand, ready.

At the top of the field, by the water tower, Shadow ran away from them.

Nasreen saw him throw the spade in anger before running into woods behind the concrete structure. "Shit! He's getting away."

Out of breath, looking for the spade, Nasreen found it and picked it up, looking for the grave. "Here, you use this," she said throwing the spade to Weekes, while she got down on all fours, using her fingers to help claw out the home secretary's daughter. "Reagan, can you hear me?" Nasreen called out, listening. There was a faint voice, muffled. Reagan was still alive, Nasreen realised, using her fingers to pull up clumps of soil.

Weekes got her back into digging, and with her help, they managed to unearth the body bag. "Call for an ambulance, quick," Nasreen ordered Weekes, while she unzipped the bag, to find Reagan not breathing. Pulling the rag out of her mouth, she asked, "Reagan, honey, can you hear me?" Nasreen prayed for Reagan to open her eyes. Lowering her ear to Reagan's mouth, she listened for signs of breathing. "Right, starting CPR."

"She was alive just now," Weekes said, kneeling next to her. "We heard her."

Nasreen got on top of Reagan – after lifting her out of the grave – put one hand on top of the other, interlocking fingers and started compressions. It was hard work. "Come on, Reagan, come back to us."

After the count of thirty, Nasreen stopped compressions, as Weekes stooped down, covered Reagan's mouth with hers and breathed. Nasreen watched her patient's chest rise and fall before Weekes carried out a second breath.

There was no response from Reagan, the home secretary's daughter.

"Please come back to us," Weekes begged.

It was the longest few minutes of her life. Nasreen started compressions for the second time and stopped, letting Weekes take over with the rescue breaths. Wanting to cry, she laughed suddenly, when Reagan choked after Weekes' third rescue breath.

"Oh thank you, thank you, thank you!" she said, patting Weekes on the back. "You did it, Weekes; you called it on the location, and you revived her." At that moment in time, all animosity between them evaporated, at least for her anyway.

Nasreen took off her jacket and wrapped it around Reagan, who was shivering from shock, and because the temperature had dropped. Using her mobile, she called in and informed her colleagues that Reagan Embry was safe, awaiting transportation to hospital, where she would be checked over.

It took the air ambulance twenty minutes to arrive. It was so noisy and windy, Nasreen thought she would take off by the time the propellers slowed to a stop. The ambulance crew, consisting of two personnel, took over, picking Reagan up and moving her onto the gurney, before wheeling her onto the helicopter. "I'm going with her to the hospital," she said to Weekes. "You're okay collecting the car and meeting me there, right?"

"I'll be fine," Weekes replied, already on her way. "I'll see you at the hospital."

Nasreen climbed on board the air ambulance, headphones dulling the noise of the propellers. She held Reagan's hand, feeling the helicopter lift off, her stomach churning at the sudden change in altitude; she hated air travel at the best of times. "Your mum will be at the hospital to meet us," she said, reassuring her patient, not knowing if it was the truth.

"Thank you, Inspector Gupta," Franks said, nodding at Suzanne Embry. "That's the best news. I'll be sure to thank Detectives Maqsood and Weekes." He hung up his phone and squeezed Embry's shoulder. "She's fine. She's being airlifted to hospital. Apparently it was touch and go for a minute. The detectives resuscitated her, but the paramedics are confident she'll make a full recovery."

There was no denying Embry's relief; it was evident in her expression. "I'll send Maqsood and Weekes a basket each," she said, picking up her bag and making to leave the station control room, where she'd been listening in to updates over the radio for hours. "Are you coming, Peter? We've got to get to the hospital. My driver will take us."

How could he refuse? He took his uniform jacket and put it on, shaking hands with the control room officers, who were as relieved as him. "I bet you're over the moon," Franks said, walking behind her, cursing his stupid comment. It wasn't surprising that she ignored his stupidity; in fact, he was grateful for it.

"Get in, Peter," she said, stepping inside her silver chauffeur-driven armoured Jaguar XJ Sentinel. "Now I can stop worrying about Reagan, we have a lot to discuss."

"Great minds think alike," he said, opening the door, getting in and fastening his seat belt. When the car accelerated, the glass separating the driver from the passengers lifted, giving them privacy.

"I met Harold the other day," Embry said, crossing one leg over the other in a very feminine display, her legs attracting his attention. Even in tights, they were lovely to look at. "And I have to say, I think you might be right. The man's falling apart; he's let himself go. He came to a meeting without shaving, for Heaven's sake. Who attends a meeting in Downing Street with stubble? The most decorated position in the Metropolitan Police Force deserves better."

Was she agreeing with Franks? He couldn't help but wonder what she was saying. Was she saying she wanted him gone? "I agree, ma'am," he said, hoping she might elaborate. "He's become an embarrassment, and if I'm honest, an empty uniform."

"Quite."

"Let me handle it, ma'am?"

All of a sudden Embry went quiet, looking away from him, out of her window.

"Be sure that it doesn't come back to haunt us, do you understand?" she said, still looking away. Then she turned to him, her pretty face serious. "Because if it does, understand this: it will only take you down. This conversation never happened."

"Understood, ma'am," he said, leaning back in the comfortable leather upholstery. He smiled to himself, knowing he could phone Astor and order Harry's death at any time he chose. A part of him felt sorry for his superior, although the majority wanted it over with; he wanted Harry gone, so he didn't have to worry about him anymore.

Weekes reached the car and got in, pleased with herself for saving Suzanne Embry's daughter, which should give her kudos in the bank for future reference. Starting the engine, she listened to the radio, which was a lot quieter than an hour earlier. Changing channel, Weekes listened to the latest song by P!nk.

Turning it down, she used her mobile to call Nevan and cancel Hazel's weekend; it wasn't like she wanted to, but she didn't have a choice. It was already quarter to three. Knowing he'd be asleep, she left him an apologetic voicemail, explaining what had just happened. "Sorry, Nut," she whispered, setting off for the hospital.

With the radio back up, helping to keep her awake, she drove along the narrow, winding roads towards the hospital, singing along to an Abba song. They were one of her favourite bands of all time. She felt her eyes drooping. To counter it, she fidgeted in her seat, before turning the music up even louder, unaware of the four-by-four behind her. Mid-song, the Range Rover behind turned its lights on full beam. "Jesus Christ!" she said, the reflection in the rear-view blinding her momentarily, enough for her to steer the car to the left, almost into the embankment. Adrenaline hitting her, she managed to correct herself. "What the hell's your problem?" she asked the car behind.

The four-by-four took to the road next to her, and matched her speed. Weekes sped up, the Range Rover matching it. She looked to her right, trying to see the driver. The driver steered right briefly, before pulling a hard left and smashing into her door.

It was when her car was forced up the embankment, Weekes realised it was Richard Pryce in the Range Rover. Her car went as high as it could on the embankment, then rolled back down onto the road, flipping onto its roof, where it remained, the radio still blaring out.

Weekes was stunned, clipped into her seat by her belt. Being upside down, the blood was rushing to her head. Trying to see Pryce, looking for him, she couldn't hear anything over the radio. The only way out was to unclip her belt. When she tried, it was stuck. Panicking, she stabbed at the release button. "Come on, you stupid–"

Her door sprung open before she could finish her sentence. A gloved hand grabbed her hair and forced her head to the side, revealing her neck. Weekes struggled with Pryce, only he was too strong, easily sinking the needle into her neck. "No! You bastard!" she cried, after he let go of her and stood back.

It was a fast acting sedative. She was quickly feeling relaxed, the world around her growing darker by the second. "I'm going... to... get... y–"

Franks could see how much Suzanne Embry loved her daughter by the way she rushed over to her bedside and hugged her for an indeterminable amount of time, while Reagan sobbed into her chest.

The poor girl would need years of counselling to recover from her ordeal, if, indeed, she ever recovered. The fear of being buried alive would live with her for the rest of her life. "I'll leave you to it," he said to Embry's back, gesturing for Nasreen to leave with him, who was holding Reagan's hand. "Detective Maqsood?"

Out in the corridor, he waited for Nasreen to join him. Walking with her to the cafeteria, he said, "Good job. You came through for Reagan; she has you to thank for her life." He was surprised when she shook her head.

"Not me," she replied. "It was all Weekes, sir. She called it on the location, and she revived her. I wish I could take the credit, but it wouldn't be right. She's the real hero."

"I see," he said, spying the cafeteria. "It's very honest of you. If Detective Weekes was here, I'd be saying the same to her. In fact, where is she?" With a success of this magnitude, he liked to congratulate his officers at the time, rather than days later. "Didn't she come with you?"

"I don't know, sir." Nasreen glanced at her watch. "She should be here by now. I came with Reagan in the helicopter; Weekes had to get the car. I hope she's all right."

Offering to pay for the vending machine food and drink, he asked Nasreen what she would like, told her to find a table and went to the machines. Since she'd started as detective little over a year and a half ago, he'd never spoken to her, not that it was strange; it wasn't the norm for commissioners to know the rank and file officers by name. Watching her while waiting for their drinks, he decided he liked her, despite busting the Harrison farm bunker case wide open. "One coffee in a plastic cup," he said, placing it in front of Nasreen.

Taking a seat opposite, he wanted to know more about her. Of course he'd read Nasreen's file, on a few occasions – most recently after she went missing, ditching a meeting with the IOPC, which had caused him a huge headache. She'd taken it upon herself to go hunting the man who'd broken into her home, warning her off looking for Daniel Rose. He asked her some subtle questions, probing when he wanted more, until they'd finished their drinks.

"I'm sorry, sir," Nasreen said, standing up, "but I'm worried about Weekes. She should be here by now. I'm going to give her a call. The car might've broken down, or something."

Franks used the time to take out his burner. "Yeah, it's me," he said into Astor's voicemail. "It's on. I've been given the green light. Can I suggest tomorrow night?" Catching Nasreen on her way back, he signed off and snuck the phone back in his jacket. "Was it a breakdown?"

"No." Her eyes scared, her complexion was paler than usual. "Some guy picked her phone up. Her car's in the middle of the road on its roof." Nasreen swallowed. "When I asked if he could see a woman, he said there was no one there, just blood. I've got to get over there, sir. She's in trouble."

It never rained; it poured. "Right, let's get going," Franks said, taking charge. "We can use the home secretary's car. She has a driver." He led their way to the reception and front doors. This was all he needed, he thought, trying to calm Nasreen. "Let's not speculate," he said, opening the Jaguar door and waiting for her to climb in. "She might be absolutely fine." He didn't believe it, not one bit.

78

———

There were blue lights flashing in the distance. Nasreen was anxious to get to the scene; she knew something bad had happened to her partner. The Jaguar came to a stop behind a panda car with its lights flashing. Climbing out, she flashed her ID to the nearest uniformed officer, who let her through. "Who did I just speak to on the phone?" she yelled, waiting for someone to step forwards.

"Me, officer," said a man in his fifties. "I was on my way to work and couldn't get past it. When I got out of my cab I thought someone had had an accident, until I saw the radio on the dash. It's how I knew it was a police car. I found this on the floor," he said, handing her the phone. "I'm sorry! I probably shouldn't have touched it."

"Are SOCOs on their way?" she asked a uniform.

"En route as we speak, ma'am," the youngster replied. "We're sealing off the road. Is there anything else you need us to do?"

Nasreen was tired. It felt like she hadn't slept in days. "No, you're doing all you can. I don't suppose you've got an evidence kit in your car, do you?" She didn't wait for a reply, before saying, "No, of course you haven't. Don't worry." It was horrible, the feeling of dread was back, only stronger; this was for her partner, not some fox hunting stuck-up home secretary's daughter. "Looks like I'm working the scene," she said to Commissioner Franks, who was stood on the other side of the road watching. "Where are you, Weekes?" she whispered.

Working the scene, using gloves she had in her jacket pocket, she inspected the inside of the upside-down car. There was no blood inside the vehicle. It was on the road. Nasreen didn't know what that meant. If she'd been injured during the crash, there'd be blood on the inside of the car as well as on the road. Maybe she put up a fight?

Another police car arrived, plain, white. Inspector Innes and Sergeant Edgeley exited their vehicle and started walking towards her. "No rest for the wicked," Nasreen said to Innes, as he stood next to her. "She's been abducted. It was Pryce."

"You don't know that," countered Innes. "She might've fallen asleep at the wheel, hit the embankment and rolled the car. She might've crawled into the woods for all we know." He made a point of gesturing woods on either side of the road. "We need to set up a search. I'll take the left; you two take the right."

"Sir, you can't be serious," Nasreen complained. "Look, her phone. I don't care how concussed she might be, Weekes wouldn't crawl into woods without it. She's gone. We need to put our heads together and figure out where Pryce might take her."

"It's too bad you didn't grab him when you had the chance," Edgeley said.

"We didn't get the chance. Reagan was already buried when we got there. Pryce knew we'd have to stop and dig her out. Then, I think he waited for Weekes to make her way to the hospital and followed her here." Nasreen walked to the car bonnet and inspected it. There was a dent on the right side. "See? Pryce rammed her off the road. I'd put money on it, sir."

"Let's stick to the plan. You two go right; I'll take the left woods. Meet back here in half an hour."

"I don't believe this," Nasreen moaned to Edgeley in a whisper, so as not to alert Franks to her insubordination, "she's not out here. We're wasting our time."

"I know." Edgeley beckoned her to follow him. "I agree, but we can't talk him out of it, so we might as well take a look for ourselves. You never know, she might be out here somewhere. Stranger things have happened."

Reluctantly, despite not wanting to leave the car, she joined Edgeley and walked into the woods with him, sighing. There was no way her partner would leave her phone unattended, no way. To Weekes, her phone was a lifeline.

79

It was dark when Weekes opened her eyes. At first she thought she'd gone blind, until she realised she was being held in the boot of the Range Rover. The accident came back to her in flashes. Remembering the car door opening and a gloved hand grabbing her, she could feel the sting of the needle going in. She wanted to rub her neck. When she tried to move her arms, her hands were tied together.

She was in the foetal position, her knees up by her chin. Trying to move her legs, she found they, too, were tied together. Her hands were behind her back. She was in trouble. Trying to break the cable ties around her wrists, she grew tired too quickly; she was still drugged. "Shit!" she cursed into the rag.

It was imperative that she break her wrist restraints. If she could free her hands, she'd be able to lift her trouser leg, open the compartment in her prosthetic leg and take out the butterfly knife and mace she had stored there. Without her weapons, she might not stand a chance against Pryce; he was a big lad.

There was a noise.

The boot opened, bright light making her eyes hurt. Weekes closed them and averted her face. When she opened them, the light wasn't so bright. Turning her head, she saw a large silhouette above her.

"Richard, you don't have to do–"

Instead of replying, Shadow bent down, gloved hands coming for her.

Struggling with her captor, Weekes was no match for Shadow's power. Before she knew what had happened, her host had stuck her with a needle for the second time. It took mere seconds for her to feel drowsy, the world around her fading into darkness again.

80

———

"Settle down, people!" Inspector Innes stood next to Inspector Gupta at the front of the room. "For those of you called back in from last night's search, my apologies; you'll get time off in lieu, as and when we're quiet enough."

Nasreen sat on the edge of the conference table, surrounded by uniforms, who'd all heard about Weekes' disappearance. Folding her arms, she waited for Innes to commence the meeting. There wasn't time; she needed to be out there, looking for her partner, not stuck at the station. It was nine o'clock, and Weekes had already been missing for at least five hours. She raised her hand. "Sir, do I need to be here for this? I want to go back to Doctor Chilvers' home; we might've missed something there."

"I applaud your dedication, Sergeant Maqsood, but if you don't mind staying, I might need your input. As you're all no doubt aware, one of our own is missing, presumed abducted." Innes explained the situation to the thirty uniforms sat and stood around the long wooden table. "We got lucky last night with Reagan Embry. We need as much luck as we can muster to find Detective Constable Weekes now. You've all been assigned an area to search. Let's get out there and find her!"

When the uniforms started dispersing, Nasreen wandered over to Gupta and Innes, who were chatting in front of the whiteboard Innes had used during the fifteen-minute briefing. "I'm going to Chilvers' house now," she said, interrupting their discussion. All she wanted was to get Weekes back; it surprised her how worried she was. "Sir, are you coming?"

"Yeah, I'm with you, Nas," Gupta replied. "Let's go!"

When she got in the driver's seat of their pool car, Nasreen saw it was almost half nine. There was a heavy silence between her and Gupta, neither wanting to talk about Weekes, about the fact she might already be dead. It was a very real possibility.

Roads were busy, even for a Saturday morning, which made her sound the horn more than was usual. Nasreen hadn't slept in over twenty-four hours. Her eyes were gritty. "I swear, when we find Pryce..." She let the comment trail off.

"You'll need to get in line," Gupta said. "Everyone's going to want a piece of this guy, including Suzanne Embry. I wouldn't want to be in his shoes when we arrest him, that's for sure. Embry's vicious." He didn't turn to look at her; he kept staring out of his window.

Pulling into Chilvers' driveway, Nasreen parked behind the vet's Range Rover. The front door still had police tape across it. Being careful not to break the tape, she unlocked the door with the key she'd taken from Yasmin and went under the cordon, closely followed by Gupta. "Where do you want to start?" she asked the inspector. "If you take the upstairs, I'll look down?"

"It's your show." He grabbed on to the handrail.

The whole house was a crime scene, and while she knew that the SOCOs had finished their cataloguing and photographing, she put on a pair of gloves. Not knowing what she was looking for, Nasreen walked around the lounge, going from one corner to the next, examining everything. Chances were high they were wasting their time, but it felt better being out, actively seeking clues than being sat in the station doing nothing.

In the dining room, she didn't find anything untoward. With a heavy sigh, she stepped into the kitchen, the room where Chilvers was attacked. Cleaners had been in and washed the lino, although bloodstains persisted, changing the colour of the flooring. Again, Nasreen did a circuit of the room, hoping to find something, anything that would help them locate Weekes. Trying not to think about what Pryce could be doing to her partner, right now, Nasreen wiped her forehead with the back of her hand and stared at a calendar on the wall.

A word stuck out to her. It was a word that had no business being written on a social calendar. Making sure her tiredness wasn't getting the best of her, she stepped up closer. It read: Oncologist. There was a time underneath it. "Huh!" She reread it for the fourth time. The good doctor had cancer? Then, she recalled the nasty cough she and Weekes had heard at the shelter, when Chilvers had told them it was her getting over a cold.

"Nasreen!" Gupta called. "You'll want to see this."

"Coming!" she said, finally taking her gaze away from the calendar. Taking the stairs two at a time, she met Gupta on the landing. He was holding a picture frame. "What is it, sir?" she asked, being given the frame. And the answer snapped into place.

"Is that, or is that not Louise Thatcher?" Gupta asked.

"It most certainly is," she replied, inspecting a happy picture of Louise Thatcher with Doctor Gillian Chilvers' arm around her, both smiling broadly. "Louise can't be her daughter. We did a background check on Chilvers. It would've come up."

"Aunt perhaps?" Gupta asked. "Whatever their relationship is, there's more to this than we know." He took the photo from her. "And it was face down in a drawer. Strange place to put a picture of the two of them, huh?"

"And she's seeing an oncologist on Tuesday. The appointment's written down on her calendar in the kitchen." When she said it, Gupta, who'd had his back to her, turned round. "Are you thinking what I'm thinking?"

"We've been looking for the wrong person the whole time." Gupta took his phone out of his pocket. "But what about the blood? There was loads of blood."

"Could it be Pryce's, or Claire Padnall? We haven't had the results back from that burnt body yet. I thought it might be Chilvers." The more she thought their suspect was Chilvers, the more doubt crept in. "But why would she kill all these people?"

"Well," Gupta scratched his head, "she's an animal lover, right? If Louise is family, her niece or what have you, maybe Chilvers found out Louise was fox hunting? Maybe she blamed the group for letting her hunt foxes, which Chilvers would detest? And maybe finding out she had cancer was the trigger? I mean, she doesn't have anything to lose, does she?"

Nasreen nodded. It kind of made sense, in a psychopathic way. "But Fiona Armstrong was mauled by a group of dangerous dogs. Chilvers wouldn't have anything to do with that, would she?" There were too many questions bombarding her tired brain. When Gupta was at a loss for words, she said, "I know who might be able to help."

81

Gillian Chilvers sat down at her mum's rickety old table and held the shotgun across her lap, an oily old cloth in one hand. It was the very same shotgun her father had used to shoot rabbits all those years ago, before she and her sister had begged and pleaded with him not to. Their pleas hadn't fallen on deaf ears. When she was eleven and her sister six, he'd hung up his hunting gear, retiring the shotgun to the barn, where she'd found it, and two working pistols a couple of weeks ago, along with several boxes of shells and bullets for the two pistols.

Massaging the shotgun with the oily rag, Chilvers thought how cruel life was.

A little over a year ago, her beautiful, talented niece, Louise, had a riding accident while out with her friends one Sunday morning. The horse bucked, apparently throwing Louise off, where she landed on her neck. It took her more than thirty minutes to die. What kind of God would let her niece suffer like that? No! She couldn't blame God. He had plans for Louise, or at least she hoped He did. It had destroyed her, and her poor sister. That had been the first real blow.

Two months ago, still grieving for her niece, she'd received a visit from Claire Padnall, an old friend of Louise's, who dropped by her house. Offering Claire a hot beverage, her visitor had pulled out a group photograph of Louise with five friends. "I'm so sorry!" Claire said, her eyes sympathetic. "I thought you should know. Louise wasn't what we thought she was." Stood by the sink, Chilvers' knees buckled beneath her, seeing Louise smiling in front of a poor, mauled fox.

There was a rage inside her, an almost uncontrollable rage. How could Louise enjoy such a vile, barbaric and cruel pastime? How could Louise visit her and Richard at the shelter, helping with the animals, and then go out with a group of her friends maiming and killing the very animals the shelter helped? A red mist grew around her. Claire had been wise enough to leave. Shaking uncontrollably, her memory of that night was hazy.

Then, six weeks earlier, she'd coughed up a bloody lump. After visiting the doctor, and being referred to the hospital to have tests done, the hospital doctor informed her that she had inoperable lung cancer. The news had almost knocked her off her chair. Why her? She was a good person; she helped animals, and people to a lesser extent. She'd never done anything to deserve lung cancer. Excusing her twenty-a-day habit, of course. No! It wasn't right, was what she kept telling herself. The results were wrong. She'd lost her niece, twice. How could she be dying? It wasn't fair!

Later that night, she'd been begging God to spare her. Kneeling in front of her bed, hands together, fingers interlocking, she'd asked Him to either spare her, or inflict pain on the fox hunting group, who'd corrupted her Louise. They deserved it. So, if He couldn't fix it for her to live, at least fix them. And then it had hit her: she would do it herself, just to make sure, to help it along.

Smiling while slowly polishing the barrel of the shotgun, she'd sent three of Louise's corruptors to meet their makers already; it would've been four had those bloody detectives not intervened. Losing Reagan Embry hurt. Having the taller detective in the boot of her Range Rover almost made up for it. She stood with the gun across her lower right arm.

When she'd been informed of her diagnosis, the first thought she'd had was to kill herself, to save herself the pain and anguish of dying a slow death at the hands of the cruel disease eating away at her from the inside. She could feel it. The first time, she'd tried slitting her wrists in the tub. It hadn't worked. Then, talking herself into it, she'd tried pulling the trigger on the pistol a week ago. Again, she couldn't do it. No, someone else was going to have to do it for her. Gillian Chilvers was incapable of killing herself.

It was time. Leaning the shotgun against the table, she began putting her chunky coat on. "No!" she said to herself, taking it off and hanging it back up. Dressed in her white vest top, jeans and white Adidas trainers, she picked up one of the pistols and walked with it to the front door.

The Range Rover was outside the large barn, the boot facing her as she walked towards it, the pistol pointed at the ground. At the boot, she slid the key in, opened it and stood back, raising the gun so that it was pointed at the detective. "No funny business," Chilvers said, leaning inside the boot. "I've got something planned for you, so I don't want to shoot you. But I won't hesitate if you try anything, okay?"

Leaving the rag in the detective's mouth, she pulled out a knife from her pocket and sliced through the cable ties around her captive's ankles, freeing her. There was no way she was going to free the impressive-looking woman's wrists. "Come on, get out." Chilvers stood back, the gun trained on the police officer's face.

"Come on! I haven't got all day," she moaned, watching the detective trying to pull herself out of the boot with her wrists tied behind her back. Grabbing her shoulders, she helped the detective out of the boot, making sure her gun was handy.

She nudged the detective with the muzzle of the pistol when she slowed. The farmhouse was approaching. "You try anything, detective, I'll put a hole in your head," she said, nudging her again. "You'd be wise to remember that."

Inside the house, she made the detective walk through the hallway until they reached a door on the right. "Open it!" she ordered.

Down a flight of twenty stairs, she walked behind the detective, until they were on the cellar floor. "Say hello to Richard, detective," she said, nudging the woman again. "Sorry to disappoint you. I know how much you wanted it to be him. But I told you, didn't I? I told you he was one of the good guys."

Sat on the floor, his wrists tied to a support pole, Richard Pryce looked up at her. "Please Gillian, don't do this," he begged. "I know you're hurting. I'm hurting; I loved Louise. But this isn't going to help."

"Shut up!" she snapped, digging the detective in the back, hard. "What do you know about hurting? She was just a silly childish crush to you, but to me, she was my world. And look what she turned into!" The rage boiled away inside her. "Sit down!"

The detective did as instructed; she sat next to the pole, back to back with Richard. The gun trained on the police officer, she pulled two cable ties out of her pocket and put the gun on the floor, before tying Weekes' wrists to the same support pole Pryce was tied to. "There!" She ripped the rag out of the detective's mouth. "Now you can apologise to Richard, can't you, detective," Chilvers said, walking back to the stairs. It would take time for this one's partner to find her, but Chilvers had faith in the fact she would... She was banking on it.

82

"Beverly, who's this?" Nasreen was holding up the framed picture of Louise and Chilvers she'd brought with her. The drive back to the station was torturous; all she'd wanted to do was find out the relationship between them.

"That's Louise's Auntie Gillian, why?" Beverly sat up. "She's not on this sicko's list, too, is she? She's lovely. Why her?"

"Don't worry, she's not on his list. Go on back to sleep." Turning to Gupta, she handed the frame to him and walked with him out of the holding cell, locking it behind her. When Beverly asked how long she was going to be in here for, she called out, "As long as you're in danger."

She strode with Gupta up the stairs to the main office, where a number of uniforms were waiting for an update. It was nearly noon. Standing against a wall, Nasreen shushed everyone, leaving the floor to her inspector, as Innes was still out looking for Richard Pryce.

"We have a substantial update for you," Gupta started, pinning the photo of Louise and Chilvers on the whiteboard. "This is now our prime suspect: Doctor Gillian Chilvers. We believe she's abducted Detective Constable Weekes, and she may have abducted Richard Pryce. We don't know. What we do know is that Dr Chilvers is Louise Thatcher's aunt. Given the fact we know Chilvers is against animal cruelty of any kind, and that we know her niece was part of a fox hunting group, we believe Doctor Chilvers has taken it upon herself to punish the group she believes corrupted Louise, her only niece."

"That's a stretch, though, sir, isn't it?" asked a uniformed constable. "She's a vet, for crying out loud. I thought we were liking a bloke for this."

"I'd have said a stretch, too," Gupta agreed, "except we've found out she's terminally ill. Cancer of some kind. This woman's just found out her niece has betrayed her in the worst way possible, and is then told she's dying. She wants to punish this group before she goes, constable."

"And Detective Weekes and I interrupted her before she could punish Reagan Embry," Nasreen said to all the uniforms. "Now we have the last two group members under our protection, she's probably pissed off about that. She'll be looking to take it out on us, or rather Weekes. Bottom line is, we need to find Chilvers before... If she hasn't..."

Gupta stepped up to her and gave her shoulder a comforting squeeze. "Now, get out there and if you find her, don't try to apprehend her without adequate backup. Consider her armed and dangerous; she's already murdered four people that we know of, possibly five. Until we get the results back on the burnt body, we won't know."

"We need everything we can get on Chilvers," she said to Inspector Gupta, after the uniforms had left. "We need to know her history, where she's been, what she's done. Everything..." Nasreen wanted to cry, thinking Weekes might be buried somewhere. Her bottom lip quivered at the thought. Gupta tried to comfort her again; she ignored it, turned and punched the wall.

"We'll find her, Nas," he said. "You'll see. She'll be back here annoying you before you know it. Come on, positivity's the key. Let's find out about Chilvers."

Nasreen remembered sitting with Weekes outside Emilian Keeble's caravan, after her leg had been shot with an arrow. She'd asked Weekes about her leg. Hang on! "I've got it!" She said, excitement permeating the air. "I know how we can find her."

"I'm listening," Gupta replied.

"Her leg," she said, as though Gupta should know what she was talking about. "Her prosthetic leg. It's microchipped, sir. If we contact the manufacturing company, we'll be able to find her through the microchip." She was so excited, she could hardly stand still.

Gupta seemed perplexed. "Her leg's microchipped? Why?"

"Because it's bloody expensive. Look, she told me her dad paid for her to have the best prosthesis she could. The manufacturer came through, but it was really expensive, so her dad took out insurance on it, and had it microchipped. Anyway, it doesn't matter why, what matters is we can find her."

"Right," Gupta said, accepting it. "Let's find out who manufactured her leg."

83

———

"How hard can it be to contact her parents?" Nasreen asked, flustered at their lack of success. "Where are they? We need this information, sir." She turned in her chair and faced Gupta, who was sat at a computer.

"I know we do, Nas. You don't need to tell me," he replied, irritably. "I've left several voicemails for her father, General Weekes. There's nothing more I can do. How've you got on with contacting her ex-husband?" He ran his hands through his hair; he looked tired.

Standing up, frustrated, she kicked the tatty carpet. "Same. Left him a bunch of voicemails. Why aren't they getting back to us? Surely they know how serious this is? It's not like I didn't tell Nevan she's been abducted. Why aren't they phoning us back?"

"Inspector Gupta," came a voice from behind them. "Nevan Vickers is in reception."

"He's here? Now?" When the uniformed officer nodded, she marched towards the reception area, leaving Gupta sat at his desk. In all the excitement, she'd almost forgotten it was Saturday. Surprised to find Weekes' ex-husband with their daughter, Hazel, she opened the reception door for them to enter. "Please, come through," Nasreen said, locking it behind her.

There was a long pause. Breaking the silence, Nasreen bent over. "And you must be Hazel," she said, a big smile disguising how anxious she was. "Your mummy's told me so much about you. I hear you like to be called Nut."

"That's what Mummy and Daddy call me. Because I'm nutty, they say. I think it's because my name's Hazel."

Wanting to chat more with Hazel – she was too cute – Nasreen had to resist; there were far more pressing matters they needed to discuss. Nasreen walked them through her temporary station, although it didn't feel temporary, and she found some paper and crayons for Hazel, to keep her amused while they had an adult discussion. "We'll be right over here, sweetheart," she said, to Hazel's nonchalant, "Okay."

At Gupta's desk, Nasreen took a seat and offered Nevan one next to her. He was as good looking as she'd expected. He and Weekes would have made a handsome couple. He had dark hair, a slight paunch that suited his years and a strong jaw. A day's worth of stubble topped the look off perfectly. "I'm so sorry we have to meet for the first time under these circumstances," she said. "But as I said on the phone, we need that microchip, Nevan. Right now, it's our best shot at finding Week... Alicia."

"I wish I could help," Nevan replied. "I really do. But she never showed me the microchip. I only remembered it was chipped when you left that voicemail. Ron will know more about it than I do; he paid for it."

"We've tried General Weekes," confirmed Gupta. "I've left messages. Do you know where he is?"

"Again, I wish. We haven't spoken since the divorce. But the microchip will be in the leg, won't it? I've got a key to Alicia's flat, and she has a spare leg. Maybe we can find out who the manufacturer is."

Excited, Nasreen stood. "Ah bugger! Her spare was shot with an arrow." Having to explain the situation to Nevan, he was concerned for his ex-wife. "She's probably sent it back to them to be repaired."

"Knowing Alicia, she hasn't," Nevan argued. "She's not known for her organisation. It's probably still at her flat." He stood, looking expectantly. "Are you coming? It's better than sitting around, waiting for Ron to call, isn't it?"

Nasreen glanced at Gupta, waiting for his answer. "It can't hurt."

Inspector Gupta got up from his seat, searched his suit jacket for his keys and joined her on their way to the staff car park, Hazel holding hands with Nevan in front. "The General has my mobile number."

84

"What more do you want me to do?" Weekes asked, still trying to break the ties around her wrist. "I've apologised five times, Richard. Please, talk to me. We need to work together to get out of this." Sat on the floor, she was getting more and more frustrated. The one item she needed was inside her leg and she couldn't get to it.

"Why bother? We're not getting out of here."

Weekes stopped wriggling. "She's not going to hurt you, is she? She loves you; I can tell. She's only kidnapped you to make it look like you killed them. Don't you see? That's why I believed it was you. All the evidence pointed in your direction."

"Nice try, detective," Pryce said, his voice resigned. "You thought it was me on sight. You kept looking at me when you came to the shelter. You really thought I was capable of murdering Myles, Verity and Fiona?"

It was the most he'd said to her all afternoon; she wasn't about to give up. "I'll level with you," she said, her voice measured, genuine. "I did. I don't trust quiet people, I guess. I think quiet people have something to hide. And you were the right height and build, or so we thought. I never suspected it was a woman. We didn't get the chance to speak to Reagan after we resuscitated her; she was in shock."

"It's not hard. Gillian's tall. All she needed to do was put on a thick coat, boots and a hood and scarf. And she's strong. She grew up here on this farm, back when it was a farm. When she grabbed me, there was nothing I could do, and I'm not small."

Chilvers and Yasmin were right. He could talk, a lot. "Yeah, well, I won't be making that mistake again. Anyway, look around for something we can use as weapons, would you? I've got an idea of how to break these ties." She used her legs to hoist her body up, her wrists wrapped around the pole. "I'm going to take my leg off."

"Huh? You're doing what?"

Without hands, it was difficult to take her leg off, but not impossible. Weekes had to shake it off, forcing the suction to release it. "Don't mind me. Keep looking for those weapons." It wasn't working. Knowing Chilvers could walk in at any moment, she shook her leg hard, so hard she felt the suction give way and her prosthesis fell slightly.

Her trousers prevented it from flying off. Carefully, she let her leg fall, trying to lift her trouser leg until it fell to the floor. "Got it!" she said, stood on one foot. Excited, she sat back down, her hand touching her leg. The only problem: moving the leg and opening the compartment. She managed to grab it.

Feeling for the compartment, she opened it and relief swept over her when she felt her butterfly knife. "I always knew this'd come in handy," she said to Pryce, who couldn't see what she was doing. Behind her back, careful not to stick Pryce, she opened the knife, tilted it the right way and started slicing into the cable tie. "Almost there."

Free, she rubbed her wrists, before replacing her leg and pulling her trouser down. "Oh shit!" she said, as the cellar door opened, light hurting her eyes. With no choice, she placed her wrists either side of the pole. The knife was between her and Pryce. She slid it to Pryce, who sat on it, hiding it from Chilvers.

Their captor walked down the stairs, carrying the long-barrelled shotgun. "It's time," she said, pointing the gun at her. "Come on, detective, up you get."

If Chilvers found out she was free, she'd be furious. It was now or never, Weekes thought, waiting for the perfect time to make her move. The vet crouched down, a knife in her hand. Weekes had to wait. "What the...?" she heard from Chilvers, as she sprung up and grabbed the confused psychopath.

The next few seconds were a blur, as Weekes fell to the floor with Chilvers, both wrestling for the shotgun, which Chilvers had dropped. She fought for her life. At one point, she was on top, punching Chilvers in the face. Then, she was the one taking the pounding.

Unfortunately, it ended with Chilvers on top, the shotgun in her hand. Weekes was out of breath, trying to catch air, while holding her hands up. "Take it easy. I made a mistake. It won't happen again."

"Too right it won't happen again; I should open you up right now." Chilvers leaned in and stuck the gun on her cheek, prodding her flesh. "But I've got something so much better lined up for you." Gesturing for her to get up, Chilvers stood back, expecting her to lunge again. "I can't wait for your partner to get here. Then the fun starts."

On her feet, Weekes walked up the stairs, occasionally feeling the gun in her back. "Where are we going?" There was no point in running, or trying to fight; her attacker had the upper hand. "Or are we not on talking terms now?"

"The barn. And I can't wait for you to see it."

"I wish I could say the same," she replied, entering the hallway and heading towards the front door. When she was outside, it was still light. With no idea what time it was, or how long she'd been in the cellar, she guessed it was late afternoon. Halfway between the house and barn, she contemplated making a run for it but the shotgun had a wide range.

"Open it up," Chilvers ordered, a safe distance away. "Go on inside."

Weekes wished she hadn't opened the doors. "What's this?"

On the floor was a raised platform. It was about four feet long, made of wood. As she walked towards it, she saw an upside down lawnmower in front of it. "So, that's it, is it? That's what you're so pleased about?" She imagined being strapped to the platform from the waist down, her body hanging over it. The lawnmower switched on, she'd have to use her core to keep her face from hitting the mower's blades. "And this is how it ends?"

"For you, it is. You won't be the only one going tonight."

"You? You want to die?"

"I don't want to. I am. There's nothing I can do about it; I can feel it inside me. The doctors have given me six months, if I have chemo. I'm not putting myself through all that. So, tonight's the night."

"Death-by-cop? That's how you want to go, isn't it?" Weekes finally understood why Chilvers started her killing spree. Finding out she had cancer was the trigger. If she was fit, healthy and had something to live for, she doubted Chilvers would have killed her niece's "friends". "Aren't you strapping me to it now?"

"Not yet." Chilvers took out two cable ties and ordered her to sit down by a support beam, where she tied her wrists together again.

85

Nasreen pulled up outside Weekes' block of flats. It wasn't an attractive build, a fish out of water compared to the prettier terraced homes on the road. Nevan helped Hazel out of the car, while she and Gupta walked up to the main door. "Please be here," she said under her breath, holding the door for Weekes' family.

No one spoke in the lift up to the second floor. Even Hazel seemed to know not to break the silence. "After you," she said, letting Nevan and Hazel out first. Waiting for Nevan to open the flat door, Nasreen said a silent prayer. All they needed was a company name.

Gupta's phone rang as they entered the flat. Nasreen watched the inspector for his expressions. She smiled when he said, "General Weekes, thank you so much for calling back." Relief swept over her. If anyone would know the manufacturer, he would. When Gupta wrote something in a notepad, she read it. It was a phone number and company name.

"When we find her, you'll be the first person I call, I promise," Gupta said, hanging up. "Don't get excited. I'll try this number, but the general said they're a Monday to Friday company. They won't be open on a Saturday. Her dad's on his way back from Baghdad."

Nasreen's phone vibrated in her pocket. It was a local Sussex number. "Detective Sergeant Maqsood," she said in greeting. It was a sergeant back at the station, telling her they'd found a property owned by Chilvers' parents. It was empty, an old farm. "You're kidding! That's it! That's where they are! We're on our way now. Give me the address!" She wrote it down, hung up and forced Gupta off his phone. "We've found her! This is her parents' farm; it's derelict now, sir."

"Looks like we won't be needing this now," Gupta said, racing with her out of the flat, leaving Nevan and Hazel behind.

Outside, Nasreen ran to the car and jumped into the driver's seat, adrenaline coursing through her veins as she floored the accelerator, switching on the lights and siren.

86

"You're a hypocrite," the tall detective said. "You know that, right?"

"How's that?" Chilvers asked, stood by the barn door, listening for sirens, or signs of intruders. She had confidence in the little Pakistani detective's ability. It wouldn't be long.

"Well, you say you're against animal cruelty in all its forms, right? And yet you used four dangerous dogs to maul Fiona Armstrong," the officer replied. "Those dogs were mistreated their whole lives. So, I put it to you that you're not anti-cruelty to animals at all."

Chilvers chortled. "Is that what you think? Really? You still haven't figured it out, have you? I didn't kill Fiona. Emile did. I couldn't go near those dogs."

"Emilian Keeble? You knew him well, did you?"

"Well enough," she replied, watching the yard. "He was Louise's dad." And she could tell by the dumbstruck silence that she'd shocked the detective. "Yeah, my kid sister was only sixteen when she first met Emile. He promised her the Earth, you know how it goes. And anyway, against my mum's wishes, she snuck out one night to be with him, and nine months later we had a screaming baby in the house."

"My sister told Louise who her dad was when she was twelve," she added. "And about six months later they met. Oh, how Louise adored him, and he adored her, too. Was he a bad man? Probably. Was he good for Louise? Absolutely, and that's all I cared about. Then, after she died, and after we found out what she'd been doing, we agreed to punish the group."

There was a long silence.

"I still don't understand," admitted the detective. "Why blame the rest of the group? Louise was a big girl; she knew what she was doing. I've seen her Facebook account. She was very much pro fox hunting."

Chilvers turned her attention to the helpless police officer, marching over to her with the shotgun in both hands. "Do you know what it's like to hate someone, detective? I mean, to really hate someone for what they've done?" Her eyes were narrow slits. "Well, that's how I feel about Louise right now. Seeing that photo, seeing her smiling behind that poor fox. It made me sick to my stomach. I shouldn't hate my niece, my sister's daughter, the girl I helped bring up since she was a baby. But seeing those people, her friends, just getting on with their lives, like she never existed... It was wrong."

"Okay, I get it."

Realising that the shotgun was pushed into the detective's cheek, Chilvers pulled back. She heard sirens in the distance. "Well, it's about bloody time." She didn't have long to get the detective in place and make it up to the attic for her last stand. "You give me any trouble, I'll just put a bullet in your head now, got it? My end isn't connected to yours." She cut the detective's restraints, then quickly tied her wrists up behind her back.

Using the pistol as persuasion, Chilvers forced the police officer to lie on her legs and waist, making sure her abdomen and chest were hanging over the edge of the platform. She tied the detective's legs to the platform, hearing the effort her captive was putting into keeping her body up. Satisfied her captive was secure, unable to move, she walked around to the lawnmower and picked up the roll of tape she'd brought with her.

The petrol mower started, the metal blades blowing air in the detective's face. Chilvers taped the starter handle to the handlebar nice and tight. Standing back, she regarded her handiwork, noting the grimace on the officer's face. In about five minutes, her core muscles would force her to drop her body and her face would hit the blades. "So long, detective," she said, picking up the shotgun.

When she opened the barn door, a plain white car was speeding towards her, blue flashing lights on top of the roof, a siren wailing. "Oh no, you don't," she said, pointing the shotgun at the car and pulling the trigger.

The recoil was strong. The small explosion reverberated through the ground.

Once the car had stopped – its bonnet peppered with pellets from the shell and its occupants hiding inside – she fired once more, emptying the weapon. Her ears ringing, she pulled a pistol out of her jeans and fired a couple of rounds at the car, shattering the passenger window. Then she ran, as fast as she could into the house, up the stairs to the first floor. She'd left the loft ladder down. Once in the attic, she pulled the ladder up and rushed over to the window, reloading the shotgun.

87

"Nasreen!" Weekes' faint voice shouted.

Covered in glass from the windscreen and passenger's window being shot out, Nasreen, huddled behind the dashboard, followed Inspector Gupta and crept out of the passenger's side. A fully equipped armed response unit was on its way, Gupta having called for assistance. Nasreen felt a drop of blood roll down her temple. Wiping it away, she glanced at Gupta. "She's in the barn."

"I know she's in the barn," he said, raising his head to take a look at the house.

A gunshot, followed by the sound of a bullet hitting the car made them both back down, out of the line of fire. "Chilvers is in the attic, right?" she asked, to his nod. "I've got to get to the barn, sir. She's in trouble; I can tell by her voice."

"You're not going anywhere until armed response get here."

With her back against the car, she swore. "Listen to her, sir," she said, itching to make a run for the barn, "she needs me!" There was no way she could sit there with Weekes calling out for her. If Weekes died because of her inaction, she wouldn't be able to live with the guilt. Getting into position, she said, "Cover me! I'm making a run for it."

Instead of running directly for the barn, she chose to run for the safety of the house. It was a shorter distance, and she could then run around the farmhouse, where she hoped the attic had only one window at the front, and make a shorter dash for the barn from behind the house. "Wait! Don't do it," she heard Gupta shout, as she ran as fast as she could.

She screamed at the roar of the shotgun, feeling the pellets whizz past her.

Before Chilvers could fire a second shot, she reached the red brick building, using it as safety from its owner. With her back against the wall, she crept around the building, all the while sirens in the distance growing louder.

From the back of the farmhouse, she could see the barn. The only problem she had was, Chilvers could, too, from the attic window. The psychopathic vet would be watching the barn, ready to fire on anyone who went near it. Taking her phone out, Nasreen called Gupta. "I need a distraction," she said, to his resigned, "Okay." Getting into position, she said, "Now!"

At full speed, she ran for the barn, hearing the shotgun fire, but not in her direction.

She reached the barn door and quickly opened it, hearing a second shotgun blast that caught the wooden door, just as she made it safely inside.

"Hurry, Nas, I can't hold it much longer," said Weekes, her face mere inches from the lawnmower blades. "Kick... this... thing!"

Nasreen, shocked that Chilvers could be this sick, watched the effort on Weekes' face.

It was clear her partner's core was the only thing keeping her face from hitting the blades.

She ran over to the mower and kicked it out of the way, as

Weekes screamed in both pain and fear, her body slumping over.

"It's okay, Weekes," she said, picking up her body and embracing her, holding her as tight as she could. "You're safe."

She held on to Weekes for as long as she could, and although her partner's wrists were tied behind her back, she could tell Weekes wanted to reciprocate.

"How'd you find me?" Weekes asked. "The microchip?"

"Actually no," she replied, relinquishing her partner and taking out her pocketknife. "Good old-fashioned police work came through. We found out Chilvers' parents own this place, or at least used to, until they died and left it to their girls." Bending over, she sliced through the cable ties and rope, freeing Weekes.

"She's not going to go quietly." Weekes rubbed her wrists, sat on the wooden platform. "She wants to go death-by-cop."

"I know. I figured it was her when I saw she had an appointment with an oncologist. Then Gupta found a photo with her and Louise Thatcher hidden in one of her drawers. But for the life of me, I can't figure where Emilian Keeble fits in to all this."

"Louise's dad. She needed him to kill Fiona. Chilvers wouldn't have anything to do with Keeble normally, except she needed him for this. And he wanted justice, too. She killed all of them, except Fiona Armstrong."

Nasreen helped Weekes onto her feet. With her arm around her partner's shoulders, she walked to the barn door, looking through a crack, up at the house, where Chilvers was holed up. "We need to get back to the inspector," she said, knowing Weekes was in no fit state to run anywhere. The sirens grew louder.

In the distance, she saw a police van and three more pandas pull up beside their peppered vehicle. Two shotgun blasts scattered the armed police officers, as they exited their van, the automatic rifles in their hands. There was no way she could take

Weekes to safety the state she was in. She continued watching through the crack in the wood.

"I'm sorry!" Weekes said, after a long silence.

"For what?" Nasreen glanced at her, then back through the crack.

"For being a pain in the arse. I just want you to know I've learnt a lot from you. And if you'll have me, I'd love to be your partner."

Nasreen knew it took a lot for Weekes to say it. "I don't think we have a choice," she said, making sure Weekes knew she was joking. "I've learnt a lot from you, too. I think we make a good team, actually. Or at least that's what I'm going to write in my report."

When Weekes smiled at her, Nasreen reciprocated, then went back to watching Chilvers.

88

Chilvers reloaded the shotgun with two shells. There were six armed officers hiding behind the van and police cars, their blue flashing lights still on. Closing the chamber, loading the gun, she aimed down at the policemen. When one dared to show his face, she opened fire, the recoil making her feel powerful, the noise making her ears ring.

One of the armed police called out to her, ordering her to surrender, to put her weapons down and walk out of the house with her hands up. The tannoy made his voice sound tinny. He informed her that she wasn't leaving here without giving herself up. But she had no intention of surrendering. She fired again, making her feelings known.

While she reloaded her shotgun, she saw two figures emerge from the barn. It was both detectives. The taller one wasn't dead. "No!" she screamed, watching them run towards their colleagues. Taking aim at them, she opened fire, missing them, and smashing a car windscreen. The second shot missed. Chilvers screamed in anger. Not only had she failed to kill Reagan Embry, she'd also failed to punish the detective.

There was a banging sound on the loft hatch. Putting the

shotgun down, she picked up one of her pistols and walked over to the hatch.

A strange whooshing noise distracted her.

A silver tube flew inside the attic, almost hitting her in the face. When it landed on the floor, smoke poured out of it. Then a second smashed through the window, landing five feet from her. It was difficult to breathe, bringing tears to her eyes. If she didn't want to suffocate, she had to leave the attic.

Dropping the hatch and ladder, holding one pistol and with the other in the back of her jeans, she climbed down. On the floor, coughing her lungs up, blood in her mouth, she walked towards the stairs, aware that the armed response officers could pounce on her at any moment. She held the gun out in front of her.

A door to her right opened so fast, it barely registered.

Something came at her.

Before she could react, she was on the floor, her face numb from being hit with something, hard. She swallowed two lumps. Feeling her mouth with her tongue, they were teeth she'd just swallowed. Blood covered her face; she could feel it dripping onto the old carpet.

"I trusted you," Richard Pryce said, holding a shovel. "How could you do this in Louise's name? I hate you. After all your lectures, you're nothing but a hypocrite." He threw the shovel down and turned his back on her.

"Wait! You're the best of us, Richard. You always were." She felt the pistol handle with her right hand, picked it up and pointed it at his back. "Don't make me shoot you. Help me up." She pulled the hammer back, until it made the click everyone recognised. "Please, help me up. I have to go outside."

She knew he would. Using Richard as a crutch, she walked down the stairs with him until she was at the front door. Through the window, she could see all six armed officers walking towards her. "It's now or never," she said to him. "I'm sorry! I didn't want to involve you in all this. Forgive me? Please?"

When he refused to speak, she shook her head and reached for the door handle.

"Please don't. Hand yourself in, Gillian, please."

Chilvers smiled at him, pulled the second pistol out of her jeans and opened the door. "Goodbye Richard," she said, stepping out onto the porch.

The lead officer ordered her to put the guns on the ground. These were her last few seconds. She thought of Louise, of her betrayal; she thought of all those she'd killed, with good reason. She thought about those poor foxes they'd taken pleasure in killing and maiming. And finally, she thought about the two detectives who'd prevented her killing the ringleader, Reagan Embry. Chilvers saw the Pakistani detective behind a police car. "Fucking bitch!" she cried, raising both guns and opening fire.

All she saw as she fired her two guns empty were muzzle flashes in front of her.

The first three bullets to hit her felt like punches, which stopped her.

Her fingers continued pulling the triggers, until a further five punches put her on her back.

They were all in her chest and stomach, all eight bullets were sucking the life out of her.

Looking up at the porch roof, trying to suck in the last couple of breaths, she remembered Louise being born; she remembered holding her sister's hand when Louise took her first breaths. Visions of her teaching Louise to ride a bike flashed before her. A smile crept over her as she saw Louise and Richard kiss for the first time, before everything went black.

89

———————

"**S**he got what she wanted." Weekes studied Chilvers' dead body.

"Yeah, and now we have to explain this to our bosses," one armed officer said. "None of us will be on duty until the inquest's held. Thanks a lot, lady."

Nasreen wanted to get as far away from the farm, and Sussex, as she could. She'd had enough of the winding country lanes, the tiny villages with lots of secrets. Definitely sick of all the driving. The city, that was where she belonged, not in the countryside. "Let's go home, Weekes," she said, encouraging her partner to join her. "I can't wait to inhale some of that smog-filled air." Nasreen laughed to herself.

"I miss it. Country air's so overrated."

"I suggest you go home, relax and enjoy your time off; you've both earnt it," Gupta said, joining them in walking to their bullet-riddled car. "I'll need your reports in asap, I'm afraid. There's a lot of work on."

"What's going to happen to Pryce?" Weekes asked.

"What do you mean? Nothing," Gupta answered. "He'll

come in and answer a few questions. He hasn't done anything wrong, as far as we know, so he's free to come and go as he pleases." He stopped walking, as they turned to him. "It's downtime now, ladies."

90

Franks sat in his office armchair, having just heard from Superintendent Bukhari that Doctor Gillian Chilvers was dead, shot by six armed officers. At least Reagan Embry was alive, mentally damaged, but alive. Now that Embry was off his back, he could focus on what was really important. His wife was out with friends for dinner, leaving him the night to himself.

Taking a sip of whisky from his tumbler, he let out a contented sigh. This was what Saturday nights were for. Getting up, he walked over to his turntable, took out a classical record and put it on, enjoying the scratchy hiss prior to the music coming through the speakers. He loved vinyl; it was the only way to listen to music.

Relaxing into his armchair, closing his eyes, he hummed along to the tune, tapping his foot. There was nothing more relaxing. "Ahhh," he said, sipping his whisky.

His burner phone vibrated on his desk. He thought about leaving it. "Damn it!" he said, pulling his heavy bones out of the chair; he was so relaxed. "Yeah?" he said, hearing Astor's voice on the other end. "What is it, Zack? I'm busy."

"Are you by a TV? Put BBC News on, would you?"

After stopping the record, Franks picked up the remote on his desk, switched on the television and changed channel. His mouth hung open when he saw a raging inferno at the marina Harry moored *The Albatross* at. The flames were so high. The aerial shot zoomed in on a boat next to the blaze; it went up, too, the explosion making Franks jump. "Is that what I think it is?"

"If you're thinking it's Harry's, you'd be right."

"But I told you not to do anything."

"I didn't. This wasn't my guys – they'd have been more subtle about it. Whoever did that wants everyone to know there was foul play."

"Shit!" he hissed. If Astor wasn't responsible, who was? The reporter was talking animatedly into his microphone, pointing at the blaze behind him, telling everyone that the fire broke out at around 11pm. According to the report, two men were seen walking away from the blaze. "Do you think Harry's in there?"

"I think it's safe to say so," Astor said. "Anyway, thought you should know."

Franks hung up and threw his phone at his armchair. Why would someone want to kill Harry? It made no sense. But doing it exactly the same way he'd planned with Astor was suspect. And burning the boat using accelerant, as they clearly had, was a sure-fire way of telling everyone that Harry was murdered.

His work mobile rang. It was Embry.

"You work fast," she said, sarcasm laced over every word. "When you suggested this, I didn't expect the towering inferno, Peter. There's no way that fire was caused by a gas leak. You've cocked this right up."

"It wasn't us, ma'am." When he'd finished explaining the situation to her, she sounded less than convinced. "But don't worry," he continued, "I'll get to the bottom of this. We'll put the best people on the case, I promise. We'll know who's responsible before you know it."

DAY 1
FRIDAY, JUNE 8TH

EPILOGUE

"We want a clean fight, ladies," Gupta said, making Nasreen shake gloves with Weekes. "I don't need to tell you what's allowed and what's disallowed, do I?"

Nasreen said no, put her mouthguard in and walked to her corner, ready for the onslaught. This time she knew it was a fight, a real fight, not a sparring session. She was going to come out of this swinging, even if Weekes was six inches taller than her; she would have to get right in there to avoid her partner's heavy hits.

Her attention turned to Bukhari, who wandered through the gym door and stood at the back, watching. His uniform was pristine; he was clean-shaven and, well, yummy. The bell rang, not that she noticed. "Nas!" Gupta shouted, interrupting her daydream. "Right," she said, focusing on Weekes, who came out of her corner like a woman possessed, throwing punches at her that she easily blocked.

The crowd of off-duty police officers, her colleagues, were cheering for either her, or Weekes, depending on who they'd backed. She may have been shorter than Weekes, but she had experience of fighting in a ring, which her partner lacked.

Nasreen brought her leg up and hit Weekes in the cheek with the base of her foot, before withdrawing. "Sorry!" she said, with a smile, watching her wipe the blood away.

It angered Weekes. She came back with a combination of punches, all of which Nasreen couldn't block. She took three punches, one to the face and two to the chest – they all hurt. Her partner had power behind her. Nasreen had tricks up her own sleeve.

Bukhari broke her concentration again when he answered his phone. Weekes jumped on it, punching her in the mouth, the mouthguard saving her teeth. Nasreen shook her head, seeing stars briefly. "Concentrate," she heard Weekes say. But she couldn't stop looking at him, even mid-fight.

"Sorry to be a killjoy, people," Bukhari said, walking towards the ring. "We just got the call. Detectives Weekes and Maqsood, you're needed. A body's been found in a ditch on the motorway. Go get changed and head down there."

Nasreen was disappointed. This was the second time their fight had been interrupted. And she was just getting started. Bumping gloves with Weekes, she took out her mouthguard, her breathing laboured. "Saved by the bell again, hey Weekes!" she said, holding the rope up for her partner to climb under.

THE END

ACKNOWLEDGEMENTS

I'd like to thank, first and foremost, you, the reader, for taking a chance on reading my book. Without you picking up and reading it, there would be no need for me writing it, or the publisher releasing it. So, thank you. If you enjoyed Bad Blood, please consider leaving a review. And if you'd like some behind the scenes information, please follow me on Instagram: @dcbrockwell or my Facebook page: DCBrockwell Author. In addition to writing, I like gardening and making cocktails, so you'll find quite a mixed bag on my Instagram account.

I would also love to thank the team at Bloodhound Books. Betsy and Fred, for taking a punt on my story, thank you so much for this opportunity to showcase my work; it's more appreciated than you know. Morgen Bailey, my editor for shaping it up, ready for publication. Also Heather Fitt and the publicity team. Thank you all for your contributions. I hope I don't let you all down.

And I can't sign off without thanking my beta readers, who often pull me up on poor choices with storylines. Extra special mention has to go to Donna Morfett for her contributions, making videos and marketing materials, and just for being a lovely person.

DC Brockwell can be found here:
Instagram: @dcbrockwell
Facebook Page: DCBrockwell Author
Twitter: DCBrockwell